Forbidden Romance

CLINTON W. GETZINGER

Forbidden Romance

(Copyright Pending)

Copyright © 2012 Clinton Getzinger

For more information:

ForbiddenRomanceAndOtherWorks@yahoo.com

This book is based on an actual event that happened in the family. The exact setting, names, and events have been changed and do not resemble actual persons living or dead and any similarity is purely coincidental.

Book cover photo design by Clinton W. Getzinger; book cover photo copyright © 2012 Clinton W. Getzinger

Printed in the United States of America

ISBN-13: 978-1478248088
ISBN-10: 1478248084

Acknowledgements

First, I wish to thank our Heavenly Father for getting me through each day and allowing me to be a writer. Next, I want to thank my friend and former coworker, Cheryl Ewart for encouraging me to begin this book almost nineteen years ago. It was through her influence that I became intrigued with writing about the Post-Civil War era. Thirdly, I wish to thank my mother, Millie Getzinger, who has always believed in me and encouraged me to be anything I aspire to be. Fourthly, I want to thank my friend Terence L. Bennett, who was very instrumental in helping to develop the description and characteristics of one of the main protagonists. Finally, I want to extend my thanks and appreciation for all my various family members, friends, former students, and coworkers who inspired me and also believed in my abilities.

Chapter 1

This time Mollie hit her face against the coarse rocks on the ground below her. She began to bleed profusely spoiling her uncommonly beautiful face. Robert had beaten her numerous times past but never to the point of near disfigurement. Watching her tremble like a helpless animal only elevated his hunger for total power.

Robert nervously led her from behind the barn down the path to the spring in order to wash the blood off her face. The bitter, icy cold water numbed her left side. Mollie felt helpless as he quickly scrubbed the blood off her face with his handkerchief. Her white blouse was stained with blood. "If mother sees me like this she'll know our secret," Mollie exclaimed nervously in tears. "You better not tell nobody about this," replied Robert vehemently. Robert knew how overbearing and speculative her mother Nancy could be.

People were beginning to talk. More often than not, Robert and Mollie were seen together. He always told his wife that Mollie needed his help to perform her strenuous duties on Nancy's 500-acre farm.

Eveline was beginning to suspect that her husband and her sister Mollie were having an affair. When she and Robert first married, she was a widow with a young son, and being the oldest daughter had the potential for inheriting the largest and most prosperous parcel of land on the Williams farm. She always knew that Robert had a hunger for power and cared less if obtaining it meant that others had to die or go into poverty. Regardless, she fell in love with him; however, when Mollie was beginning to grow older and become more and more attractive, Robert paid less attention to her and made various excuses to go visit Mollie and stayed gone for many hours each day. Naturally, she suspected that perhaps some kind of immoral relationship was developing between her husband and her youngest sister. She did not blame her sister at all, because she knew that any woman was helpless in the hands of her husband and had no choice but to comply with his demands.

Before their father died, during the War Between the States, Eveline helped on the farm. As far as she could recall, there was nothing to prevent Mollie from doing it on her own. Isaiah and Nancy Williams' children performed backbreaking duties, but that only made them stronger. Nevertheless, why were they always together? They must be having an affair. What else could it be?

Robert took off his frock coat and handed it to Mollie. "Put the coat on to cover up your bloodstained shirt. Go in the house and change your blouse. Don't stop for nothing' and don't tell your mother about this. If you do, I'll kill ya!" he cried as he turned to go home. He never threatened her like this before. Although she was too embarrassed to tell anyone anyway, she grew more frightened than ever before. "It's all my fault. If I was ugly, maybe

I'd be left alone. Oh, I've got to get outta this, but how?" she said to herself.

Mollie walked from the barn to the back of the two-story log house making sure that her mother did not notice her. Nancy was sitting on the front porch reading her Bible and smoking her long, thin black pipe. It was about four o'clock in the afternoon and all of the chores were complete. Her mother had no reason to look up as she passed by her. Mollie did not take any chances and walked as quickly as she could. She stepped upon the boardwalk and slowly and carefully opened the creaking back door. Next, she climbed the ladder up to the second floor where she had an enclosed bedroom. Quickly, she took off Robert's frock coat and changed blouses. Then she threw Robert's frock coat into the bottom of her wardrobe for safe keeping.

Poor Mollie was so exhausted after her ordeal that she just collapsed on her bed and fell fast asleep. Thankfully, her mother was still outside on the front porch sitting on her rocker.

"Mollie, where are you? Supper's ready and you didn't help me," shouted Nancy waking up Mollie after about two and a half hours. "Coming, Mother!" She could surmise that her mother was rather angry with her right now by her tone of voice. Mollie stepped onto the boardwalk and walked quickly from the house to the kitchen. Whoa, did Nancy have a spiteful look on her wrinkled up face! "Where have you been? I've been lookin' fer you the last two and a half hours. You knew it was yer turn to cook supper. And, why are you wearin' that old tattered blue blouse? What happened to the beautiful lacy white one you had on earlier? And why's yer cheek so red?"

"Uh, Mother, don't worry. I'll clean up the kitchen and wash the dishes after supper. I just fell asleep and I'm still very tired. Can we talk about this some other time, please?" stated Mollie. The whole time they were eating Nancy just stared and scowled at Mollie. All Mollie could do was look down at her plate and ponder what happened earlier. The whole time she had the strangest feeling her mother could read her thoughts.

After supper, Nancy got up from the table and walked back to the house not uttering a single word. The kitchen was a mess, but Mollie began to clean up while at the same time reflecting upon her earlier encounter with Robert. Then she returned to reality and said, "I've got to do somethin' about this. I can't continue to live in fear. There must be somewhere I can go where nobody knows me."

An hour later, Mollie had washed everything and put it in its proper place. She blew out the oil lamps, closed the kitchen door, and slowly walked back to the house. It was late fall and had grown dark earlier. The house was completely dark, and Nancy was already in bed, thankfully. Mollie climbed the ladder once again and went into her bedroom.

As she sat down on her bed, she began to daydream about how her affair with Robert had transpired. The first time she ever saw him was at her father Isaiah's funeral in January of 1865 when she was eight years old. The entire community knew that Isaiah's sizeable estate would soon be divided. Robert desired obtaining as much or all of it that he could, and he knew it was rich in minerals and valuable timber. His mother Susan Sutherland and her mother Nancy were childhood friends and now distant neighbors. One thing she specifically remembered was the way Robert eyed her older plain-looking sister Eveline and could not keep his hands off her. She felt even then that Robert was planning something unethical. At eight years old, Mollie was clearly the most beautiful daughter out of Isaiah and Nancy's four daughters, and Robert realized it.

It was not until April of 1873 after years of surveying that Isaiah's estate was finally settled. Robert and Eveline had been married six years by this time, had a son, and Eveline had inherited the largest portion of the estate. Mollie had received the second largest portion as she was Isaiah's favorite and was still unmarried.

Then in August of 1874 Robert and Eveline attended Mollie's seventeenth birthday celebration. While they were eating lunch, Mollie noticed that Robert continually stared at her with lustful eyes. Rather than cause a scene with the family she simply ignored him. After an hour had passed, Mollie got up from the table and announced to her mother she was going into the woods to be alone. Nancy and the three older sisters were busy cleaning up the kitchen and discussing all the local news in the community. Knowing no one heard her she just went on her way.

"Would you be a good boy and wait for yer mother? I need to go into the woods fer a spell," Robert told his five-year-old son.

"But Daddy, I wanna go with you!" cried Isaiah. "Sorry, Son, but I need to do this alone. You'll be all right here in the yard waitin' for yer mother," exclaimed Robert. "Aw right, Daddy!" replied Isaiah, "Come back soon!" Robert quickly left and went in the direction of the woods.

Mollie had strolled to her grandparents' abandoned old log house where she liked to be alone and reflect on the beautiful scenery. It was located only a couple of hundred feet from the edge of the woods. As she was sitting on the porch steps singing a hymn, she heard someone approaching as he walked through some crackling leaves. She trembled and called out, "Who's there?" Robert shouted, "Don't worry, dear, it's only me, Robert." He immediately walked up to her from behind the house. Although she was not very fond of Robert, she was relieved it was someone she knew.

"What're you doing here, Robert? I thought you'd have been gettin' ready to go home by now?" she exclaimed.

"Oh, uh, there's actually somethin' I've been meanin' to say to you for years now, and it can't wait no longer."

"What could this possibly be about? Why's he actin' so nervous?" Mollie stated to herself.

"I'll just go ahead and say it."

"Say what?"

Finally, he worked up enough courage to say, "Mollie, you're a beautiful woman, and I've admired ya for years. You're so beautiful and so kind and thoughtful that I would like to start courtin' ya."

"What? Are you mad? You're married to my sister! Get away from me and don't ever come near me again!" sobbed Mollie loudly, "Go away before I scream!"

Robert, afraid his in-laws might hear them, quickly rushed back to the Williams' farm. He went into the kitchen and told Eveline that he needed to go home immediately. They quickly said their goodbyes and the Sutherland family loaded themselves onto their wagon heading for home. The whole family had planned to stay until late that evening. Mollie's sisters Polly and Carrie and their spouses decided maybe they too should go home and wait until another time to find out what was going on.

This was not the last time that Robert tried to make advances towards Mollie. A few days after her birthday Robert met her in the cornfield offering to help her. "I thought I told you to stay away from me," cried Mollie angrily.

"I just came to apologize to ya. I's mesmerized by yer beauty and just said the first thing that entered my mind. Mollie, I'd never intentionally hurt ya. Can I help ya finish hoein' the last five rows a corn?" exclaimed Robert convincingly sorrowful.

"I appreciate your apology and I accept your kind offer with gratitude. It's a lotta work to do, and I do need some help," stated Mollie with relief. It was extremely hot out as she was working up a sweat, and she was eager to have assistance no matter who was giving it.

After more than an hour when they were finished loading the wagon with corn, Mollie was exhausted and drenched and needed to sit on the ground. Robert sat down beside her and instinctively embraced her. Her first thought was to shout at him, but she found herself actually liking it. The last time she had been embraced by another man was by her father the day before he was killed. Robert's warm touch actually felt good and reassuring. After a few moments, she collected her thoughts and took out her father's solid gold pocket watch. She noticed it was after one o' clock and had missed eating the basket lunch she had brought. Before telling Robert goodbye, she found herself inviting him to stay and share her lunch of ham sandwiches with her. For some strange reason she did not feel the least bit uncomfortable in his presence. She even found herself liking him. Never before had he treated her with such kindness and respect.

After they had each finished the sandwiches and the last of the water, Robert prepared to go home. Just before he mounted his horse, he grabbed Mollie in a moment of her weakness, embraced her, and then kissed her on her lips. Not giving her a chance to reply, he climbed onto his black mare, Fancy, and rode away. She just stood in awe as he rode away into the distance. "Maybe I should become a little friendlier with Robert. Maybe, it won't hurt me a bit," she thought to herself with a smile on her face. Suddenly, she came to her senses and realized what she was thinking was immoral and had a look of concern.

During the next several weeks as Mollie was finishing the final fall harvesting of corn and wheat, Robert came to her rescue to assist her. It was hard to believe, but she found herself actually falling in love with him. His kindness towards her was overpowering and irresistible, and she did not want it stopped. He was different from the Robert she knew all her life.

Finally, the day before the last day of fall harvesting, Mollie built up enough courage to say, "Robert, I really have appreciated all the help you've given me over the last several weeks."

"I've enjoyed assistin' ya."

"Hold on, Robert, please let me finish what I'm tryin' to say."

"Yes, Mollie?"

"Over the last several weeks somethin' really strange has happened to me that I can't really explain."

"Go on," said Robert.

"You're married to my sister, but at the same time I've fallen in love with you, and I believe you've fallen in love with me," exclaimed Mollie.

Robert thought for a moment and realized that his plan to woo her had finally taken full effect. He knew then that it would not be long before he could take over her property. His plan had worked.

"What do ya think we oughta do about this?" stated Robert, "You know we could meet secretly and nobody'd ever find us out."

"No, Robert, you must tell Eveline that we love each other and then you can divorce her. We must be honest with her. She deserves to know the truth."

The thought of losing all of Eveline's land began to frighten him as the deed was in her name. He had neglected to have it put into his name solely. No, he could not let this happen. He also knew that Nancy would probably come after him with one of her shotguns. His mother-in-law was not the least bit fond of him anyway, especially since he had cheated her husband out of some land over in Smyth County before the war. In addition, he had fought on the side of the Union.

"Mollie, I think for the time being we oughta keep this a secret. You know how much it might hurt little Isaiah. He might not never trust either of us again. Why, I bet even your own mother would begin to hate ya," explained Robert slyly.

"Oh, it never occurred to me how many people we might hurt this way. Oh, you're right, Robert. We oughta keep this a secret for now," replied Mollie nervously.

As the weeks and then months passed, they continued to meet in secret in the woods. She enjoyed being kissed and embraced by Robert. Every time they met; however, in the back of Mollie's mind she still felt guilty for hurting her sister. The problem was she felt her sister had no idea she was being hurt and that made things seem worse for her conscience.

One day Robert exclaimed, "Mollie, now that you and I love and trust each other don't ya think you oughta consider havin' a man protect the rights and interests of yer property?"

"What do you mean?" cried Mollie.

"I mean that ya need somebody to guide and protect ya from foolishly allowin' somebody to take yer land. Anybody could come and take advantage of a poor unmarried woman," chimed in Robert.

"Robert, does this mean what I think it means? Does this mean we're goin' to tell your wife about our affair so that we can get married and start a family of our own?" asked Mollie.

"No, it don't. I just think ya oughta allow me to be yer power of attorney and put my name on yer deed. It's only for yer own pertection," stated Robert.

Then Robert took his hand and slapped her across the face and cried, "Don't you dare breathe a word of this to Eveline or it'll be worse next time."

Suddenly realizing what he had done, he apologized to Mollie for slapping her. He knew he had better be careful or he would never gain control of the land. Despite Robert's apology, she still felt very uncomfortable as the stinging pain lingered.

More weeks passed and Robert and Mollie continued to see each other. Eveline was becoming suspicious as to the whereabouts of her husband. He seemed to be gone more than he was at home.

If it had not been for their children to help around the farm things would have been worse. Finally, Eveline asked, "Robert, where've you been goin' the last several months? Poor Isaiah has to do more than his share of chores around here and stays tired. You're hardly ever home."

"I've been helpin' Nancy and Mollie on their farm. You know there ain't no other men around to help them," explained Robert. Although she felt uneasy knowing what he was really doing, she dropped the subject.

The next day Robert met Mollie in the woods, as usual, in her grandparents' old log house. "You told Eveline our secret didn't ya!" roared Robert as he slapped her so hard the ringing sound echoed in the trees.

"No, I haven't told anyone, honest," sobbed Mollie.

"Well, if I do find out ya told, you're gonna find out how much you're really gonna hurt," exclaimed Robert.

Mollie was perplexed. She did not know what to do. She did not know whether to keep seeing Robert or risk telling their secret. Regardless, she was beginning to feel uncomfortable around him each time they met. His temper grew shorter and shorter. Then a thought struck her and caused her to think of one of the most foolish things she could ever do. She decided in her mind if she put Robert's name on her deed then he would trust her, love her even more, and ask Eveline for a divorce so they could get married.

"Robert, I've decided we oughta make arrangements this winter to have your name put on my deed. That oughta prove to you that I love you and you can trust me forever." Roberts' quest to control most of the Williams' farm was now well on the way to becoming a reality.

The following morning as Robert prepared to leave for the Williams farm, Eveline asked him, "Robert, are you havin' an affair with my sister?" Ignoring her, Robert stormed out of the house slamming the door in a fit of rage. He went to the edge of the woods where he spotted Mollie. Then he quickly walked up to her and hit her so hard she fell to the ground hitting the rocks.

Suddenly, Mollie stopped daydreaming realizing that it was almost ten o' clock at night. After today's ordeal, she knew she could not let Robert have her land and needed to figure a way out of this situation. She needed to find a way to get out of town for a while and think of how she could let her family know about her affair with Robert. Mollie did not wish to hurt her sister but thought she deserved to hear the truth. She also knew that Robert did not love her but only wanted her land. How could someone who beat her to near disfigurement possibly love her?

Chapter 2

Early the next morning Mollie arose at 4:30 as usual to get ready for the day's chores. Naturally, she felt extremely weary from yesterday's events, but knew she could not disappoint her mother. Quickly, she poured water from her blue and white delft ceramic pitcher into the matching washbowl sitting on the dark pine washstand. Then she took a cloth dipping it into the cool water in the bowl and washed her entire body. Next, she took the bowl and poured water out of it out of the bedroom window onto the bushes below.

After putting on her work clothes, she climbed down the ladder slowly and went to the back door. She could smell the aroma of freshly frying bacon and eggs wafting through the air from the kitchen. Her mother always arose about a half hour earlier to cook breakfast and get ready for the day.

As soon as she entered the kitchen, Nancy very kindly announced, "Good mornin', Mollie. I hope ya slept well!" Mollie did not know what to think. She was puzzled and assumed her mother would still be angry with her about yesterday. Nancy did not always allow herself to forget anything and usually held a grudge for a couple of days anyway. Perhaps, she had a good night's sleep without a lot of aches and pains and that was why she was extra cheerful.

"Mother, is there anythin' I can help ya with?" cried
Mollie. "No dear. The table's already set and the bacon and eggs
is done. Just sit right cheer at the table and rest yerself. We's got a
long day ahead of us," stated Nancy. Nancy placed some bacon
and eggs on each of their stoneware plates and then took a knife
and sliced them each two pieces of light bread. Then she poured
them each a cup of coffee into their china cups with saucers.
Although her mother was in a very good mood, breakfast time was
still rather quiet.

"Mollie, after ya milk the cows, churn the butter, and grind
some flour at the mill, I need fer ya to go into town fer a few
thangs." "Sure Mother. I don't mind." It was Wednesday, and it
was about time for Nancy to need more baking soda, tobacco, and
salt. She knew she would also need to go to the post office and
pick up any mail they might have.

Nancy was forty-six when she gave birth to her last child
Mollie. Now in her sixties with graying hair, many wrinkles, and
chronic rheumatism she relied heavily upon her daughter's help.
Although she could still cook fabulous meals and clean the house
and kitchen, it was too difficult for her to go into town, milk the
cows, chop the wood, or do any of the other backbreaking chores
on the farm. Fortunately, Mollie had developed into a very strong
woman after years of such drudgery. She was a stunningly
beautiful woman. Mollie had beautiful, long dark hair, dark brown
eyes, and was five foot seven. Her beauty and stature resembled
her father's side of the family. Her three sisters were shorter, had

light brown hair, blue eyes, and had average features like their mother. Mollie was a definite catch for any man as she was an extremely attractive young woman.

After breakfast was over Mollie went out to the barn and left her mother to clean up the kitchen. There was still dew on the ground, and she could feel the cool morning breeze as it blew through her hair. She knew it was going to be a beautiful day. Entering the barn, she found that her favorite Holstein cow Rose was already in her stall waiting to be milked. Rose mooed loudly as Mollie approached her.

As she was milking Rose, she kept pondering about how she was going to leave town and at the same time worried about leaving her aged mother who needed her by her side. Although she knew she had to escape Robert, this would take a lot of serious consideration. She hated him so much now she could not bear to remain here much longer. No matter how much she tried to resist him he always visited her in the afternoons. She dreaded seeing him today.

Later after she had milked the cows and had churned the butter, it was time to walk to the mill and grind the wheat. Twenty years before the War, her father Isaiah and his father had built a gristmill along Williams Creek to serve the Pine Mountain community. The mill was only a mile from the farm. Some people as far away as Smyth County brought their corn and wheat to be ground here. The Williams family always charged fair prices for their work and never cheated anyone. They were only open on

Wednesdays and Fridays, however. Sometimes, people were already there very early awaiting Mollie's return to the mill.

Mollie stayed at the mill for the usual four hours to grind her mother's wheat, some corn, and that of the others who drifted in steadily. Although it was strenuous labor, she enjoyed every opportunity to see people she normally would never see any other time. One of her favorite Wednesday customers was dear old Mr. Jacob Mills. Mr. Mills was a widower, about eighty-two years old, and originally came from London, England and lived on the border of Grayson County and Smyth County. Each visit he always shared a joke with her and always commented on how pretty she was. Despite being humble and modest, she greatly appreciated his kind words. Before he left, he handed her a quart of red clover honey as a bonus to his usual pay and with a big smile on his face said, "Stay just as beautiful as you are, my dear. Cheerio, then!"

Time had passed quickly, and it was time to close up the mill. She swept up the wheat straws that had fallen on the floor and pushed them out the door onto the ground. Pine Mountain Mercantile and the post office were just two miles away, but she needed to get there soon. After she finished sweeping, she grabbed her large oval shopping basket, pulled out her skeleton key and went out the mill door locking it with a large padlock. Then she strolled over to her gentle brown stallion, Prince, and tied the basket to the side of his saddle. "There's my sweet boy! We're goin' into town." After talking to Prince and making him feel more comfortable, she mounted him and proceeded on her way.

The two-mile road to town was rather picturesque. All of the trees had changed to their brilliant autumn colors of red, yellow, and orange. Farmers on both sides of the road had stacked their hay in perfect beehive shapes. The day was still pleasant as a cool breeze continued to flow through the air.

In the distance, she could see the livery stable on the edge of town owned by her sister Carrie's husband, Hiram Gehring. She decided to stop and see Hiram for a few minutes. Fortunately, Hiram was not busy now and afforded her the chance to talk. "Good day, Mollie! Did you hav a prosprous day at ze mill today?" cried Hiram with a smile.

"Howdy, Hiram! Yes, I had a wonderful day, thanks. That dear Mr. Mills was extra humorous today. Anyway, do ya have time to talk with me about somethin' important," exclaimed Mollie with a serious look on her face.

"Anyzing for my faverit zister-in-law," laughed Hiram.

"Hiram, I'm goin' to need to go away for a while. I don't know how long I'll be gone, but I might even have to sell my share of the farm," remarked Mollie gravely.

"Zis zounds zerious. Hav you told your mutter about it?" replied Hiram looking somewhat puzzled.

"No, she knows nothin' about it, and I don't know how I'm gonna tell her. She needs me, but I need to go away for a while. Please, don't ask me why," stated Mollie, almost sobbing.

"Would you be willin' to buy my land if I ever need to sell it?"

"I zink so. Carrie and I set aside zom money zat could be used. Don't vorry. Your secret vould be safe wis us."

"Thank you, brother dear! I'd even sell it to you at a fair price on one condition." "Vat? Iz zere somting wrong?"

"Dear Brother, would you be willin' to ask your oldest son Jacob to move in with Mother and help her around the farm? I'd even set aside a few acres for him in exchange."

"Are you zertain you vant to do zis? I'm fairly zertain Carrie and I could convinze Jacob to help his grandmutter. He already plans to farm inshtead of helping me here at ze livery."

"Thank you. That's wonderful! I knew I could count on you," replied Mollie happily. She looked at her pocket watch around her neck and noticed it was almost 1:30. It was time to get to the bank before it closed at 2:00. She quickly remounted her horse and cried, "Goodbye, Hiram. I got to be on my way and thanks again."

"Don't mention it!" he shouted as she rode away towards the bank kicking up dirt.

Mollie stopped in front of the bank, climbed down from her horse, and tied him to the post. "I'll just be a moment, Prince." She went inside and presented fifteen dollars to the banker, Mr. James. Mr. James quoted her current balance, which pleased her. He asked her if she wanted to keep out some money to go to the mercantile. She then thanked him for reminding her. They exchanged parting greetings and Mollie left to go to the mercantile across the road.

Before crossing the road, she told Prince to wait for her, as she would be back soon. Prince neighed gently.

As she opened the door of the mercantile, the pleasant, welcoming bell rang. Upon entering the owner, Mrs. Maggie Mueller greeted her and asked if she could be of any help. "Good day, Mrs. Mueller. My mother needs a pound of soda, a pound of salt and a large tin of pipe tobacco. Here's my basket," exclaimed Mollie.

"Before I forget thar's a letter here fer yer mama all the way from Kansas. I think it's from yer Uncle Joseph Williams," retorted Mrs. Mueller as she gave her the mail.

"Thank you. I know my mother'll appreciate it." While Mrs. Mueller was measuring out the baking soda and salt, Mollie heard the bell ringing. Entering the store were her sister Eveline, Robert, and their three young children. Cheerful as always towards her Eveline cried, "Greetings, Sister. It's always good to see ya."

"And it's always good to see you and the three children," replied Mollie. Robert smiled at her in anticipation of meeting her later in the woods. Mollie did not relish the thought of her clandestine meeting later that day.

"That'll be ninety-eight cents," stated Mrs. Mueller as she handed the basket back to Mollie. Mollie handed her the coins and then proceeded to leave. Before she opened the door, she told Eveline and Robert that she would be helping her mother make quilts and would not have time to stroll in the woods. She knew that would anger Robert but avoided looking directly at him and

23

left the store quickly without saying goodbye. Mollie crossed the road hurriedly, tied the basket to the saddle making sure the lid was fastened tightly, and remounted Prince. Then she rode away as fast as Prince could gallop. As she passed the livery stable she told Hiram goodbye, and he waved back to her.

It was now about 2:30 in the afternoon and Nancy would be eager to have her back home. Mollie arrived home and walked Prince into the stables. She could see her mother sitting on the front porch smoking her pipe, rocking back and forth, and heard her singing a hymn. "You're sweet to do as you're asked, my Dear. I'm grateful fer what ya do fer me. A beautiful young lady like you oughta be marred by now, but ya choose tuh stay and help me. Yer the best!" stated Nancy affectionately. Mollie was beginning to feel extremely guilty for what she was planning to do. Why did she have to say such nice things about her right now?

"Mother, would it be all right if we worked on those quilts ya started last spring? For some reason I feel like doin' some quiltin' about now," retorted Mollie.

"That'd be fine, my dear. We really oughta get them done for winter commences. That's an excellent suggestion!" cried Nancy. Nancy got up from her rocking chair and went into the house and into her bedroom. She opened her trunk and took out quilt squares, pieces of cloth, sewing needles, thread, and spread them out all over the floor. Next, she picked up all the supplies and carried them into the sitting room. Meanwhile, Mollie got up from her chair and walked to the back of the house towards the kitchen

24

carrying the basket. Upon entering the kitchen, she put the basket on the table. She began putting the soda and salt into their proper stoneware crocks. At the same time, she could not help glancing down at the letter from her Uncle Joseph. What could be in it? They had not heard from him or Aunt Elsie since year before last when they left Virginia for Kansas. Anyway, she finished up and left the kitchen en route to the house.

As Mollie entered the back door, Nancy asked her if there was any mail today. She handed the letter to her mother hurriedly in anticipation of the news. They both went outside in the front of the house to sit down. After they sat down, Nancy began to read the letter aloud:

Dear Nancy,

We're both well and finally settled completely. Our 160-acre tract a land's very beautiful. We planted many trees and still had more than 150 acres left to farm. I sold $1,000 worth a wheat this fall and a herd of cattle. We used part of the money to buy sheep so we can sell the wool in the spring. As much as we miss our old home, there's no future there for us. The re-growth in the South is to slow. Elsie says hello. Come see us.

Sincerely,
Your brother-in-law Joseph

Chapter 3

Uncle Joseph and Aunt Elsie Williams had taken advantage of the 1873 Timber Culture Act in Kansas. If they were willing to plant trees, they were granted 160 acres to farm. They were tired of the slow economic growth of the South during Reconstruction. Conscript soldiers had hit land hard and there did not appear to be much of a future left. Joseph and Elsie were too old to wait any longer, so they left for a better opportunity.

Nancy and Mollie were glad to learn that Joseph and Elsie were succeeding. It had been so long since they had heard from them and they did not know what had happened to them. "Mollie, I think it's time we started on them quilts," stated Nancy.

"Yes, Mother." Both women got up from their chairs and went into the sitting room where Nancy had carefully laid the quilt squares, cloth strips, and thread on the wooden floor. Mollie took a needle, threaded it, picked up some quilt squares, and began sewing them together. As she sewed, she remembered that she had broken off her meeting with Robert. She knew how furious he must be by now, but more importantly, she had to think about leaving Virginia.

Until they heard from Uncle Joseph, Mollie had forgotten all about the 1873 Timber Culture Act. Although she was not interested in planting trees, perhaps she could buy a small farm in Kansas and start a new life there. After all, her relatives could take her in until she found something permanent. If she could not find anything immediately, she could return home and figure out something else.

The more she pondered the more Kansas appealed to her. This would be the perfect place to escape from Robert and his advances. His interests would remain in Virginia and he would forget all about her. "I have to do this! I got to do this if I want any kind of life without the hardship of a troublesome man," she said to herself.

Hours later Nancy and Mollie finished working on enough quilt squares to piece a large quilt. It was growing late and it was time to start supper. Mollie got up from her chair and placed the quilt pieces into her mother's trunk. Next, she went out the back door onto the boardwalk straight to the kitchen. Once in the kitchen she went to the cupboard to get the ingredients to make dumplings for the chicken and dumplings, her mother's favorite meal.

As she measured out the flour, she began to think about how she planned to tell her mother she was leaving soon. Her mother would be coming out to the kitchen soon and she dreaded facing her. It was wrong to keep this from her any longer, but at the same time, she did not want to hurt her emotionally.

Next, she mixed the flour with lard and milk to make sticky dough. Then she set it aside on the table and walked to the cellar entrance. She went down the steps into the deep cellar under the kitchen where they stored their salted meats, preserves, and other canned foods. Her mother had plucked a chicken earlier that day and left it hanging down there to stay cool. Mollie grabbed the chicken and climbed up the steep steps where she found her mother sitting at the table snapping green beans. "Oh, Mother, I didn't hear you come in. I got the chicken to de-bone and get ready to boil," stated Mollie. Nancy nodded her head and continued working.

While she was finishing the chicken and dumplings, she focused again upon how she would tell her mother about leaving. She decided to wait until they were already sitting down to eat.

Time had passed and everything was ready to serve. Nancy set the table with their best dishes and silverware and Mollie placed the blue and white bone china tureen with chicken and dumplings on the table. Next, she placed the brick red stoneware bowl of green beans cooked with bacon beside the tureen. Her mother had already sliced the bread and spread butter on it.

Nancy said a prayer to have the meal blessed. As soon as she finished Mollie planned how she was going to explain her need to leave. She must not wait any longer and wanted to get it done. After about fifteen minutes of eating quietly Mollie said, "Mother, I've been thinking about this for a long time now, and I've decided to go away for a piece." Nancy stopped eating halfway, dropping food out of her mouth. "What do you mean yer goin' away for a spell? How am I s'posed to run this here farm by myself?" stated Nancy with sadness in her voice. "Mother, please let me finish," cried Mollie. "Whenever I do go away I've asked Hiram to buy my share of the farm and persuade Jacob to come help ya."

"What made ya decide ya had to get away? Is it somethin' I 've done or said to make ya hate me enough to leave me here alone? Do ya think I didn't notice that yer my pertiest daughter and might wanna leave someday?" stated Nancy angrily.

"No, Mother. It's somethin' else completely, and I can't tell you why right now," said Mollie with tears in her eyes. Nancy could ascertain that something was seriously disturbing her but respected her wishes not to ask any more questions.

"Have ya thought about whar you're plannin' to go? Winter's almost here ya know," stated Nancy in a much calmer tone.

"I'm riding out to see Hiram tomorrow morning and make the necessary arrangements. He told me he had cash money in hand to pay me," replied Mollie excitedly. Not wanting to discuss this anymore both women continued eating quietly.

Mollie told her mother to go into the house and she would clean up the kitchen. Nancy bid her goodnight and went away. She thought her mother took the news better than she expected but realized that she was heartbroken too. There was not as much to clean up, so it did not take her nearly as long as usual.

After such a tiring day it did not take Mollie long to fall fast asleep once she hit the bed. All night she dreamed about what a better life she would have in Kansas. Of course, she had never been there but had heard stories about the plains and smaller settlements there. This would definitely be the perfect place to escape from Robert and not worry about too many people knowing her.

Early the next morning Mollie arose as usual at 4:30 to bathe and get ready for her daily chores. She dressed quickly and started right away so that she had plenty of time to visit Hiram. This morning she skipped breakfast in anticipation of selling her land as quickly as she could. Hurriedly, Mollie went out to the barn to milk the cows.

While Mollie was about to finish milking the last cow she heard someone opening the creaky barn door. Thinking it was her mother she shouted out, "I'll be finished in a few minutes, Mother!" Expecting her mother to shout back she was surprised to see Robert walk towards her.

"Why didn't ya meet me in the woods yesterday? I waited for ya for o'er an hour," exclaimed Robert frantically.

"You heard me tell Eveline I'd be helpin' Mother make quilts," said Mollie angrily.

"I thought ya were just makin' up excuses in case Eveline needed to stop o'er," stated Robert calmly. "By the way, why're ya in such a hurry? Ya never finish milkin' the cows this blamin' early."

"How'd you know when I'm done? Have you been watchin' me while I work?" replied Mollie nervously.

"Yes, I've been watchin' ya but patiently," cried Robert confidently. "I've seen ya at work fer several months now. Eveline thinks I'm out in the fields tendin' our bulls. Since ya missed me

30

only yesterday I'll forgive ya. Just don't let it happen again. Do ya hear?" stated Robert forcefully. "Make sure ya meet me at the log house at 3:00 today. I'll be waitin'," shouted Robert as he left the barn.

Now more than ever Mollie knew she was making the right decision. When she and Robert first started seeing each other as lovers, he was much less violent. At least then, she admired him for his good looks as Robert had coal black hair, wore a short beard, and kept a neatly trimmed moustache. His eyes were piercing blue and very stunning to gaze at. Mollie also appreciated the fact that he was over six feet tall, strong, and muscular. Although she still considered him very handsome, she detested him now for his rough treatment of her, and by no means would she really consider meeting him in the afternoon. She knew that she could make some kind of excuse to avoid seeing him.

Knowing that winter was soon approaching, she decided she had better wait until early spring to travel to Kansas. In addition, she knew she had to write her Uncle Joseph telling him that she would be there by the end of April.

As soon as she finished milking the last cow, she carried the pails of milk to the spring to keep it cold. The spring was about 300 feet from the barn in the direction of the woods. Isaiah had constructed a trough in which the cold water flowed through it. Mollie poured the milk into the milk cans standing inside the trough. Even in the hot, humid summer, the spring stayed icy cold. It also helped that her father built it near the edge of the woods

31

where the tall oak trees shaded it. When she finished she rinsed the pails in the spring and hung them inside the barn once again. Next, it was time to go chop some wood for winter.

Once she completed all of the chores Mollie went into the house to get ready to go to town. She washed off quickly with a wet towel and then put on one of her best frilly Sunday dresses. Next, she laced up her boots and put on a black bonnet to finish off her outfit. As she climbed down the ladder, she heard her mother stirring in the sitting room. She went in and told Nancy she planned to sell her land to Hiram and Carrie today. Although Nancy still did not understand why, she bid Mollie goodbye and to have a safe trip into town.

Mollie went out the front door and out to the barn to saddle up Prince with a side saddle. As she neared him, Prince neighed loudly in the excitement of seeing her. Very carefully, she fastened the saddle and mounted him not wanting to spoil her best dress and rode on towards town.

As she approached town she could see that the livery stable had several customers waiting. "Mollie, I'll be zrough wit zese gentlemen in a few minutes," exclaimed Hiram. "That's fine brother. I ain't in no hurry," replied Mollie patiently. She climbed down from Prince and tied him to one of the support beams of the stable. While she waited, she fed Prince some carrots that Hiram had piled on a table for the other horses.

After about fifteen minutes, the last man left with his carriage. Hiram did not expect to see Mollie but always enjoyed her company. "Vell, Sister, vat can I do for you today?" exclaimed Hiram cheerfully.

"I'm here to sell you my land, if you're still willing," cried Mollie anxiously.

"Vouldn't you rather vait until spring? You might get a better price zen," stated Hiram. "Yes, I know, but I want you to have it as I trust you to protect us all," cried Mollie. "A stranger might not want to allow us to have access to the surrounding areas." In her mind, she knew that a stranger would probably be in reality Robert.

"Vell, in zat case I'm prepared to offer you ze sum of $700 for ze entire tract. Does zat sound fair to you?" exclaimed Hiram.

"That is more than fair, but I'd still like to save back a portion for Jacob for takin' care of Mother for me," replied Mollie with a smile. "Tomorrow mornin' I'll ride over to the courthouse and have my uncle, Judge James Greene draw up the papers."

"Vonce again, Mollie, are you zure zis is vhat you vant to do?" stated Hiram.

"Yes, more than anything else in the world I need to sell my land and leave town," replied Mollie. "As soon as I am settled I'll write you and Carrie and explain everythin'."

Hiram was reassured by the tone in her voice that everything would turn out all right. They continued talking with each other for more than an hour and lost track of the time. Just as the stage rode by both realized neither had eaten lunch.

"Well, Brother, I've enjoyed talkin' with you, but I gotta get home and help Mother with lunch. Goodbye!"

"Goodbye, Sister dear! Zee you tomorrow afternoon!" Mollie walked over towards Prince, untied his reins, and mounted him. As she rode out of town, she waved goodbye to Hiram. Hiram waved back with a big smile across his face.

As Mollie approached the farm, she could see smoke rising from the chimney above the kitchen. She could smell a delicious odor of roasted chicken wafting through the air. Since she was already extremely late, she stopped at the picket fence in front of the house and tied Prince to one of the posts. Mollie almost dreaded facing her mother. Nancy loved her youngest daughter dearly, but at the same time expected her to be on time and tardiness annoyed her fiercely most of the time.

Mollie entered the kitchen with slight apprehension while Nancy was engrossed in her cooking and paid no attention to her. She sensed that her mother was upset but set the table to help ease the situation. Next, she strolled over towards her mother and helped her carry the food to the table.

Both women sat down quietly and Nancy uttered a prayer asking God to bless their meal. Nancy served herself first and then Mollie began after her. While she served herself Nancy asked angrily, "Did ya sell yer land?"

"Yes, Mother, and I received a fair price for it," replied Mollie. "And don't worry. I don't plan to leave until March or April." From that moment on, there was less tension in the air. As desperate as she needed to leave town and get away from Robert, she realized that travel to the west could be difficult because of the harsher weather approaching this time of year. Also, with the weather changing Robert would be unable to make as many excuses to help her on the farm, and she would be able to avoid him more until spring. All of the wood they needed for winter was close enough to home, and any supplies she needed that they were unable to grow in the winter she could buy in town. For the time being she felt safe from Robert.

Chapter 4

The fall months had finally passed and the harsh winter was upon them. Mollie had cut and stacked more than enough wood to last them until the arrival of spring. In a few days, it would be Christmas Day. It was also Nancy's sixty-fourth birthday. Everyone in the Williams family would gather to celebrate Christmas here. Nancy and Mollie always had a quiet birthday celebration after the family members returned home. "Nothing could spoil my last Christmas in Virginia," thought Mollie to herself. She had already sold her portion of the land to Hiram, and she now had $700. In a little over three months, she would be on her way to Kansas to stay with Uncle Joseph and Aunt Elsie.

Suddenly, she remembered she needed to check on the huge, white-feathered, domesticated tom turkey in the turkey pen behind the barn. Walking steadily from behind the house where she had stacked the last pieces of wood she headed towards the painted white barn. In the distance, she could hear the chickens clucking and the turkeys gobbling. It was feeding time for all of the farm animals, but she wanted to feed the fowl first.

As she approached the holding pen, the chickens outside of the henhouse were clucking louder in anticipation of Mollie feeding them. All four of the turkeys, the three wild hens and the big white domesticated tom, began gobbling louder too. The tom turkey had fattened himself up very nicely. Mollie knew that tomorrow morning was the day to prepare the tom for Christmas Day just three days away.

Mollie began to reminisce about the years when her father Isaiah had the duty of chopping off the turkeys' heads. The first time she ever saw it done was when she was four years old. As soon as the sharp axe hit the tom's long fat neck and blood spurted everywhere, Mollie screamed and ran inside to her mother. Isaiah immediately looked for her and calmed her fear. She recalled her Daddy assuring her that it was just a way of life and that was how they always prepared for the Christmas meal. Mollie was much less frightened but still did not want to go behind the barn for many days afterwards.

In the years following Isaiah's death, Mollie was accustomed to asking her brother-in-law Hiram to kill the tom. Poor Nancy's stiff arthritic hands could no longer grasp a sharp axe safely. Besides, Mollie was still afraid and although she wanted to assist her mother in any way possible, this was not one of those occasions.

Now that she was finished feeding the turkeys she moved on to the chickens by the henhouse. She bent down to pet her favorite hen Sally for a few moments. Sally ate a few kernels of feed out of her hand very carefully. "Sorry to have to leave ya, Sally, but I gotta go feed the cows and horses," said Mollie sadly thinking of never seeing her again. She proceeded into the barn from the rear door. Rose immediately began to moo loudly at the prospect of seeing Mollie. "There's my sweet Rose!" called Mollie affectionately. Next, she strolled over to Rose's stall and patted her gently on the head. Rose mooed to show her approval. Then, Mollie gave Rose some hay and went across the barn over to the horses' stalls. After feeding the horses, she unlatched the side gates to allow them to trot into the fenced pasture.

****

Christmas Day was finally here and Nancy was cooking in the kitchen singing her favorite hymns. Mollie could hear her as she was climbing down into the cellar to get the smoked turkey, some white potatoes, and yellow apples for the dinner pies. It was 5:30 A.M. and both women wanted to complete the meal by noon. As she was ascending the ladder back into the kitchen, Mollie remembered something wonderful. Robert, Eveline, and their children planned to spend Christmas with his mother, his sister and brothers, and all of their families. She quickly said a short prayer thanking God for allowing her to have a day without consequence.

Hours later, the wonderfully fragrant smells of baking turkey and spicy apple pies filled the kitchen. In just about another thirty minutes Hiram, Carrie, Abraham, and Polly would be arriving with their families. Mollie placed a crocheted lace tablecloth on the long English beechnut table, a 100-year-old heirloom from Nancy's paternal side and set out the fine bone china, an heirloom from Nancy's maternal side. "Thank you my dear. I know this'll be a wonderful last Christmas together," stated Nancy lovingly. She smiled back at her mother.

It was now time for the various family members to arrive. This year both sets of grandparents would be joining them for dinner. Although she loved all of her grandparents dearly, she felt a much closer bonding with her Grandmother Williams. Grandmother Williams was a tall, lean, gentle woman and affectionate. These were characteristics similar to her father Isaiah. She was now one hundred years old but still as spry as a twenty-five year old and retained her youthful dark brown hair with virtually no trace of gray. Her dear grandmother did not have arthritis or any other physical ailments. Grandfather Williams was turning 105 on December 27. He was about six feet four inches tall, gentle, lean and wore a long white beard and moustache. Mollie always thought he resembled Father Christmas. Unfortunately, Grandpa Williams suffered from rheumatism, partial blindness, and hobbled with a cane.

Mollie put on her long black shawl and walked outside towards the front of the house. She stepped up onto the front porch and sat down on the Windsor rocker waiting for the company to arrive. Her favorite cat, a black one named Pandora, hopped onto her lap, lay down, and purred loudly. Pandora's back left leg had been severed from being hit by a carriage; however, she was completely well now and walked with a limp to get sympathy. "Howdy, my sweet girl! Waitin' for the folks too?" cried Mollie lovingly. Mollie knew she was fine but played along with her.

Suddenly, Pandora quickly jumped down from her lap and ran under the porch. Mollie looked up and could see her sisters and their families arriving in wagons one behind the other. Abraham and Polly were the leaders of this lovely procession. Behind them followed Hiram and Carrie who brought with them Grandpa Joshua and Grandma Agnes Greene. The Greene homestead adjoined theirs and naturally was on their way.

Grandpa Greene stood a mere five feet two inches tall and wore a short-cropped gray beard without a moustache. He served as a lieutenant in the War of 1812 and was proud of his service to his country. Most family members avoided discussing politics with him as his views usually differed from others. Despite his eighty-two years, he still stood and walked as straight as a soldier walks. On the contrary, poor Grandma Greene stooped over and walked with a cane. She too was eighty-two years old but stood only five feet tall. Her eyes were a stunning light blue that stood out from her head of snowy white curly hair. It almost looked like she had no eyes at all they were so light. Both Greene grandparents were extremely contrary and stern in demeanor and one knew immediately if nothing suited them. They both had married at seventeen and required permission from their parents to wed. Nancy was their oldest child from this early union and was the favorite child. Grandpa and Grandma Greene always wanted to spend Christmas Day with her as long as they were physically able.

Since Grandpa and Grandma Greene were aged, Abraham let Hiram advance ahead and stop in front of the Williams farm. Hattie, aged five, and Peggy, aged twelve, jumped out of the wagon before it even came to a complete stop followed by their mother who waited for it to stop. Next, Jacob, aged eighteen, climbed down to help Grandma get out of the wagon. Soon Hiram climbed down to assist Joshua and Agnes. "Don't forget my pumpkin pies, Hiram," shouted Agnes. "Ya, Grandma, I von't," called back Hiram slightly annoyed. She must have reminded Hiram about twenty times along the way not to forget her pies. Grandma Greene always brought along enough pies to feed Lee's army. Her pies were some of the best in the county, and she vowed she would never share her recipe until they buried her.

Abraham and Polly finally climbed out of their wagon along with their twin sons Karl and John. Karl and John were twelve years old and were extremely helpful to their parents on the farm. The twins immediately ran over to Peggy since they were all the same age and had a lot in common. All three giggled and ran to play behind the kitchen until their parents called them for dinner. Hattie tried to follow them but they told her to stay with her mother. She cried for a few moments and then stopped and began to smile, because she saw Pandora slowly limping in the yard and ran over to play with her.

After her sisters and their husbands went inside the house, Mollie continued to sit on the porch in anticipation of the arrival of her Grandpa and Grandma Williams. Jacob sat down beside her and brought up the subject of her leaving town. "If you don't mind Jacob I'd rather wait until after dinner to discuss my partin'," stated Mollie.

"Yes, Mollie, I'll respect yer wishes," answered Jacob. Just as they finished their brief discussion, they could see the grandparents coming down the lane.

Granny Williams was pulling the reins of her black leather phaeton carriage. It was made of white oak and upholstered in black leather including the top. She kept the leather well-oiled and in tiptop shape thanks to her son David, Jr. who lived on an adjoining farm. David, Jr. replaced the wheels just in time for winter. Leading the phaeton was Granny's favorite horse, Diamond. Diamond was a five-year old palomino dobbin and was a fifth generation farm horse. Granddad Williams had purchased Diamond's ancestor from a neighbor in 1792 after his honeymoon.

"Oh, Granny, it's so good to see ya!" cried Mollie with a big smile on her face. "Granddad, I'm very glad to see you too!" shouted Mollie as she ran towards them. The grandparents climbed out of the carriage slowly and Mollie embraced them both at the same time. Besides being overly zealous about seeing them Mollie had more than just height and looks in common with them. Granny Phoebe Williams was a former teacher and had taught school for forty years in addition to farming. Their sons David, Jr. and Isaiah were also teachers, and Isaiah was teaching until he joined the Confederate cause. Being bright like her father and grandparents, Mollie had recently received her teaching certificate to carry on the tradition.

"Before we git too close to the house, my dear, we've got a gift for you," exclaimed Granny. "If ya look behind the carriage you'll see a medium-sized box tied to the back. That box is our special Christmas gift to you. Take it up to yer room right now before dinner. Jacob can help us inside."

"Thank you, Granny and Granddad. You're always so good to me!" cried Mollie as she untied the box. Quickly, she strolled into the house, climbed the ladder to her bedroom, and put the box on her bed.

After a few moments, Mollie climbed back down the ladder and then went out the back door. As she walked across the boardwalk, she saw her mother coming out the kitchen door. "Oh, thar you are, my Dear. I was just a comin' after ya. We're all ready to sit down," declared Nancy. She strolled over towards her mother, gently grabbed her arm, and smiled at her.

They entered the kitchen together and found their empty seats at the table. After they sat down, Granddad Williams, being the oldest family member present, stood up clutching his cane. He prayed, in his deep voice, to God to bless their meal. When he finished, he carefully returned to his seat and waited for the meal to begin.

Abraham quickly stood up and began to carve the huge turkey. As always, Nancy insisted that the children eat first and then the oldest family members followed by the younger adults. Everyone took turns passing a plate down each side of the table until every person received a plate.

Hours later, it was time for everyone to leave. Nancy and Mollie both put on their long black shawls and black bonnets and went outside to say good-bye. Hiram, Carrie, Jacob, the young girls, and the Greene grandparents all said good-bye and climbed into their wagon and rode off first. Next, Abraham, Polly, and their children said good-bye, climbed into the wagon, and then left. Finally, Granddad and Granny arose from their chairs on Nancy's front porch and walked towards Nancy and Mollie. "Thank you, Nancy, fer another wonderful Christmas dinner. Everything's perfect," exclaimed Granny. Granddad concurred.

"It's great seein' ya both today. I'll make my reglar stop next week to see ya. Goodbye," cried Nancy. As Nancy went inside after telling them farewell, Mollie walked with her grandparents to the phaeton carriage. Mollie hugged and kissed both of them, said farewell, and cried as they ascended into the carriage.

"Come see us next week when yer Mother drops in," said Granny.

"I will, and thanks for the gift. I love ya both dearly," stated Mollie sadly. As they drove off Mollie waved continually until they were no longer in sight.

She walked over to the wide gate of the picket fence, opened it carefully, and latched it back. As she stepped onto the porch, she suddenly remembered the unopened gift and went into the house quickly. Mollie pulled off her shawl, untied her bonnet, and threw them on the chair. Then she went to the back of the house and ascended the ladder to her loft bedroom. Next, she walked over to her ornately carved cherry wood bed, stepped onto the stepstool, and sat down on the bed.

Mollie carefully lifted the lid off the wooden box. Inside on the very top was a letter folded in half. She opened the letter and read it slowly. In the letter, her Granny had explained that she wanted her to have her revolver, an 1836 Colt revolver, to take with her for protection in Kansas. Deeper inside of the box was a medium-sized book that Granny had wrapped securely with a crocheted doily. Next, Mollie unwrapped it to find that it was a leather bound Bible ornately carved. The letter further stated she wanted her to have her own grandmother's personal Bible that she carried to church. Then she looked inside and found a copyright date of 1700. Inside on the following page written in German were the following words: To my devoted granddaughter, Anna Kinsler, on her eleventh birthday, August 5, 1701, from your loving grandmother, Martha Schenkel. Mollie remembered that her Granny had mentioned having a grandmother named Anna. Never in her wildest dreams did she think she would inherit two wonderful family treasures. Thankfully, Mollie had learned enough German to understand most of the more important scriptures.

It was growing dark outside, so Mollie went to the kitchen to help her mother clean the dishes. She was also eager to tell Nancy about the wonderful gifts her Granny gave her. "Mother Williams always did have an extry special place in her heart for ya. You were born the same month that yer Daddy's sister Mollie died. It was a comfort to her that just as God took a life a new child was

45

born," stated Nancy with a tear in her eye. "Yer Granny lived in the log house, their summer home, on our property when you was born. She and Granddad helped me care fer ya fer the first year of yer life. As a matter fact, she always told me ya looked just like her own Mollie." Mollie knew her grandparents had a special bond with her.

Now that they had washed all of the dishes and put them away, Mollie told Nancy to sit down at the kitchen table. Mollie went down into the cellar but returned a few moments later with a beautiful frosted cake. "Happy Birthday, Mother!" exclaimed Mollie.

"Ya remembered as always my dear," stated Nancy. They continued to celebrate together until the clock struck 9:30. Both women blew out the oil lamps, left the kitchen, and went towards the house to prepare for bed. It had been a long but wonderful day.

Early the next morning while still in bed Mollie could hear a wagon driving up the lane. The hunting dogs were barking fiercely. Until Nancy became crippled, both women enjoyed hunting and fishing together. Suddenly, a man stopped in front of the house, climbed down, and preceded towards the front door. Nancy heard a loud knock and got out of bed. She put on her black shawl and hobbled over to the front door. No one ever came to visit them this early, and Nancy was slightly annoyed. She opened the door to find that it was her brother-in-law, David, Jr. "Good mornin', David. Is thar anythin' wrong?" asked Nancy.

With tears in his eyes David answered, "It's Father. He fell down on the floor in front of the bed. We think it's his heart. Dr. Kinsler is with him right now. Mother wants ya both to come back with me."

"I'll call Mollie down cheer right away," stated Nancy.

"I'm here, Mother. I'll go get dressed quickly," shouted Mollie down from the loft. Both women rapidly put on their work dresses along with an apron. Next, they laced up their boots, put on their shawls, and tied on bonnets. All three left the house, climbed onto the wagon, and road away.

David and Phoebe Williams lived on a 100-acre farm about four miles away on the other side of town. Their son David lived on a modest farm directly across the main road that separated the two farms. David, Jr.'s log house lay across from his parents' front porch. The elder David's home was a two-story painted white house with a porch that wrapped around on three sides. Downstairs there were two large bedrooms, a parlor, a large kitchen, and a formal dining room. Upstairs there were four large bedrooms and a large staircase leading to the full-size attic. Now that they were advanced in age, they used the largest downstairs bedroom beside the kitchen.

The whole time Mollie was in the wagon she tried to picture in her mind the wonderful times she spent at her grandparents' home. Her Granddad was like a second father to her. Sometimes she looked at him and wondered if her father would have looked just like him at this age. David and Nancy remained silent the entire trip. Finally, they turned down the long road that separated the two farms. As the wagon came closer, Mollie could see the doctor's black phaeton carriage parked in front. Soon they pulled into the lane and stopped in front of the house. It was a long lane with cherry trees growing on both sides. Mollie quickly climbed down and ran into the house. David helped Nancy down and together, holding hands, walked into the house. Already, Mollie was sitting on a chair at Granddad's bedside. Granny was sitting on another chair on the opposite side. Dr. Kinsler asked Phoebe, David, and Nancy to follow him to the parlor while Mollie stayed behind.

In the parlor Dr. Kinsler began talking, "I called you in here to update you on David's condition. Yes, he's sufferin' from heart trouble, and his heart's weak. Phoebe, I'm sorry to say, but I ain't expectin' him to make it before the first of the year." David and Nancy began to cry while Phoebe held back her tears. "I know that when he dies I'll see him again someday," exclaimed Phoebe bravely.

Dr. Kinsler continued, "All that we can do now is keep him as comfortable as possible. If ya need me anymore, I'll be down the road at Jake Chatwell's place. His wife's expectin' their baby any day now. I'll go get my bag and see myself out."

Meanwhile, Mollie was having a conversation with her Granddad. "Don't worry Granddad. Mother and I'll stay here overnight if you need anythin' at all." In a very weak stammering voice Granddad replied, "Th-thank y-you, m-m-my d-dear. I l-love y-y-you." Granddad closed his eyes and went to sleep. He began to snore but very quietly. Mollie poured some water from the water pitcher onto a cloth. Then she placed the wet cloth on his forehead. Phoebe, David, and Nancy entered the room quietly. "I had better go home and feed the cattle and fowls. Let me know if there's any change. Nancy, I'll send my son over to yer house to milk yer cows and feed all of the animals," stated David.

Nancy went into the kitchen and started to make dinner. Phoebe stayed beside her husband and read Isaiah 53, from their family Bible. Mollie put another log in the fireplace and then went outside to feed the chickens and Granny's horse Diamond. As she fed the animals, she remembered that Robert and his family were returning home tomorrow from Flatridge where his mother lived. She began to feel depressed but remembered she needed to stay cheerful for her Granddad's sake.

Just as Mollie was putting away the chicken feed, she could hear Nancy calling her name. It was time to sit down for dinner. She put away the feed and latched the barn doors. Next, she strolled over to the back door of the house. As soon as she opened the door, she could smell the delicious pungent scent of vegetable soup and warmed buttered light bread toast. Granny preferred tea to coffee, so Nancy made tea in Granny's favorite delft blue teapot. Her mother had brought it with her when she came to America from Germany. Nancy placed some food on a serving tray and carried food into Granny and Granddad's bedroom. After a few

49

minutes, she returned to the kitchen and sat down with Mollie. Mollie offered a word of prayer, and then they began to eat.

Hours later, it was time to go to bed. Nancy and Mollie went into Granddad's bedroom to tell the grandparents goodnight. "If you need anything call me, and I'll come," exclaimed Nancy.

"Yes, I'll help you too, Granny," replied Mollie.

"Thank you, my dears. Good night!" stated Granny. Mollie and Nancy left the bedroom and then ascended the stairs to go to bed.

As soon as Mollie's head hit the pillow, she fell fast asleep. It had been quite an eventful day, and she was exhausted. She began to dream about the day Robert had thrown her against the rocks, and he had threatened to kill her if she revealed the affair. Fortunately, in the winter he left her alone. Just as she was about to get up from falling in the dream she felt someone grabbing her shoulder and a familiar voice calling her name. Mollie woke up to find her mother standing beside the bed. Nancy was carrying a small oil lamp and was acting very strangely. "Mollie, your Granddad's died. Your Granny says he died in his sleep with a smile on his face," stated Nancy sadly. It was 3:30 a.m. and both women quickly descended the stairs.

Mollie and Nancy went into Granddad's room and found Granny sitting on a chair beside him. "I'm very sorry that Granddad died, Granny," stated Mollie with a choked up voice and tears streaming from her eyes.

"He's at peace now and no longer sufferin'. I'll see him again someday," replied Granny calmly and assuredly. She ran over to Granny and hugged her tightly for several moments. Then she kissed her on the cheek and told her she loved her.

Although it was still very early in the morning, everyone stayed up to plan for the funeral early the next day. Mollie volunteered to sit with him to keep the cats away. Meanwhile, Granny and Nancy met in the parlor to talk about all the preparations. There was no need to buy a casket since Granddad had built caskets for himself and Granny when they were in their seventies. Granddad was an expert carpenter and built a lot of things on the farm and for his neighbors and was always out in his barn using his tools since he had retired. He stored the caskets out in the barn up in the loft. Granddad never expected to live this long as his own parents only lived to be in their sixties, as did his grandparents.

Since it was Granddad's 105th birthday, David, Jr. came over to check on his father. He always walked inside without knocking since he usually helped his parents tend the farm. Knowing that his father was ill he promptly went into his parents' bedroom. He was surprised to find Mollie sitting there alone with him. David walked closer to the bed and realized that his father was dead. Tears formed in his eyes and dropped profusely. He ascertained that the funeral would take place tomorrow, and he would need to go to the barn and bring down the casket. Before going out to the barn he went into the parlor to see his mother.

Nancy and Phoebe were discussing ways to arrange the furniture for all of the visitors.

Though it was Sunday and they normally attended church, they knew their minister would understand their absence. All of the children and grandchildren would be at church and come over afterwards for the celebration of Granddad's 105th birthday; however, Mollie decided to attend church and inform the family of his death. David, Jr. planned to put Granddad in the casket and store it and the body in the barn until tomorrow. There would be no need for Mollie to sit with the body any longer, and she was free to attend church.

Soon Mollie washed up to get ready to leave. Fortunately, her grandparents had a windmill that pumped water into the attic and then into pipes to give them running water indoors. Next, she went outside to the barn, saddled up Diamond, and rode off into town. When she arrived at church, she noticed that her three sisters and their families were already inside, and she dreaded telling them the news. Ugh! Robert was there too. As quickly as she went inside, Carrie looked at her and could ascertain that something was troubling her. "Mollie, what's the matter?" stated Carrie. She ignored her and approached the pulpit where Reverend Fletcher was standing. "Reverend, I've an announcement I'd like to make to the whole congregation," Mollie whispered into his ear.

"Go ahead, my dear. Take as much time as you like," replied Reverend Fletcher.

Mollie stood behind the pulpit and everyone was in awe seeing her stand there. "Friends and family I've a very important announcement to make. Granddad David Williams died early this mornin' on his birthday. The doctor says it was his heart," stated Mollie with tears streaming down her cheeks. "His funeral's tomorrow." She looked in the direction of her three sisters, who were sitting together, and they began to cry. Immediately, she walked over to sit with and help comfort them. Reverend Fletcher returned to the pulpit, made a few statements about their Granddad, and began to preach his sermon about deliverance.

Thirty minutes after the sermon, it was time for singing the closing hymn. Reverend Fletcher changed the hymn to "Amazing Grace" in memory of Granddad. For some reason the congregation seemed to put more heart into their singing. Once the hymn was completed, the reverend delivered the benediction. Then, as they began to leave, the organist played Bach's "Sheep May Safely Graze." The four sisters remained seated and waited for Reverend Fletcher to say "Goodbye" to the last church member.

"Well, my dears, I'm truly sorry to hear of Mr. Williams's passing," stated Reverend Fletcher quietly. "If you don't mind I'll come over to your Granny's house after dinner. My wife'll be waiting for me and then I can explain what's transpired." The reverend had a short word of prayer and then bade the young women "farewell." Mollie and her sisters climbed down the front steps and walked towards their wagons. Robert was sitting in the front of his wagon and was staring at her with hungry eyes. She quickly turned her head and focused her attention to her three sisters standing together talking and crying.

"Granny says she still wants all of you to come over at six this evening for supper. She said that's what Granddad would've wanted," cried Mollie. Next, Mollie mounted upon Diamond, waved "Goodbye," and rode on her way.

It was now almost 1:30 in the afternoon and Reverend Fletcher and his wife were driving up the lane in their wagon. As soon as they stopped in front of the home, they climbed out and walked to the back of the wagon. Mrs. Fletcher reached into the back and brought out four peach pies. She always baked some of the best peach pies this side of the county. Mollie had heard the wagon drive up and opened the front door. "Good afternoon, Reverend and Mrs. Fletcher. Thanks for coming over. Mother and Granny are waitin' for you in the parlor, Reverend. Mrs. Fletcher, I'll help you carry the pies to the kitchen," stated Mollie. Mrs. Fletcher set the pies on the kitchen table and then took off her long black cloak and untied her bonnet. "Mrs. Fletcher, if you don't mind cuttin' one of the pies I'll make us some tea," said Mollie. The two women set the kitchen table with a crisp, fine white linen tablecloth and then set out china dessert plates, forks, spoons, cups, and saucers. Mollie placed the tall, footed square honey dish in the middle of the table. She was getting ready to call the others, but they began walking into the kitchen.

"Oh, my dear Mollie, the table looks lovely! Thank you!" shouted Granny. "You're welcome, but Mrs. Fletcher helped out lots," replied Mollie. The group sat down to enjoy the peach pie and drink tea. While they ate, they talked about the plans for the funeral. Everyone decided that the funeral should take place at 10:00 in the morning in the parlor. The burial would follow at 10:30 in the family cemetery behind the barn. Reverend Fletcher stated that his wife and other women in the community would bring food for the family at dinnertime. When everyone finished eating Mollie and Mrs. Fletcher cleared the table and began to wash the dishes. The others retired back into the parlor. After twenty minutes had passed, Mollie and Mrs. Fletcher joined them where Granny and Nancy were quoting some of their favorite scripture passages.

Granny's German clock, made in 1695, struck three times. "My dear friends, it's time that my wife and I return home. We need to go around the community to help get organized for tomorrow. Until then," said Reverend Fletcher.

"Thanks so much for all that you've done for us, Reverend," stated Granny smiling. Reverend Fletcher kissed her hand and went out the door on his way. His wife followed him out to the wagon. "Good-bye," shouted Mollie. Mollie and the other women went back into the parlor where Granny sat down and started to play hymns on the piano and Nancy began to sing along. Overcome by a feeling of sadness Mollie strolled quietly into the kitchen and sat at the table weeping. She could not get the thoughts of her Granddad out of her mind. Remembering that her sisters would arrive in less than two hours she collected her thoughts and focused on helping Granny and Nancy prepare the evening meal as soon as they finished making music.

Granny stopped playing just as the clock struck 3:30. "Nancy, we oughta go into the kitchen and help Mollie prepare supper."

"Yes, Mrs. Williams, I agree," replied Nancy. With three women working diligently together, the meal would be ready in plenty of time for the guests. All of a sudden, they heard a wagon approaching. Mollie looked outside from the back porch and saw that Hiram and Carrie were arriving early. She went back inside the kitchen and told Nancy and Granny.

Hiram and Carrie stopped in front. Jacob jumped out and walked towards the back of the house to look for Mollie while his parents and siblings went inside the front door. The small children and Hiram went inside the parlor and Carrie walked back to the kitchen to help. Granny's parlor was the most lavishly decorated room in the entire house. Most of the furniture was Hepplewhite from the 1700s and looked as good as new. The Gehring children knew that Granny expected small children to sit quietly when they were in the parlor. In this room, family made important decisions and Granny entertained her company here. Meanwhile, Jacob helped his grandmothers cook and talked with Mollie about her upcoming move. Mollie whispered into his ear, "When your aunts and their families arrive later do not mention to them I'm movin'. I don't want to tell them until the day before I leave."

"I can't imagine why you don't want them to know, but I'll honor yer wishes, Mollie. All I can say is that when that day comes I'll miss you terrible," exclaimed Jacob. Being about the same age, they had grown up together and sometimes played together. Often Nancy took care of them both at the same time when they were toddlers.

Time passed and it was time for the others to arrive. They could hear wagons in the distance, and David and his family were walking across the road in front of the cherry lane. Even David's grandchildren carried food in their little arms. The wind began to blow and the clouds grew grey. Soon snowflakes began to fall slowly and lightly dust the ground and roads. Fortunately, everyone was almost to the front door.

Inside of the parlor, David Junior and his son Albert had placed several benches in three rows facing where the coffin would lie. Next, they placed a cherry wood catafalque in front of the first row. Albert draped a large blue cloth over it, and together they placed the coffin on the cloth. In only about fifteen minutes the family would seat themselves in the two front rows. The third rows seated their friends. Everything was now in its proper place. David and Albert waited for the rest of the family.

Soon Phoebe, Nancy, Mollie, and all of Nancy's daughters entered the room and sat down in front. The men in the family came and sat by their wives followed by the grandchildren, great-grandchildren, and the two great-great-grandchildren. Phoebe decided the funeral would be private for the family and a select few good friends. Finally, the friends from church walked into the room and sat down in their seats in the back rows.

Reverend Fletcher stood up and offered a word of prayer. He then began to read a background of Granddad's long life:

"David Williams was born on December 27, 1769, in New York City, New York to Albert and Mary Griffith Williams. He spent his early life attendin' grammar school as a young boy and later helpin' his father at his law office. In 1788, at the age of eighteen he followed in his father's footsteps and became a full-time attorney practicin' alongside his father. Then in 1791, after practicin' law fer three years he decided it was time to settle down, marry, and raise a family.

One day while he was out deliverin' depositions, he entered the home of Anton and Ada Haase Steg, German immigrants who spoke little English. Sittin' in the corner at her spinnin' wheel was their seventeen year-old daughter, Phoebe. She was one of the most beautiful women he'd ever laid eyes upon." Phoebe smiled as he said this. He continued:

"As time passed, David made frequent visits to the Steg home deliverin' deeds, etc. One day when he'd worked up enough courage he asked Phoebe if they could start courtin'. Her parents consented and so began the start of a long and happy relationship together. On March 31, 1792 on Phoebe's eighteenth birthday, they married.

"Four years later they had their first child Mary also called Mollie. In 1798, their first son, David, Jr. was born. They began to think they'd never have another child when in 1811, their second son, Isaiah, was born. Their last child and third son, Joseph, was born in 1814. Together with their four children they moved to Grayson County, Virginia in 1815.

"Phoebe's parents owned a 1,000 acre tract of land near Pine Mountain Township that they gave to them as a weddin' present. One of Anton's business partners came from Grayson and recommended the property. This family continually prospered as they added on 3,000 more acres stretchin' west towards Smyth County.

"We can be thankful what a close family they remain even up to our dear Mr. Williams's death. Let us pray again."

In conclusion, Reverend Fletcher told everyone what a kind, Christian man he was even to the last. Ladies from the church sang a hymn to conclude the service. Moments later, everyone rose up from their seats and strolled out through the front door. David, Jr., Albert, Hiram, Jacob, Abraham, and Robert serving as pallbearers lifted the casket, carried it out the front door, and placed it on a wagon by the front steps. Afterwards, the funeral procession advanced to the family cemetery located atop a hill one thousand feet behind the house. Phoebe and Nancy were the first ones to descend their carriage and wait beside the plot.

Mollie alighted from her horse and walked towards her father's grave. She began to weep thinking of her father's funeral a little over ten years before. This was the first burial in the Williams' Cemetery anyone had been to since Isaiah's death. She did not want to leave her father's grave but heard the wagon with her granddad's remains approaching.

The six pallbearers marched over to the funeral wagon. Next, they slid the coffin to the front and lifted it carefully. Finally, they walked towards David's plot, stood together for a moment of silence, and lowered the coffin into the grave. Phoebe's two great-great-grandchildren placed dried flowers on top of the casket and then ran to her and each held one of her hands. Reverend Fletcher said a final prayer and then everyone began to disperse.

While everyone else returned to the house to prepare for lunch, David and Albert stayed behind to fill the grave. After they finished they looked around the cemetery to make certain none of the markers were in disrepair. One particular stone caught the eyes of David and caused him to begin crying. It was the grave of his dearly departed first wife, Susannah. She had died just a week before his brother Isaiah, and although it was so many years ago he still missed her terribly. Snow began to fall heavier, and the men knew they must leave the hill before the road iced over.

Chapter 5

In early March of 1875, Granddad Williams's will was probated. Everyone in the family was summoned to Granny Williams's for the reading of the will. Uncle Joseph and Aunt Elsie were unable to attend due to the harsh winter, as the plains were still covered with snow and ice and prevented travel. Everyone else waited in anticipation of the arrival of the family attorney, Lorenzo Dow Mueller.

Suddenly, Granny's dogs began to bark uncontrollably. Granny rose from her chair and looked out the window. Mr. Mueller was arriving in his black phaeton carriage. It was still bitter cold outside, and you could see his warm breath before it dissipated into the air. Without a moment to spare Mr. Mueller climbed down carrying his papers and then made his way to the door.

David answered the door and showed Mr. Mueller into the parlor. "Good day, Lorenzo!" cried Phoebe.

"You're looking well today, Phoebe," replied Lorenzo. Lorenzo sat down and began to read Granddad's will. Mollie could not believe all that was contained within and how eloquently written it was until she recalled that Granddad had been an attorney until he was ninety years old. The farm and the adjoining 1,000 acres were jointly left to Granny and David. He would inherit the house and other buildings and any cash upon Granny's death as long as he cared for her in her last years. The remaining

3,000 acres were split between Uncle Jedediah Morgan (Aunt Mollie Williams Morgan's widower), Nancy, and Uncle Joseph Williams. Jedediah and Nancy inherited their spouse's portions with the stipulation that they would never sell them and upon their deaths their children would inherit the land. Granddad was determined that the Williams property would always remain in the family. Lorenzo finished the will and instructed the heirs to come into town in two weeks to sign their deeds. Uncle Joseph appointed Hiram as his power of attorney.

After Lorenzo left all of the women excluding Phoebe, who dozed off in her chair, went into the kitchen to prepare lunch. Robert sat in a corner quietly pondering how he could acquire Uncle Joseph's tract cheaply or free of charge. His hunger for more power began to consume him once again. He arose from his chair and left to look for Mollie. All the other men and the children were outside by now working.

Mollie was in the barn feeding the cows and horses. Suddenly, she heard the side door creak and then slam shut. It was Robert! "Hello, Mollie my dear. Is there anything I can do to help ya?" exclaimed Robert faking a pleasant tone. She ignored him and continued to work. Quickly, Robert marched in her direction and grabbed her arm holding it tightly. "I asked you a question, woman. Answer it!"

"Let go of my arm, or I'll scream," shouted Mollie. Immediately, he released her arm but refused to leave her side.

"Mollie, you've not been to the old cabin all winter, and I miss our meetins."

"Well, I've been busy helpin' Mother and Granny a few days each week," answered Mollie.

The thoughts of taking over Mollie's land clouded anything else in his mind. He must find a way to get his name on her deed. Robert had no inkling that Mollie had already sold her land to Hiram last year and Mollie's tract bordered the property that Uncle Joseph inherited. Somehow, and he was not exactly sure yet, acquiring Mollie's property would help him in his quest to take over Joseph's acreage. The more land he owned the greater his power would be in that part of the county.

"Is there anythin' I can do to make ya love me more and better gain your trust?" asked Robert.

Avoiding his question Mollie replied, "Mother and Granny both need my help even more now that spring is almost here. I just have too many chores to do, and I hate to disappoint Granny, because she specifically asked for my help." While Robert looked at Mollie about to say something, Jacob walked in and announced that lunch was ready. Mollie whispered in Jacob's ear, "Thank you!" Not understanding why she said that they left the barn arm in arm with Robert trailing behind them with a great scowl on his face.

After lunch Granny asked Mollie to go talk with her in her bedroom. All through lunch Granny perceived that she had a great look of concern and sadness on her face. "Come in and close the door, my darling," uttered Granny. "I noticed all day today that you've looked rather sad. Are you thinkin' of your Granddad? Is that what's botherin' you?" She was extremely reluctant to reveal the truth to Granny, but she realized she needed to confide in someone. Granny could be trusted to keep secrets, and she never judged anyone no matter how evil he or she might be. No one ever heard her say a single cross word about anyone. Instead, she tried to find the good in everyone.

"Granny, what I am about to tell you may come as a shock," cried Mollie.

"Go ahead, dear," interrupted Granny.

"You do know that I've got plans in April to go stay with Uncle Joseph and Aunt Elsie, right?"

"Yes, my dear, but I never questioned any reason why you'd leave us," stated Granny. "I know I'll be very heartbroken when that day comes. You look so much like my own dear Mollie." Granny tried to fight back tears, but a few streamed down her cheeks anyway.

"Well, I've a great confession to make, and I find it too humiliatin' to reveal to you," exclaimed Mollie almost in tears. "Last year I had an affair with Robert. He forced himself on me at first, but then for a while he changed, and I thought he really loved me. Then before winter he changed and started mistreatin' me and threatenin' me to silence. In the winter it were'nt too hard to avoid him, because I was able to stay busier inside helpin' Mother and you and Granddad." Granny looked at her with pity but said nothing and allowed her to continue talking without interruption.

"Finally, I got so disgusted and sore afraid that I decided I needed to leave Virginia for good. I sold my portion of Daddy's land to Hiram and Carrie. Like you and everyone else they never questioned my actions."

"Mollie, I've known Robert since he was a baby, and he was always trouble for his parents. When The War broke out he joined the Union, and that really upset his whole family. Some say he did it out of spite, because he hated his very own father. Even up to the day his father died, I never heard that Robert apologized to his father. His poor father died a brokenhearted man.

"What I'm tryin' to say, dear, is I've no doubt that what you tell me is true. I do got one question for you. Did you lose a child that was Robert's?"

Why would her dear Granny ask her such a question? She did say she trusted her and answered her question. "There were many times I thought I was a goin' to have Robert's child, but I guess I must be barren. Granny, I just don't think I'll ever have a child of my own," replied Mollie with tears in her eyes and a choked up voice. Granny comforted her and told her she would never reveal her secret to anyone. Although she would miss her so much, she told her that her decision to go to Kansas was a wise one.

Both women walked together into the parlor and joined the rest of the family. Granny had a big comforting smile on her face, so no one asked why she and Mollie were gone for so long. The day was growing late and everyone needed to return home. Everyone arose and said their goodbyes to Granny and left her alone with David, Jr.

As soon as Nancy and Mollie arrived at home, they remembered chores they needed to complete before nightfall. Nancy went to the kitchen to prepare for supper, and Mollie went to the barn to put away the horses and the wagon. No sooner had she entered the barn when she heard a man whistling near the cow stalls. Oh no! It was Robert!

"Good day again, Mollie. You didn't think I'd give up that easily did ya?" stated Robert. Robert's presence startled her immensely, and she needed to think of a way to get rid of him.

In the nicest tone of voice Mollie replied, "Robert, Jacob's coming over to have supper with me and Mother tonight. He said he'd be here at 6:30, and that's in thirty minutes." She put her watch back in her pocket. Robert did not want to confront Jacob, and knew he detested him greatly. He told her goodbye and walked home through the woods.

Jacob Gehring was almost six feet five inches tall. He had light blond hair, blue eyes, and was very muscular. This young man was truly a catch for any single woman in the whole county. He despised Robert, because he was his teacher in school and treated him horribly almost daily. Young Jacob grew five inches after he finished school, and this made Robert terribly afraid Jacob would seek revenge and beat him to his death. They avoided each other at all costs.

Mollie went to the kitchen to help her mother prepare supper. She could hear Jacob's wagon pull into the yard. He was bringing his personal belongings in preparation of moving in with Nancy. Jacob walked into the kitchen carrying an apple cake that his mother Carrie had made.

"Good evenin', Jake. So good to see ya," exclaimed Nancy. She kissed him on the cheek as he handed her the cake.

"I'm happy that you'll let me live with you, Grandma," replied Jacob.

After supper everyone went to bed. Until Mollie moved out Jacob would sleep on the hay in the loft of the barn.

Early the next morning before breakfast while Mollie was milking the cows, Robert, not knowing Jacob was living there, entered the barn. Very quietly he strolled over by Mollie who was humming her favorite hymn. "Good mornin', my dear Mollie. I'm here to invite ya to the log house after breakfast. It'd be great to cuddle together again after being apart so long. I've missed our times together."

"What do you mean you've missed yer times together?" stated Jacob with disbelief in his voice. Robert began to tremble unaware that his nephew was nearby putting away farm tools.

Mollie, who did not wish to reveal her secret, spoke up, "What Robert means is that he's missed spendin' time with me and Mother because of the hard winter." Jacob did not believe her, because he heard their entire conversation here and the time he caught them together at his great-grandmother's place. Looking over at Mollie he ascertained that there was apprehension and fear in her body language, but he did not question her. Jacob was an intelligent man and surmised that Robert and Mollie were having an affair. They were his uncle and aunt, so he did not utter a word. Robert hurriedly excused himself and left the barn as quickly as possible to avoid any further altercation.

"Jacob, I suppose I do owe you some sort of an explanation. After all, you've now seen me and Robert together twice in a rather compromisin' situation," stated Mollie embarrassed.

"Oh Mollie, you don't have to explain. It ain't none of my business," cried Jacob calmly.

"Well, I do feel like I can confide in you, since you'll be takin' care of Mother. Ever since last summer your Uncle Robert and I've been in an affair. Most of the time we met at the old log house to have romantic interludes together. At first, he was extremely kind to me, and I thought he'd truly loved me.

"I sincerely believed he'd divorce Eveline and marry me. Yes, I know we were committing adultery, but I was confused by what I thought was true love. Then a few weeks or maybe it was a whole month before winter, Robert started becomin' violent. He threatened my life if I told anyone about this or tried to break it off.

"Probably, what convinced him not to kill me was his interest in controllin' my share of Daddy's land. Robert's got no inkling that I sold my share to your parents. Jacob, I beg you to never mention this to anyone. You and Granny are the only ones who know."

"So that's why you're leavin' fer Kansas the end of this month. That explains a lot. Father and Mother only told me you'd be leaving. I had no idea they didn't know the real reason either. How does Grandma take it?"

"Mother's sad that I'm leavin', but she hasn't questioned my decision. I'm afraid she couldn't withstand the truth. You know her heart ain't very strong," replied Mollie.

Mollie and Jacob went to join Nancy for breakfast. Nancy had cooked some oatmeal that was rather lumpy and toasted some bread she baked yesterday. The kitchen aromas wafted out the door as they entered. "Good morning, Grandma. The food looks wonderful!" exclaimed Jacob.

"Thank you, Jake. Please give the blessin' before we et," answered Nancy.

While everyone was sitting down to breakfast, Robert was at the edge of the woods almost home. He was thinking out loud, "What's Jacob doing over there? This ruins my plans to catch Mollie alone today. I wonder how long he plans to stay. Well, there's one way to find out fer sure. I'll send Joshua over thar to find out fer me. He never fails me when I need anythin'.

Joshua Thomas was Eveline's adult son she had by her first husband, Ephraim Thomas and was devoted to Robert. He was now twenty-one years old but never knew his father. Ephraim was an older brother to Polly's husband Abraham and was on a turkey hunting trip in Wythe County with Robert when Joshua was only four months old. Robert and Ephraim got into an argument and Robert shot him dead. In a state of panic, Robert dragged Ephraim's body to a nearby cliff and threw the body down the side of the mountain into Wood's River. So that no one would suspect him, Robert threw Ephraim's rifle down the mountain as well which no one ever recovered. Robert told everyone that Ephraim slipped and fell on his own. At Ephraim's funeral his casket had to be closed because his skull had been crushed by the rocks near the river.

Robert prayed and made a promise to God that if he married Eveline he would treat Joshua as his own son and love him with all his heart. From that day forward Robert and Joshua became close and no love was ever lost.

As soon as he arrived home, he told Joshua to go visit his grandmother and find out how long Jacob would be staying. Joshua loved his stepfather and was always eager to please him. In one way, Joshua took after his great-grandmother Phoebe, in that he tried to always find the good in people. He never suspected that Robert had evil intentions. Despite being a truly terrible man Robert, remarkably had genuine love for Joshua, and Joshua sensed it at all times.

Nancy was outside hanging up clothes when Joshua arrived. Joshua was Nancy's oldest and favorite grandchild. He brought her a loaf of rye bread that his mother baked discreetly wrapped up in a reddish cloth placed in a basket.

"Hello, Grandma. Can I help with that?"

"That's all right, my dear, this be the last dress."

"Mother sent ya this loaf of rye bread to eat with yer dinner," replied Joshua.

"When ya go home after dinner you tell Eveline I thank her very much. Also, tell her to come help me with the quiltin' now that spring is a comin'," cried Nancy. Joshua knew better than to argue with her when she told him to stay for the midday meal. Nancy always made sure no one left her home hungry, and if you left without eating it was your own fault.

Together Joshua and Nancy went into the house to visit together and catch up on the latest news. Mollie and Jacob were also inside cleaning up the sitting room. "Good day, Joshua. What brings you here?" stated Mollie.

"Oh, I'd been so busy with my farm chores lately I thought I oughta come see Grandma," answered Joshua. Nancy smiled at him. "What brings you here, Jake? You're not usually over here this early of a day," continued Joshua.

Knowing that Joshua's parents would hear about it later that day Jacob chimed in, "I've decided to move in with Grandma and Mollie and help out with the heavier farm chores and harvestin'." Nancy decided to change the subject and talked about her plans for quilting and spring cleaning.

After lunch Nancy gave Joshua some quilt pieces to leave with Eveline. Joshua bade everyone goodbye and then walked towards the woods to go home. Robert was already waiting for him near the old log house. "Howdy, son. Did ya find out why Jacob's been thar so much?"

"I sure did, Father. Jake say he's moved in to help Grandma and Mollie with all of the backbreakin' farm chores." This news angered Robert immensely, but he tried not to show it in front of his son.

"Well, Son, let's go home and finish up our work before it gits too late." All the way home Robert grew angrier and angrier realizing that as long as Jacob was present, he would never be alone with Mollie. He thought to himself, "What am I gonna do? How'll I e'er gain control of her property?"

Mollie decided to write a letter to her Aunt Rebecca Patton, who lived in Chattanooga, Tennessee. Aunt Rebecca was Nancy's sister who was just a year younger. Her husband, Increase Patton, was a successful iron master and built a fine mansion along the Tennessee River. Although they were extremely affluent people, they chose to help the poor in any way possible. No one had seen them since before the War, but they sent letters to the Williams family each month.

Aunt Rebecca was a kind, caring, and generous person, and no one would believe she was a very wealthy woman until you visited her home. Mollie decided to write her and ask permission to stay with her a few days on her way to Kansas. As far as Nancy knew, there would be no reason why her sister should say no. There was still another whole month before she would embark on her journey out west. Surely, she would hear from Aunt Rebecca before she bought her train ticket. Regardless of the news, Mollie began packing her belongings in preparation of the trip.

Chapter 6

The first two weeks of April had come and gone, and Mollie still had not received an answer from Aunt Rebecca. She decided to go into town and purchase some items from Mueller's Mercantile. Naturally, while she was there she planned to collect any mail.

It was a beautiful April spring day. Only days before it had rained almost nonstop. The outside of the Williams home was surrounded by yellow and red tulips that Granny Williams had originally brought with her from New York. Granny had given bulbs to Isaiah and Nancy when they first built their homestead. Robins, cardinals, and blue jays were singing from the apple trees. The flowers and the music from the birds made it a perfectly cheerful day to go into town.

Mollie mounted Prince and rode swiftly into town. Before going to the mercantile she stopped by the livery stable to chat with Hiram. "Good day, Sister dear. Tomorrow is ze big day!" cried Hiram.

"I dread leavin' behind all my loved ones, but I'm eager to begin a new life in Kansas," replied Mollie.

"Carrie, ze twins, and I'll be over zis evenin' to spend your last evening meal at home vith you." Mollie smiled at Hiram, remounted Prince, and rode off to the mercantile.

When Mollie approached the store, Mr. Mueller was outside wearing an apron and sweeping the porch stirring up dust.

As Mollie walked past Mr. Mueller she coughed after getting dust caught in her throat. He graciously and humbly apologized. She continued to walk inside, and Mrs. Mueller, behind the counter, greeted her faithfully.

"Greetings to you, Mrs. Mueller," stated Mollie, "I need to purchase one pound a salt, a pound a soda, and ten pounds a coffee."

Mrs. Mueller smiled at Mollie and said, "I'll get the order together right away. Things are kinda slow today, and I'm betting people are enjoyin' a rain free day."

"Before I forget is there any mail for us, Mrs. Mueller?"

"Oh yes, there's a thick envelope addressed to you from a Mrs. Patton from Chattanooga, Tennessee."

It was exactly what Mollie hoped and prayed for to arrive before she boarded the train tomorrow. She was much too excited to wait until she got home and sat down on a chair. "Mrs. Mueller, take your time with my order. I want to go ahead and read the latest news from Aunt Rebecca." Mrs. Mueller nodded and continued to finish up the order without speaking.

Quickly, Mollie opened the envelope, unfolded the letter, and began to read:

April 7, 1875

Dearest Mollie,

I'm very pleased to hear that you wish to visit me for a few days on your way to Kansas. Your Uncle Increase and I discussed it, and we'd be happy to entertain you here as long as you want. The last time we saw you, you were only two years old. Now that you're almost eighteen, I'm certain that you're a beautiful young woman. Before you board the train at Rural Retreat send us a wire so that we'll know when to pick you up from the train station.

Love always,

Aunt Rebecca Patton

Enclosed with the letter was another letter addressed to Nancy. Mollie folded it up with her letter and put them into her basket. Next, she paid Mrs. Mueller for the supplies. As she left the store, Mr. Mueller apologized to her again for all the dust. She told him it was all right and remounted Prince. As she rode out of town she waved to Hiram as she passed the stables.

Knowing that it was her last full day at home, Jacob completed all of the chores while Mollie was in town. The only thing she needed to concern herself with was to finish packing. Nancy was in the kitchen preparing the evening meal with help from her mother.

Mollie dawdled a little on her way back home. The farms on either side of the main road were covered with tall green seedlings. She saw Mrs. Mueller's father, William Hatfield, walking in his fields pulling weeds. Mr. Hatfield tipped his straw hat as she rode past. "Good day to you, Mr. Hatfield," cried Mollie as she halted Prince. Then she climbed down and walked towards the split rail fence. Mr. Hatfield straightened up from being bent over yanking weeds and strolled towards Mollie slowly.

"I hate it that ya won't be a runnin' the mill anymore. You're the kindest miller in the county since your father used ta run it," stated Mr. Hatfield. He was one of Nancy's closest childhood friends and the family trusted him with Mollie's secret trip.

"Thank you, Mr. Hatfield. I'll miss all my regular customers. Of course, my nephew Jacob'll run it for Mother now. He makes a good replacement for me. Well, I gotta get on my way as I've some last minute packing to do." She remounted Prince and urged him to gallop away.

As soon as home was in sight, she saw Granny's black phaeton carriage parked in front. The mere presence of it made her cry; because she knew she might not ever see Granny again once she left Virginia. Suddenly, she smelled roasted chicken wafting through the air, and it made her smile to think that her mother cooked her favorite meal.

Granny was sitting on the front porch rocking and humming, "Bringing in the Sheaves." Mollie walked towards her and embraced her firmly with tears in her eyes. "Now don't cry, my child. I'll try to write you at least once a month, and I'll say a prayer for you every night before I go to bed," exclaimed Granny.

"Oh Granny, I'm going to miss you so much that I can hardly stand it. I wish you'd go with me," said Mollie.

"My dear, now that I am 101 years old I'm much too old to start a new life. I feel fine inside, but I don't think I could stand a long trip," exclaimed Granny. On March 31, they had celebrated Granny's 101st birthday outside in front of her home. Over 100 of her descendants and family friends had attended her party from all over the state.

Beside Granny on the porch was a large basket overstuffed and covered with a white hand woven bedspread. She reached over and picked up the bedspread carefully. Then she placed it on her granddaughter's lap. "I was a workin' on this just before your Granddad died. When I heard you were a leavin' I decided to give it to you and asked David's wife to help me finish it in time for yer trip." David had remarried after his first wife died.

"Thank you so much, Granny. I'll always treasure it," stated Mollie. She examined it carefully and noticed along the hem Granny had embroidered the words, "To my dear Mollie, from your loving Granny, Phoebe Williams, April 2, 1875." Mollie smiled and embraced her again tightly.

Next, Granny reached inside of the large oblong basket and pulled out a thin object wrapped with brown butcher paper and tied with white twine. She handed it to Mollie and asked her to unwrap it immediately. Mollie noticed that it was slightly heavy. Carefully, she untied the string and then tore off the paper. Tears filled inside her eyes once again. Inside was an 8x10 ornately hand-carved frame with an ambrotype photo of Granddad and Granny taken for their sixtieth wedding anniversary behind very thick beveled glass.

Granddad had carved the frame out of walnut wood and carefully carved tulips all over it. "This is for you to remember me each day while you're in Kansas." Mollie's face beamed with joy as she held the photograph close to her heart. Both women continued to sit on the porch singing their favorite hymns.

Hours later, it was almost time to go eat supper in the kitchen. Hiram and Carrie and their children were arriving up the lane followed by Abraham and Polly and their family. Robert, Eveline, and their family went to his mother's for supper and knew nothing about this gathering. Mollie was more at ease knowing she would not have to embellish the truth about her morning departure.

Together holding hands Granny and Mollie walked over towards the kitchen. The odors of roasted chicken, fresh whole wheat bread, and dried apple pies rushed out of the kitchen door and the open windows. Granny and Mollie welcomed the enticing scents as they entered the kitchen and sat down at the table. Grandma Greene had already set the table and was sitting down waiting for the others.

Soon they heard the laughter of the small children approaching the boardwalk. As each person entered, the floor creaked. Polly and Carrie both went over to their mother and hugged and kissed her. The men helped all of the children sit down right away.

After everyone sat down, Grandpa Greene stood up and asked the blessing. Everyone held hands until he finished. Various family members asked Mollie questions about what she planned to

79

do as soon as she settled. She smiled back and cordially responded. This last meal together was filled with laughter and sometimes tears but a night they would certainly remember years from now.

It was getting late and the children were beginning to fall asleep sitting on the floor. Usually everyone retired to bed by 9:00 each night, but since it was Mollie's last night they stayed until almost 11:00. Everyone got up and said their farewells. Mollie persuaded Granny to spend the night and Granny willingly obliged.

Once everyone was gone Mollie went up into the loft to her bedroom. Granny slept with Nancy. All three were exhausted and fell asleep immediately.

Chapter 7

Mollie awoke the next morning to find a breakfast tray beside her bed. She lifted it and found that the food was still warm and smelled heavenly. On the tray was a small note written in Nancy's handwriting, "I wanted your last morning to be in comfort."

Moments later, Nancy was at the bottom of the ladder calling up to Mollie, "Time to git ready, my dear. Hiram'll be here in an hour to take ya to meet the train over thar at Rurl Retreat."

"I'll be down in a minute, Mother," replied Mollie who then hurriedly gulped down some of her breakfast and leaving the rest on the tray.

Nancy returned to the kitchen where Granny was helping to make Mollie a basket lunch for the trip. Meanwhile, Mollie was busy packing her clothes into her Saratoga trunk. Carefully, she placed all of the gifts from Granny inside and her leather-bound photographic album that had photos of all of her family members. She paused to think about all that she would be leaving behind. Most of all, she would miss her mother and the wonderful times they spent together. Nancy always treated her equally and valued her opinions even as a small child. Tears started to stream down her cheeks.

Finally, Mollie had gathered together everything she needed for the trip. Now she would go downstairs to spend her last hour at home with her dear mother and Granny. As she climbed down from the loft she could hear the voices of Nancy and Granny talking and laughing outside in the yard. Mollie soon joined them. She handed Nancy the letter she forgot to give her the day before. Nancy accepted it and kissed Mollie on the cheek.

The three women strolled to the front and sat on the front porch. "Mollie, don't worry about yer trunk. I've already asked Jacob to bring it down fer ya," stated Nancy with a smile. She smiled back at her mother and grasped her right hand firmly.

"Oh Mother and dear Granny, I don't know what I am a going' do without you both. I could always count on your sage advice and your listenin' ears," sobbed Mollie.

"Don't worry, my dear. We can always write each other, and I'll pray fer you every day. Despite our distance our love fer each other'll remain just as close," replied Granny. She embraced Mollie and kissed her on the cheek.

"Yes, my dear daughter. Ya can count on me and Granny to keep ya in thought as ya also think of us," exclaimed Nancy. Nancy kissed her daughter on her other cheek.

Hiram's wagon was finally approaching. Carrie was with him as well as the twin sons, Karl and Gottfried. Jacob walked across the yard from the barn to fetch Mollie's trunk. He waved to his parents and then went upstairs.

Hiram climbed down from the wagon and went to assist his oldest son. Carrie walked carefully as the twins ran over to Nancy and Granny. "And how're my two little boys?" exclaimed Nancy.

"We're just fine, Grandma," answered the boys in unison. Nancy gave each one a stick of candy from out of her sewing basket. She always kept candy wrapped up in brown paper and hidden for the youngest ones. Meanwhile, Mollie and Granny were talking about the trip to Chattanooga.

Minutes later Jacob and Hiram carried the Saratoga trunk and loaded it onto Hiram's wagon. It was time for Mollie to leave. She walked over to her mother and whispered in her ear, "Mother, I love you very much, and I'm sorry for leavin'. Someday, I'll let you know everythin'." Nancy and Mollie both had tears rolling down their cheeks. Then she moved over to Granny and hugged her tightly and told her she loved her. Granny smiled back and had tears in her own eyes.

"Vell, Mollie, ve've got to get going. Ve hav to send a vire to Aunt Rebecca to tell her you're coming," stated Hiram.

Everyone said their parting words, embraced, cried a little, and laughed some. Hiram and Mollie climbed into the wagon and rode away. Mollie waved to everyone as they stood in the yard while the twins ran behind them saying "Goodbye" over and over.

The scenery on the way to Rural Retreat was breathtaking. Some wildflowers were blooming and pointing their faces towards the bright warm sun. Their pure, clean scents were hypnotic to the senses. Farmers were in their fields too busy to notice anyone traveling on the road.

Suddenly, it began to thunder and the clouds were growing darker and darker. Small raindrops started falling in delayed succession. "I better put up ze canvas before ve get soaked to ze bone," stated Hiram.

"I'll help ya so we can get it in place faster," answered Mollie.

When they left home the clouds looked just fine, so they thought the trip would be without consequence. Within a few moments the canvas was in place.

All the way to Rural Retreat it stormed heavily. The roads now covered with mud proved to be cumbersome. Hiram had to slow down the wagon to avoid an accident. "I hope ve can still make it on time to send ze vire," exclaimed Hiram with a worried look on his face. Mollie was not the least bit worried, because she had complete trust in Hiram's driving ability.

Hours later they arrived at the train station with only about twenty minutes to spare. Mollie climbed down from the wagon and strolled over to the telegraph office.

"I'll take your zings and buy ze ticket. Ve need to hurry," cried Hiram. Hiram found a porter to help carry her heavy trunk to the platform near the train to Bristol. Next, he went to the ticket counter to purchase a ticket to Chattanooga with a stop in Bristol. Meanwhile, Mollie sent a telegraph to her Aunt Rebecca.

Minutes later, Mollie found Hiram standing by the train. "All aboard!" cried one of the conductors.

"Thank you, Hiram, for all that you've done for me. I'll never forget you for this," stated Mollie tearfully. Hiram kissed her on the cheek with tears in his own eyes.

"Ve vill all miss you terribly. Write us ven you get to Kansas and send us a vire ven you arrive in Chattanooga," replied Hiram. Both parties bade each other farewell as Mollie boarded the train.

As soon as the train was well underway, Mollie unpacked her lunch from her square lunch basket that her father had woven. An elderly woman, dressed in red from head to toe, sat beside her and read from her Bible. "Would you like one of my sandwiches? I've got more than enough for me," asked Mollie.

"Thank you, dear child. Bless ya fer yer kindness," exclaimed the woman grasping Mollie's hand.

"My name's Mollie Williams, and I'm from Pine Mountain Township."

"Pleased to meet ya! I'm Charlotte Padgett from Danville. My son lives in Bristol, and I'm a goin' to spend a few weeks with him. Whar you a goin', my dear?"

"I'm stoppin' to visit my aunt in Chattanooga on my way to Kansas. I've decided to start a new life," replied Mollie.

"You're a very brave young woman to embark on such a journey. That's quite a burden for someone without a husband," exclaimed Mrs. Padgett.

"I don't mind so much. It's time to leave my problems behind. Someday I hope to be as happy as I was as a child," said Mollie.

"If ya don't mind me a askin', are you a tryin' to leave a lost love?" stated Mrs. Padgett.

"Since we *are* strangers and you're kind I'll tell you a little about it. I'm leavin' behind a man who I loved at first but turned out to be a horrible person. He only wanted me for my land and wouldn't consent to marriage. At first, he was extremely kind, but as time went on he became abusive," stated Mollie sadly.

"Oh, you poor dear! I hope ya find someone someday who'll love ya fer yerself. I've got a feeling things'll work out well fer ya. You got a strong head on yer shoulders, and you're generous and kind. Mollie, you remind me of myself at yer age," exclaimed Mrs. Padgett with a big smile.

Mollie smiled back. They had talked so long that they were almost in Bristol. The conductor came down the aisle announcing that they would be arriving in fifteen minutes. She had never been to Bristol but knew it must be a very pretty town.

The Bristol train station was of course larger than the one at Rural Retreat. On the platform were several well-dressed people waiting for passengers. One of the children was playing with a long stick hitting it against the tracks. She heard a man yelling at the child telling him to stop. Mollie giggled to herself quietly.

"That's my grandson, Charles. He's always inventin' ways to get himself in trouble. My son Frank, his father, acted just like that when he was that age. We thought he'd never outgrow it," said Mrs. Padgett laughing.

"I'll get your bags fer ya, Mother," stated Frank.

Mrs. Padgett sat on the bench with her grandson who adored her and behaved in front of her. Mollie went to the ticket agent to find out when the train was leaving for Chattanooga. The next train was not leaving until the following morning at 8:15 am. She found out the afternoon train had been canceled due to problems with the engine and should be repaired by morning.

"Mollie, you can come spend a night with us at my son's home. He lives just a few streets down from here, and I know he'll not mind bringin' ya back to the station," exclaimed Mrs. Padgett.

"I 'preciate your kindness, Mrs. Padgett, and I accept your most generous invitation."

Frank returned with the bags and put them in the back of his wagon. His mother asked a porter to help him put Mollie's things in the back, as well. "Mother, I hope you don't mind, but I invited my old friend Robert over fer supper. He's in town on business and will also stay the night," stated Frank. Molly felt slightly uneasy at the mere mention of anyone named Robert.

"I don't mind at all. It'll be nice to see him after all these years," cried Mrs. Padgett.

All four climbed into the wagon and rode away to Frank's home. When they arrived moments later Frank's wife was in the front yard tending her flowers and cutting a few stems for the dinner table. She waved to them but said nothing. Mollie was beginning to think that her host's wife was rather rude, but she made no complaints. After all, she was a guest in their house. Mrs. Padgett, Mollie, and little Charles walked inside holding hands. Frank carried his mother's bags up to the guest room. His wife came after him with her flowers for the table still very silent and on her way into the kitchen.

In the distance they could hear the sounds of another wagon approaching. "It must be Frank's friend," thought Mollie to herself. She went into the kitchen to ask her hostess to help with supper. Once again she ignored her. Charlotte happened to be standing in the doorway and heard everything.

"Dear Mollie, Hannah won't answer you because she's deaf and dumb. The poor thing was in an accident three year ago and lost her hearin' and ability to speak. Since that time Frank and Charles have learned signin'."

While they were talking they heard a knock at the front door. Frank answered it and led his visitor into the front parlor. Charlotte and Mollie stayed in the kitchen to help Hannah prepare supper. Charles was in his room playing until someone came for him.

Two hours later supper was ready. Charlotte persuaded Charles to set the dining room table for six people using their best china. Hannah brought the roast duck and placed it in the center of the table. Mollie carried the potatoes to the table. Charles rushed back to the kitchen and returned with a pitcher of cold water. It was now time to sit down to supper.

"Charles, would ya please go fetch your father and his friend?" cried Charlotte.

"Yes, Grandma!" replied Charles loudly.

Hannah and the other women sat down and waited for the men. She smiled at Mollie and signed a hello to her and a thank you for her help.

The men arrived and Mollie had a surge of fear build up in her body. Frank's friend was none other than her own terrible brother-in-law. Robert was just as shocked to see her there too; however, he hid his anger behind a fake smile and said "Good day" to her.

"Oh, do you know each other?" asked Frank.

"Robert's married to my oldest sister, Eveline," replied Mollie nervously.

"Well, what a coincidence that you two met in Bristol," laughed Frank.

Frank and Robert sat down and Charlotte said the supper blessing. Suppertime was quiet except for the occasional exchanging of words between Robert and Frank.

Hours later, it was time to go to bed. Charles had already been in bed for an hour. "Mollie, you can sleep in my room," stated Charlotte.

Robert quickly glanced at Mollie with a look of disappointment. He had hoped to go into her room after everyone else had retired for the night. "Please excuse us, folks. I need to take Mollie outside fer a minute to tell her somethin' in private," stated Robert.

Mollie did not want to accompany him even in church but did not want to arouse any suspicion.

"What're you doin' here in Bristol? Nobody told us you were plannin' a trip," exclaimed Robert.

"I'm goin' to visit Aunt Rebecca Patton over in Chattanooga tomorrow," replied Mollie.

Robert raised his hand and slapped Mollie across the face. "I told ya to ne'er leave town or I'd kill ya. Don't ya e'er listen to what I tell you? Your mother's a goin' to find out about our affair, because I'm a goin' to tell her you threw yourself at me," cried Robert.

Mollie held her face tightly and sobbed quietly to herself too afraid to speak. Unknown to them Hannah was outside by the garden pouring the dishwater on the flowers. She had witnessed the entire incident and was afraid to move right away.

Both Robert and Mollie went back inside to get ready for bed. Charlotte noticed that something was wrong with Mollie but did not wish to pry. Robert had a devilish grin on his face as he ascended the stairs up to the extra guest room.

"Come with me, Dear, and we'll go up to bed too," said Charlotte jovially. Charlotte led her upstairs to her room. Inside was one of the most lavishly carved beds that had a headboard so tall it almost reached the ceiling. On either side of the bed were marble-topped Hepplewhite nightstands. Each table had a pressed glass oil lamp etched with roses on it. Hannah had placed a bowl of fruit on the table beside the settee near the window in case they were hungry in the middle of the night.

Charlotte fell asleep rather quickly, but Mollie lay awake worried about what Robert might do to her; however, she knew as long as she stayed close to Charlotte no harm would come to her. She sprang out of bed and bolted the door, just in case. Her roommate began to snore lightly which made Mollie giggle to herself. Finally, after an hour of thinking to herself, she dropped off to sleep.

Early the next morning, Mollie awoke to the smells of coffee, fresh biscuits, and sizzling beef bacon. Robert and Frank were outside feeding the livestock and Hannah was tending to the delicious breakfast aided by her mother-in-law. Mollie got out of bed, washed up, and put on her traveling clothes. "Breakfast's ready!" shouted Charles.

After breakfast, it was time to return to the train station. Frank had the team ready and Robert had already left the premises. Charlotte, Charles, and Hannah waved goodbye to Mollie as she rode away. "Thanks for everythin!" shouted Mollie.

Minutes later they returned once again to the train station. They still had a whole hour to spare before the train left, and Frank decided to wait with her. She felt like she had known him all her life he was so easy to talk with. "I appreciate your kindness to me. This is my first time travelin' alone, and I was sore afraid to spend the night in the train station," exclaimed Mollie.

"That's perfectly all right, Mollie. Anybody who shows kindness towards my sainted mother can't be all bad," stated Frank in a jovial manner.

It was time to board the train. Frank handed her the square basket refilled with sandwiches Hannah made for her. "Feel free to come stay with us again next time you're a passin' through," exclaimed Frank.

"Many thanks for the kind offer, but this may be the last time I ever see Virginia," replied Mollie.

Robert happened to be in the crowd hoping to catch a glimpse of her before she left and overheard what she expressed to his friend. "I wonder what she meant by that?" thought Robert to himself about to boil with anger, "I'll find a way to bring her back from Chattanooga. Nothing's gonna stop me."

The train left right on time bound for Tennessee. Sitting beside her was a young couple holding a set of twins no more than a year old. They hardly made a fuss as the train went on its way. She smiled at the couple and they smiled back.

Time passed quickly as Mollie and the couple conversed together. Five hours hardly felt long enough to them as they enjoyed one another's company so well. "We're approachin' Chattanooga," cried out the conductor. Mollie had never been to Chattanooga, but she was eager to become better acquainted with her Aunt Rebecca.

Chapter 8

When the train arrived at the station there was already a footman waiting by the platform. As the train came to a complete stop Mollie noticed him right away. The footman was not easily avoidable. He stood over six feet tall, was dressed in a formal black suit, and had skin like mahogany. His hair was long of pure white tied in the back beneath his footman's hat.

After Mollie descended the steps of the train, she approached the footman. "My name's Mollie Williams, and I believe you're here to take me to the Patton home."

"Yes, Madam. I'm Pierre. Show me your bags and then we'll be on our way," stated the footman. One of the porters assisted Pierre as he carried the trunk over to the black brougham carriage. Some of the passengers stared as Mollie, dressed in her plain clothing, entered the brougham, because very few middle class people could afford one.

The road in the country to the Patton Plantation was rather picturesque. As they traveled down the road it followed along the beautiful Tennessee River. Several small fishing boats scattered it in both directions. On the opposite side of the road there stood half a dozen plantations with stately mansions dotting the landscape. Mollie was in awe as she tried to take in the wonderful sights. No matter how impressed she was, she still preferred her simple home life back in Virginia.

A half hour passed and they neared the entrance to the Patton home. The lane was aligned on both sides by willow trees. Aunt Rebecca's home looked somewhat minuscule in the distance, as it was half a mile from the entrance to the main road. As they got closer, the mansion grew in size and proudly displayed its beautifully manicured gardens in front against its humongous walls. Mollie sat in awe, once again, of what looked like a home of at least fifty rooms.

When the brougham stopped by the stone stairs at the entrance, a very tall, Negro man wearing a powdered wig standing totally erect in a butler's uniform stood at the top of the steps. Pierre motioned for the butler to come help with the trunk and her other personal belongings. "You may call me Vincent, and I'm here to assist you in any way," stated the butler in a perfect English accent.

She surmised that he was probably from England or Africa originally but really had no interest in asking him. He was after all a servant and only there to do his duty.

Aunt Rebecca came rushing out of the house and grabbed Mollie embracing her tightly. At the same time, Pierre and Vincent carried the trunk inside and on up to Mollie's guest chamber. "Look at you, my dear niece! You're so much differnt now and very beautiful. I think you was just two year old the last time I saw ya and holdin' yer daddy's hand ever so tight," exclaimed Aunt Rebecca joyfully.

"Yer Uncle Increase will be so pleased to see ya when he gets home from his office."

"Yes, I'll be happy to see him too. I can't remember much about him, I'm sorry to say. If I could be so bold as to say, 'What're we havin' for supper?' I'm kinda tired and hungry after the trip," replied Mollie.

"Go on up to yer room and take a short nap before supper. I'll send Vincent after you in due time. Cynthia, our cook, is preparin' a scrumptious beef roast along with many delectable vegetables. For dessert we've got a delicious raspberry torte," stated Aunt Rebecca, "I got that there recipe from the Governor's wife." Mollie's mouth watered at the thoughts of those tasty dishes. She almost hated to take a nap but knew it was needed. Aunt Rebecca told her that her room was the first room at the top of the stairs on the right of the grand fireplace.

The grand front hall had marble statues of various Greek and Roman deities. Above the marble staircases hung a massive majestic crystal chandelier inlaid with gold. This was clearly the most luxurious and most beautiful home she had ever seen in her life. She ascended the staircase to the right of the enormous fireplace and went to her room to wash up and take a nap. In the corners of the room stood ancient Chinese vases which surrounded a fireplace so large, a six-foot tall man could stand straight up inside of it. The floor was so shiny it reminded her of polished glass.

Two hours later, Vincent knocked on the door announcing that supper was almost ready. "Thank you, Vincent."

"Yes, Madam."

Vincent and Mollie descended the stairs and on in the direction of the dining room. He led her to her seat at one of the largest tables she had ever seen. The legs were eagles' claws clasping balls. There was enough room to easily seat thirty-two people. This table was bedecked with the finest white linen, eighteenth century blue and white china, and sterling silver flatware. At each plate was a crystal footed salt cellar with a miniature sterling spoon. The crystal water goblets were filled to the rims with water from the spring house.

Aunt Rebecca and Uncle Increase had already seated themselves at the end of the table near the fireplace. As soon as Vincent helped her sit down beside them, Uncle Increase prayed for the meal to be blessed. Uncle Increase did not believe in conversations during the meal, so they remained quiet until everyone was finished with dessert. Just as they were about to get up, Vincent announced, "Tea will be served in the conservatory."

Once inside the conservatory Aunt Rebecca had a surprise to reveal to Mollie. "Now Mollie, there's something I wanna do fer ya before ya move to Kansas, and I'll not take 'no' for an answer."

"Go ahead, Auntie. I'll listen," replied Mollie.

"Tomorrow, I want us to go into town and purchase fer ya some new dresses. Thar's a dress shop on Main Street that sells all the latest fashions," stated Aunt Rebecca eagerly.

By the look on Mollie's face, Aunt Rebecca could tell she wanted to refuse her offer. "I just want ya to look yer very best out on the frontier. Please don't deprive yer dear Auntie of showin' her love fer her dear ones."

Mollie smiled back at her and thanked her. The three persons began to enjoy the tea that Vincent served to them.

After tea time it was growing late and everyone was ready to retire for the evening. "I really am pleased that you'll be stayin' with us a week," exclaimed Uncle Increase with a slight smile on his face. Uncle Increase usually did not smile a lot due to having a lot of aches and pains inside; however, he continued to bless God each day for another day of life and strived to find ways to help those less fortunate. Rebecca and Increase's only child Kathleen and her husband Lawrence Hairston were on a missionary trip to Africa to carry on the family passion for helping those in need.

"Good night dear. It's been a great day talkin' with you, but tomorrow's our big shoppin' day," stated Aunt Rebecca pleasantly and yawning afterwards.

"Vincent'll make sure that you wake up in plenty a time to wash up and get dressed before breakfast," said Uncle Increase.

"I appreciate all that you do for me and more," replied Mollie. She kissed them and embraced them before going to her room. Once inside of her room she realized how totally exhausted she really was. Despite being tired she had great difficulty falling asleep in a strange bed.

Mollie's room was huge. It was almost as large as her mother's entire home. On both sides of the bed there stood ornately carved marble top tables. On the left bedside table was a crystal water carafe in case she became thirsty during the night. Near the large bedroom window with scarlet red velvet drapes sat a Chippendale settee and matching style coffee table. On the table was a cut glass bowl filled with fresh fruit and in another bowl beside it some of the finest chocolate money could buy. Seeing those wonderful things put a beaming smile on her face and a warm and cheerful feeling on the inside. "They're really very good to me," thought Mollie to herself.

Early the next morning, Vincent knocked on Mollie's door about 5:30. "Time to get ready for breakfast, Madam."

"Thank you, Vincent," exclaimed Mollie.

She arose and climbed off the bed to prepare for the day. One thing that impressed her was the fact that her bedroom had its own water closet with a full-size bathtub. Never in her life had she partaken of such a luxury. Most people used a washstand with a bowl and pitcher and towels. This was something she definitely could grow accustomed to.

Breakfast was served at precisely 6:30am. Vincent led Mollie into a separate breakfast room that adjoined the kitchen. The meal consisted of three types of sausages, omelets, wheat and rye toast, various jams, and orange juice. Mollie was eager to taste a little of everything as the food tempted the eyes. As always, the meal was quiet and no one conversed until breakfast was completed.

"Before we go to the dress shop we gotta stop by the church. I need to make arrangements for the dinner we're havin' next Sunday after service," exclaimed Aunt Rebecca, "It shouldn't take us long. Since it is such a beautiful day today, I think we'll have our lunch in town at one of the restaurants."

"Whatever you decide, Auntie, will be perfectly fine with me. I've never eaten at a fancy city restaurant before, and I think that'll be most enjoyable," stated Mollie. Just before they left Mollie went to her room to get some writing paper to write some letters while she waited for Aunt Rebecca at the church.

Uncle Increase went into town in his own private brougham with his own driver. Aunt Rebecca and Mollie entered Aunt Rebecca's brougham driven by Pierre.

Later on, the drive to the church was rather long, but the scenery was absolutely breathtaking. Fields of spring wheat were still a lush green tint. Other fields of wildflowers produced a soothing aroma.

Along the way to the church they passed a tavern and who should be standing outside ready to leave it was none other than Robert Sutherland. Mollie and Rebecca did not notice him, but he saw Mollie and recognized her immediately.

Robert proceeded to follow them but kept a safe distant pace so as not to draw attention. He was determined to approach her and discover a way to convince her to come back to Virginia and deed her land to him; however, he knew he needed to devise his plan to treat her in a delicate manner. Already, he had hurt and abused her numerous times, and he was afraid she might never trust him again.

Moments later, they were within sight of the church. Pierre parked the brougham by the front steps, climbed down, and helped Mollie and Aunt Rebecca out of the coach. "Return for us in half an hour," stated Aunt Rebecca, "I'm a goin' to meet with the reverend's wife and the other ladies of the church. Mollie, you can go wait in the reverend's office to write yer letters."

"See ya later, Auntie. I wanna get started right away on these letters to Mother and Granny."

"Give them my best and all my love."

"I will."

Aunt Rebecca left her alone in front of the reverend's office. Meanwhile, Robert was stopping in front of the church in anticipation of finding a moment alone with Mollie. He stealthily entered the church making little noise in search of Mollie. Quickly, but carefully, he walked past the reverend's door which was ajar and caught a glimpse of a woman's dress. Thinking it must have been someone else he continued on down the hall looking inside of the Sunday school rooms and then the sanctuary. Inside the sanctuary the women's committee was holding its meeting.

"Are you a lookin' for anybody in particular, Sir?" stated the reverend's wife.

"Uh, no. I was just havin' a look round. I just might start attendin' church here," exclaimed Robert lying though his teeth. Aunt Rebecca had not seen him in fifteen years, so she did not recognize him. His voice was slightly familiar to her, but she had no time to ask about it. He then went back down the hall to the office. Next, he opened the door quietly peeking in to see the woman at the desk. It was Mollie!

Mollie was seated in the corner writing her letters unaware that she was being watched. Suddenly, she heard the door close and looked up. She began to have a feeling of uneasiness. "Robert, what're you doing in Chattanooga?"

"I'm here on business. Eveline sold some cattle to a friend a mine livin' here. We met in Bristol, and he invited me here fer a spell." She found it so hard to believe his story but tried not to show any emotion.

"Why'd ya leave me alone all this time? I've been miserable without ya. It's been so long since we spent a lot of time together," cried Robert.

"I just wanted to get away for a while and think about what I'm a goin' to do for the rest of my life," stated Mollie nervously but convincingly.

"Come back home with me tonight. I promise I'll be good to ya. Why, I'll even help ya farm yer part of the land to make things easier fer ya and yer mother," exclaimed Robert.

"Jacob's there to help Mother while I'm gone. In a week or so I'll be going home and things oughta be back to normal. Robert,

I promise you we can work things out somehow when I get back," said Mollie in a persuasive tone of voice. Robert appeared to accept what she said was sincere and from the heart. At the moment, he had no reason to disbelieve her and was completely satisfied.

The women's meeting was beginning to disband and they heard some of the women coming down the hall. Before he left; however, he told Mollie that he looked forward to her return. He kissed her directly on the mouth and embraced her tightly. Mollie wiped her mouth. Hurriedly, Robert left the office and made his way outside to leave. In his mind he began plotting ideas to take over her deed. Once he had her land and Eveline's together it would be easier to control the water rights and then force their sisters to pay for them.

Mollie went into the hall and her Aunt Rebecca said, "We can go into town to the dress shop now, dear."

"I *am* looking forward to getting new clothes and store bought at that. All of ours were stitched by hand," cried Mollie excitedly but still nervous after her encounter with Robert. They strolled outside together and found Pierre waiting for them. He climbed down and helped them enter the brougham and then they went on their way.

Chattanooga's city center was very impressive. The street was booming with wagons traveling in both directions. Several shops along the main street had potted plants neatly arranged in front of them. Some of the shopkeepers were busily sweeping in front of their stores awaiting their first customers.

"Good morning, Mrs. Patton," shouted Mrs. Martin, the dress shop owner. Peering out of the window Aunt Rebecca shouted back to her, "Greetings to ya, Miss Martin. My niece and I are here to purchase goods from ya. I want the very best for her."

Mrs. Martin smiled back at Aunt Rebecca. She ascertained that she was going to make a considerable sale with her. After all, the Pattons were one of the wealthiest families in Chattanooga, if not the wealthiest. Mollie and Aunt Rebecca exited the coach and walked towards Mrs. Martin. Mrs. Martin went into her shop with Mollie and Aunt Rebecca following close behind her. Never in her life had Mollie seen so many elegant and fashionable dresses. Aunt Rebecca told her to select five complete outfits which included matching bonnets, stockings, and shoes. All of the dresses in this particular shop were either made from silk or linen and there was such a large assortment that Mollie had trouble making a decision.

Later, Pierre met them by the door to carry the large packages to the brougham. Mollie's face beamed with happiness as she left the store; however, at the same time she felt guilty about accepting such expensive gifts even from a wealthy relative. She had been reared to accept what she had in life no matter what her station was. Not wishing to hurt her aunt's feelings she made certain that she had an outward expression of gratitude. Several times she thanked Aunt Rebecca for her generosity to reassure her that she was pleased.

Before going home they drove to an elegant restaurant situated on the main street of the business district. A man in a uniform greeted them as they stopped near the entrance. Next, he helped the ladies dismount the coach and then led them inside to where the manager was standing. Mollie had never in her life eaten in an expensive restaurant and felt slightly overwhelmed by its fancy décor.

The manager who knew Aunt Rebecca seated them at one of the best tables in the restaurant. "Good to see ya again, Mrs. Patton. I hope you'll enjoy yer stay with us. Don't hesitate to ask fer my personal assistance at any time." He left them with one of the best and friendliest waiters on duty.

"Good aftanoon, ladies. My name's Bue, and I's here to serve ya. May I begin by pourin' ya a glass a water?"

"Thank you, Bue. My niece and I'd like a few moments to make our decision about what we wanna eat."

"Yes, madam."

Bue was a young Negro man almost six feet tall with a slim, toned build. He had a short moustache that was almost shaved off and had short dirty brown hair. Mollie paid no attention to him despite his handsome appearance. Growing up she was conditioned to think of Negroes as second class citizens.

"My dear, Bue Cunningham's been my own special waiter fer the last four years. I don't think I've ever seen a more dedicated, hard-workin' young man in my life. He'll always be special to my heart, because four year ago he risked his life to save mine when a robber came in a shootin' up tha place.

Bue pulled me down to the floor just in time missin' a getting' a bullet himself."

Aunt Rebecca was so grateful to Bue that she decided to add him in her will. He had no idea she did this but always appreciated her continuous kindness towards him.

He returned and told them about the specialties of the house. The ladies decided to order steaks with baked potatoes and fresh tomato and cucumber salads. For dessert they ordered an apple strudel. Bue brought them each a china teacup filled with orange spiced tea.

"If ya need anythin' else I'll be right cheer."

"Thank you, Bue. We oughta be fine for now," exclaimed Aunt Rebecca.

Mollie and Aunt Rebecca ate their lunch and then their dessert. Both women had a wonderful time together talking about their families as they drank their piping hot tea.

The afternoon hours were passing quickly and they needed to return home before Uncle Increase came home. Aunt Rebecca left a most generous tip on the table, and then they told the manager farewell and went out to their coach. Pierre helped them in and then they went on their way. Seeing the packages again rekindled her utter joy at receiving such beautiful clothes.

Days later, it was time for Mollie to prepare for her trip to Kansas. In order to save her some money Uncle Increase prepaid her ticket to Kansas City, Kansas. He also paid the extra money so that she could sleep in a parlor car in between stops to save time. As a final gift Uncle Increase and Aunt Rebecca gave her $500 to help in her quest to start a new life. Finally, they told her if she needed anything else to contact them immediately by telegraph and they would send her whatever amount she needed. Mollie thought to herself that she had no intention of further imposing upon their generosity but embraced them and thanked them cordially, regardless.

Early the next morning, Mollie arose early to her last chance at bathing in an indoor water closet. She decided to soak in the bathtub an extra twenty minutes. Although she could do without the luxurious home and furnishings she sorely missed the bathtub already.

After she climbed out and dried off she put on one of her new dresses with a matching hat and stockings and shoes. The dress was deep navy blue linen with a matching jacket. She looked absolutely regal and could rival even the wealthiest woman in the country. Mollie looked in the mirror and could not believe she was looking at herself.

Moments later, she descended the back stairs to the breakfast room. Uncle Increase and Aunt Rebecca were already waiting for her but had not been served yet. They waited for Mollie and she was slightly early anyway. Since it was her last morning there the cook made her last breakfast extra special and extra-large.

"Uncle and Auntie, thank you again for all that you've done for me. I'll never forget you for this."

"You're most welcome, dear niece," exclaimed Uncle Increase, "We love and adore ya very much and we'll miss ya terrible."

"Once ya get settled we want very much to come visit ya. I don't think our travelin' days are over just yet," stated Aunt Rebecca chuckling.

As soon as breakfast was over it was time to leave. Before the three left Aunt Rebecca took out of a table drawer a current tintype photo of Uncle Increase and herself. "This is fer yer album and a remembrance of us."

In addition, she handed Mollie a bundle wrapped in brown butcher paper and tied with twine. "This is a small lap quilt I made fer my sister Elsie. Please give it to her when she meets ya at the train station in Kansas."

"I certainly will. I know she'll treasure it always as I will everything you've given me."

The happy trio went out to the brougham and embarked on their journey to the train station. It was a beautiful spring morning and the birds were singing in the trees. The sky was a beautiful bright azure blue with a few puffy clouds. Mollie enjoyed the picturesque countryside on the way to town. All along the sides of the road she could see the breathtaking blue, red, purple, and orange wildflowers.

107

Soon they approached the train station and Mollie began to feel sad at the thoughts of leaving her aunt and uncle. They still had at least an hour together before the train departed. Pierre helped his passengers out of the brougham and then took the trunk and other luggage with the aid of a porter to the platform. Uncle Increase, Aunt Rebecca, and Mollie found a bench to sit on before the conductor requested the boarding of the passengers. Very discretely, Uncle Increase handed her the extra $500 for the start of her new life. This combined with the money she received from Hiram would be a splendid beginning.

"Be sure and send us a wire the moment ya arrive at my sister's home near Fort Leavenworth," stated Aunt Rebecca, "We wanna know ya made it thar safely."

"I sure will. Mother'll wanna know too. She and Granny asked me to send a wire," replied Mollie.

"Are ya sure ya got everythin' ya need?" stated Uncle Increase.

"You've done more than enough for me."

The conductor announced the final boarding of the train. Everyone embraced one another one last time. Mollie boarded the train and waved farewell. A porter showed her to the luxury cabins. Several minutes later the train began to hurry along down the tracks. The conductor glared at a passenger who continued to stand blocking one of the passages. After he spoke to him he finally sat down.

Now Mollie would have to make things a little more comfortable. St. Louis, the next major stop, was greater than four hundred miles away. Naturally, there were several stops at various minor towns along the way. From Chattanooga to Kansas she was completely alone, because none of her family members or friends were scattered in any of these settlements or small towns.

Mollie looked in her small satchel where she had placed her grandmother's Bible. Underneath the Bible was a large, thick book wrapped in butcher brown paper that she did not remember placing there. Immediately, unwrapped it and caught a letter that fell out of it. She unfolded the letter and began to read:

My dear Niece:

I thought you might enjoy havin somethin to read on yer long journey.

Love,
Aunt Rebecca

Aunt Rebecca had given her a signed copy of Louisa May Alcott's book, *Little Women*. For a few years now she had always intended to purchase this acclaimed novel but never had time to read it even if she had the time.

This arduous journey was now less lonesome with a good book to read along with her Bible. At the same time she tried to imagine how things were back home now that Jacob was looking after her mother. She missed her mother and Granny terribly and wondered if she would ever see them again. As long as Robert still lived she dared not return as he would probably live a long full life. "How does someone as corrupt and evil as Robert continue to live without somebody killin' him?" she wondered to herself.

In some ways, she felt sorry for her poor sister Eveline. Now that Mollie was gone he probably would take out his frustrations on his wife and subconsciously blame her for Mollie's disappearance. Robert never relinquished a grudge he held against others and never allowed Eveline to stand in his way. Besides, strangely enough, he fell out of love for Eveline about the time their twins were born. The major reason he remained married to her is he knew as long as they were together he controlled her land. Upon her death the land reverted to him as her legal representative, because he was the sole heir in her will. Eveline's health was not the best lately and it was only a matter of time before her health declined even more. Robert was tired of taking care of her. He daily wished for her death and even sometimes pondered ways he might kill her without getting caught.

Meanwhile, Mollie decided to relax by beginning to read her novel. The trip almost seemed endless as the hours passed too slowly. Sometime the next day the train was to stop in Memphis for a few hours. This was also where she needed to change trains to journey onto St. Louis. "There's too many stops in between the larger cities," thought Mollie to herself.

Early the next morning the train arrived in Memphis. There was more than enough time to do a little sightseeing before boarding the next train. It was an absolutely beautiful spring day. The sky appeared almost as blue as a sapphire and the clouds were huge and white and puffy like enormous stretched balls of cotton. Robins were hopping across the ground with worms in their mouths. The ground was slightly saturated and obviously the birds were reaping the rewards of a wonderful spring rainstorm.

The man who had stood too long when the train was leaving Chattanooga argued loudly with one of the conductors. He complained that his sleeping quarters were too cramped and the food was horrible. Mollie hardly believed what she was hearing, because she thoroughly enjoyed the food and believed her quarters, identical to his, were more than adequate. She also overheard the man to say he intended to take the stage to the next stop. She felt relieved that the man was not continuing on the same train. On the entire trip his face appeared to have a cemented frown no matter where she saw him.

Around the corner from the train depot stood a mercantile surrounded in front with beautiful golden and purple crocuses all along the perimeter of the building. Once inside the huge store Mollie perused the counters but became extremely interested in the book section. She finally found some magazines and decided to purchase the latest issue of *Harper's Bazaar*. "This'll be perfect for the trip," she muttered to herself. While she held the magazine in one hand and looked at others she heard an elderly couple arguing back and forth speaking in German with one another. She chuckled to herself because all they seemed to talk about were the high prices of all the merchandise and how cold it was outside. The elderly woman frowned at Mollie for laughing while her very embarrassed husband pulled her by the arm towards the register.

"Well, I guess that's the extent of my entertainment for today," thought Mollie to herself smiling and trying not to laugh out loud again.

Mollie opened up the pocket watch pinned to her jacket bodice. Now she only had just over an hour before the train left for St. Louis. Just as she was going to the counter to pay she heard the heavy rain begin to pour once again.

"You poor dear! That beautiful expensive outfit you're a wearin' will surely get drenched out there," cried the clerk. She had a parasol but had left it on the train. The ones in the mercantile were not too costly, so she elected to buy a new one.

"It never hurts to have more than one," stated the clerk.

She was accustomed to worse storms back in Virginia and decided to proceed back to the train depot. Fortunately, it was located just around the corner and there was not a lot of mud from the previous storm. Lucky for her the outfit she chose to wear was a dark, navy blue suit and any dirt would not be too revealing.

This sudden storm caused the platform to be extra crowded with passengers. She hoped to be able to board before time to leave as the people were moving ever so slowly. Mollie pictured in her mind snails in clothing creeping much faster in her mind and began

112

to chuckle quietly to herself. As she stood quietly waiting to board she noticed the elderly couple from the mercantile was climbing aboard the same train. "I suppose they'll think I'm following them so I can laugh at them again," exclaimed Mollie in a seemingly low voice. A man standing in front of her looked at her astonished and then looked forward again. She did not realize anyone heard that and from that moment on tried to keep her comments in her mind.

Finally, after fifteen minutes of waiting she reentered the train. As she strolled down the aisle to her own private compartment she passed the elderly German couple entering their own quarters. She walked as quickly as possible trying to avoid contact with them as soon as their backs were turned.

An hour and a half later the train doors closed and they were again on their way. For some reason the train departure was delayed which Mollie figured was due to the storm somehow. By now she was hungry and rose up from her seat, left her compartment, and went towards the dining car. Once inside she found one table free. Quickly, she sat down before anyone else took the table. All of the others were completely filled with people. Just as she glanced down at the menu the elderly German man asked her in broken English if he and his wife could join her. She did not even hear them come in. Although Mollie wanted to sit alone she refused to be selfish and deprive them of the only available seats in the entire car. "Yes, you may sit here with me." The old woman was unable to speak any English and refused to even glance at Mollie. She inferred that her husband most likely told her it was foolish to get upset with her for chuckling over a silly little argument.

In an effort to make polite conversation Mollie asked them the usual questions such as where are you from and where are you going? Early on she decided to introduce herself. "My name's Mollie Williams, and I'm a travelin' east from Pine Mountain, Virginia."

"Nize to meet you. I am Jan Schulz ond zis iz my vife Gertruida," stated the elderly man. Gertruida wryly smiled out of shame more than distaste, as she determined that Mollie was a rather kind young woman. She also believed her to be a person of breeding since she had wonderful poise and dressed elegantly.

Mr. Schulz had a little bit of difficulty understanding the menu with its fancy calligraphic lettering, so he asked Mollie to assist him. While they waited for the food they talked more about their final destinations. Gertruida was totally lost in the conversations because she was unable to understand English.

The Schulzes were from Baltimore and lived with their oldest son. They were taking a trip to Kansas City to visit their youngest daughter awaiting the birth of her own first grandchild. Mollie listened quietly as Jan slightly struggled to put sentences together that halfway made sense. Finally, the meal was ready and they all stopped conversing.

Chapter 9

Days later, the big moment arrived when she neared the train depot in Kansas City. The conductor announced loudly they were pulling into the Kansas City train station as he walked up and down the aisles in each of the cars. Slowly, the train came to a complete stop. It was very late in the afternoon and no one appeared to care that most of the day was gone. Mollie told the Schulzes farewell in German and wished them a safe visit in Kansas. Together they disembarked from the train and went their separate ways.

Uncle Joseph walked up to Mollie who looked to him to be slightly bewildered and lost. "Mollie? You're the spittin' image of my dear departed sister Mollie. It's so good to see ya after all these yars," said Uncle Joseph who began to embrace her tightly. Standing beside him holding onto a cane was Aunt Elsie who resembled her mother. Both were modestly dressed in comparison with their niece's elegant outfit and made Mollie look incongruous standing with them. Strangers likely surmised that they were not from the same place.

"It's so good to see you both. I'm a lookin' forward to a spendin' time with you folks as I get settled in the west," declared Mollie as she reached to embrace them both at the same time. She towered over both of them slightly which did not bother anyone in the least.

The trio proceeded to Uncle Joseph's wagon not too many feet away from the station. Mollie was impressed with their solid black horses which shimmered in the late afternoon sun; however, there was nothing special about Uncle Joseph's wagon. His prairie schooner was covered with a canvas and the green paint on the sides was flaking off. Clearly in her mind the horses made the wagon look extra plain. Although it was late in the afternoon, Mollie sweated slightly and she wiped sweat from her left cheek as it trickled from her forehead. Uncle Joseph knew his niece was ready to leave.

"Since it's so late in the day we'll wait til morning to go home to Fort Leavenworth," exclaimed Uncle Joseph.

"We can stay at one of the hotels just outside town. If I was thirty years younger we could sleep in the wagon," chuckled Aunt Elsie.

They drove onto a quaint hotel on the main road to Fort Leavenworth. The hotel had flowers in pots all around the front near the steps. All three noticed the odors of apple pies, fresh bread, and steaks wafting in the air from the open windows downstairs in the restaurant.

"I think we've arrived just in time fer an early supper," remarked Uncle Joseph who knew that Mollie was likely famished. Uncle Joseph helped Aunt Elsie and Mollie down from the wagon and then proceeded on to park along the side of the building with the other wagons. Both women climbed up the steps and sat down on the painted white bench near the restaurant door awaiting Uncle Joseph's return.

While they waited Mollie noticed a few Negro couples leaving the building. She was not accustomed to seeing them frequenting the same establishments as whites. They appeared to be very content with their surroundings and did not seem the least bit apprehensive mingling with the whites. Aunt Elsie noticed a look of concern on Mollie's countenance and said, "Joseph and I were a bit shocked when we first came to Kansas but now we're more adapted to the whole idea; however, I still won't invite no Negroes in tha house."

"Shall we go inside, ladies?" cried Uncle Joseph interrupting his wife. The trio went inside and found an empty table. A middle-aged woman in a crimson red dress, a white apron with ruffles, and a red bow at the neck approached them to take their orders. Her dark brown hair with streaks of gray was pulled in the back in a bun. She somewhat reminded Mollie of one of her mother's first-cousins. After taking their orders she went back into the kitchen to bring them some coffee.

Mollie began telling them about her trip and how things were back home before she left. Elsie and Joseph alternately asked her questions about how their parents really coped from day-to-day. They were worried about them because of their advanced ages. She related that Granny Williams was as healthy as a woman half her age, but Grandpa and Grandma Greene were slowing down more and more each day.

117

After supper they went upstairs to the rooms Uncle Joseph had already reserved prior to picking up Mollie from the train station. Mollie adored the simplistic style of her room, as it reminded her of her loft bedroom at home. Someone had put fresh yellow flowers on the dresser in a cut-glass vase which brightened up the otherwise plain room and made her smile. Then tears began to fill her eyes because she thought about being home with her mother. Seeing that she probably wanted to be alone, Uncle Joseph and Aunt Elsie went to their room. Everyone needed to arise early so that they could leave before five o'clock in the morning. Fortunately, someone started preparing breakfast as early as 4:30 am at this hotel, so they would not go hungry in the morning. Although it was only 7:00 pm, they wanted to retire early for the night since the trip to Fort Leavenworth took most of a day.

Morning almost seemed to creep upon them quickly just after they lay down. They could smell the early morning breakfast all the way upstairs. Mollie and her family dressed rapidly and packed all of their belongings. All three proceeded downstairs to the restaurant. Uncle Joseph took their bags to the wagon while Aunt Elsie and Mollie found a table. Moments later they sat together and ate breakfast.

As soon as breakfast ended, Uncle Joseph paid the restaurant and hotel bill and rejoined the women who were waiting on the front porch. "Thanks, Uncle Joseph for the wonderful meals and allowin' us to stay in such a cozy hotel. I slept better than I have since leavin' Aunt Rebecca's," exclaimed Mollie.

"You're quite welcome, dear Niece. It pleasures us to have ya stay with us as ya start a new life in the West," replied Uncle Joseph.

Everyone got into the wagon and began their journey north to Uncle Joseph and Aunt Elsie's farm. The Williams farm was located just outside of Fort Leavenworth. Now that it was spring they needed to hire someone to help shear their large flock of sheep. Until Mollie found a job she intended to help them on the farm. This wagon trip lasted almost the whole day because their land was nearly forty miles away. In some ways Mollie dreaded the trip due to being on the road so long; however, riding with her aunt and uncle made it less burdensome.

Along the way they encountered various animals that Mollie recognized from Virginia. Two animals she had never seen before other than in books were the prairie dog and the buffalo. As they went down the road she saw some of the prairie dogs cautiously peering out of the holes of their settlements. She thought they were as adorable as could be. Every so often when they approached any buffaloes most kept their distance and out of their way.

"The buffaloes have been known ta charge after people fer apparently no reason," stated Uncle Joseph noticing Mollie's interest in them and stopped the wagon for a moment. "I once saw a man try to feed one and the silly animal chewed off a couple his fingers. You never did hear a man scream and yell so much."

"I think I'd rather enjoy them from a distance," replied Mollie with a sound of nervousness in her voice. Her uncle laughed a little and then continued to drive on.

Hours later, Mollie noticed in the distance a large paddock with sheep grazing inside of it. Behind the paddock was a large red barn and beside it was a small wooden structure that resembled a house. As they drew closer and closer she became aware that the gray weathered boarded home appeared to have at least four rooms with a covered porch in front. In the back of the house stood a windmill to pump water from deep inside of the ground. Surrounding the house were more than twenty cottonwood trees and in front of the porch were various orange, red, and blue flowers. Despite the crudeness of their dwelling, Aunt Elsie was determined to make her humble abode as presentable as possible. One of the main roads passed by their property, and she did not want them to be ashamed or look to be in need. Someday she hoped to build onto the house to make it larger and look like one of the finer homes in Virginia. But for now they were content with their home.

"Here we are, ladies. It ain't much to look at, Mollie, but we call it home," stated Uncle Joseph who then smiled. He helped them down from the wagon and then went to help Mollie get her bags out of the back. "We can get the trunk out later when our neighbor Elijah Benson stops by to borrow my plow. His plow is broken and he'll use ours until they get some new ones in at the mercantile. He's a nice young fellow and I know he won't mind.

Dr. Benson trained in medicine over in Europe, but he don't get a chance to practice much in these parts," exclaimed Uncle Joseph.

Mollie thought it was rather odd that as much as people needed doctors on the plains that he did not have much work, but she had nothing to say about it to them. Regardless, it was comforting to know that a doctor was living nearby.

Aunt Elsie went inside to light the oil lamps and the stove so she could make some coffee and start supper. Uncle Joseph led Mollie into the spare bedroom. It was the smallest room in the house but more than adequate for the present. The bed was a rope bed that Granddad Williams's father had carved in the 1700s. On the marble top table beside the bed stood a ruby red glass oil lamp that Aunt Elsie had lit moments before. Aunt Elsie had filled the pitcher on the washstand with fresh water and placed a clean towel on the handle of the stand. Mollie was ever so eager to freshen up after riding the dusty dirt trail from Kansas City to Fort Leavenworth.

After freshening up Mollie unpacked her bags and placed her Bible and other books on top of the small dressing table near the lone window. Hanging above the dressing table was a painted portrait of Granny Williams's parents. Both of her great-grandparents were dressed in traditional German clothing. Mollie knew immediately who they were without a doubt because of their attire, blue eyes, and platinum blond hair. Suddenly, she heard the front door close, so she knew Uncle Joseph had finished putting away the horses and wagon and it was time to get ready to sit down for supper.

Mollie went into the kitchen and sat down at the table where Uncle Joseph was waiting. Aunt Elsie was just bringing the fried sausage to the table before she sat down. As soon as everyone was settled Uncle Joseph asked the blessing of the food. While they ate they discussed various ways that Mollie could help until she found a teaching position and possibly a home of her own.

"There's an empty homestead between us and Dr. Benson that's been deserted since 1868. The last owners left just about a year after Dr. Benson moved in with his wife who was a carryin' their first child. It was the strangest thang after a bein' there five year. Ain't no one shown much interest in it so the owner said they'd make a sacrifice and take only $500 fer it," stated Uncle Joseph.

"It's worth at least $2,000, but really nobody ever come out to look at it," exclaimed Aunt Elsie. Land that is worth $2,000 and the owners sacrificing $500 for it sounded mighty strange to Mollie. What was wrong with this tract of land with a house sitting on it? The bargain price was very tempting to Mollie to buy it for herself. She was just about to ask her uncle and aunt what was wrong when she heard a horse galloping out front.

Uncle Joseph got up from the table and peered out the window. "It's Dr. Benson here to pick up the plow for his spring plantin'."

"Joseph, he's a little early ain't he?" said Aunt Elsie who then began to laugh and said, "No, he's actually not early. We've been a talkin' so much we forgot the time."

Dr. Benson dismounted his white stallion named Othello and knocked at the door. Aunt Elsie rose from the table and walked over to the door and opened it. "Good evening, Dr. Benson. As always it's so good to see ya."

"The pleasure's all mine, Miss Elsie," responded Dr. Benson. Mollie was taken aback when she saw him. There standing in front of them was a Negro man wearing brown leather boots, blue jeans, a white long-sleeved shirt, and on his head a brown leather hat. "This just can't be the doctor," thought Mollie to herself. Why were they being so friendly towards a Negro? Also, she remembered her aunt saying at the restaurant she would never invite a Negro in her home. What was so special about this man?

Elijah Benson was five feet nine inches tall and weighed about 150 pounds. He was obviously slim but had a defined body. His skin was a silky smooth caramel complexion and had chestnut brown eyes. On his face was a killer smile with almost perfect white teeth that gleamed with the likeness of pearls and his high cheek bones that would let anyone who questions it know that he was also of Black Foot Indian descent.

"Won't you come and sit a spell while Mollie and I clear the table and wash up the dishes," cried Aunt Elsie. Elijah and Joseph went into the sitting room and began talking to each other about spring planting, irrigating, and other things concerning their farms.

"I'll bring the coffee and some cake for ya shortly," shouted Aunt Elsie.

"I'm much obliged," exclaimed Elijah.

"Ain't he a handsome young man, Mollie dear?" asked Aunt Elsie.

"I can't believe how friendly you and Uncle Joseph are towards this Negro. One would almost think you were the best of friends the way all three of you were a conversin'," replied Mollie. Aunt Elsie surmised that Mollie still held the attitude of many southerners that Negroes were considered to be inferior to Whites. She once had the same attitude but felt in her own mind that times were changing.

"Mollie, I don't wanna offend you, but you're wrong about Elijah Benson. Before we met Dr. Benson we'd have never had nothing to do with Negroes. Poor man lost his wife and daughter in childbirth just after they settled here after the War. I wouldn't have blamed him if he'd been a very bitter, cruel man, but he's a man of compassion and a man who's after God's own heart. He's very forgivin' towards those who mock him. That's what keeps him a goin' strong ever day. Elijah's a very successful cattle rancher and wheat farmer. This man has been a growin' wheat so well for years that other farmers watch him to know when to plant, when to fertilize, and when to harvest. Also, dear Mollie, here on the plains thangs are a little differnt than back home in Virginia. All races of people got daily struggles and must be a little more kind towards each other if'n we expect to survive out cheer."

"But you keep a callin' him Dr. Benson. Who's ever heard of a Negro doctor? That's impossible," stated Mollie.

"Let me tell you what Elijah has told us about that. His parents were former slaves who moved to New York. Their former master, a very wealthy planter in North Carolina, was a kind man and realized the potential in Elijah and sent him to the University of Montpellier Medical School in France. He left for Europe when he was just sixteen year old and returned just in time to serve in one of the New York regiments in the last yar of The War. Once The War was over he married a beautiful young woman, and they came out cheer to take advantage of the 1862 Homestead Act. Our mutual neighbors didn't like the fact that they got Negroes a livin' next ter them and just took up stakes and left. That's why the house over thar's still empty. Nobody'll touch that house and land now. Although Elijah's a better doctor than anybody we got around here most white folks don't take kindly to the idea of a Negro doctor. People's attitudes about Negroes are some better, but they still won't abide by a colored doctor. Joseph and I are just happy to have anybody a livin' that close since we're both a getting' on in years."

Elsie told Mollie as much as she knew about her trusted neighbor. By no means was she even attempting to force Mollie to be his friend, but she wanted her to be aware that the relationship between Negroes and Whites in Kansas was slightly better than the

South. Just looking at her dear niece's face and hearing her words she ascertained that it would take a very long time for Mollie to adjust to their newer way of living. Chances are her parents and her sister Nancy might be offended that she had befriended a young Negro. In spite of that, her mother-in-law Phoebe accepted people no matter what their background or ethnicity might be.

Aunt Elsie took the coffee on a wooden serving tray in the sitting room for the two gentlemen. Mollie joined her and the two ladies sat on the couch beside Uncle Joseph. Dr. Benson sat on a matching red velvet gentleman's parlor chair with claw foot legs. Uncle Joseph and Dr. Benson did most of the talking while the two ladies sat in silence. It utterly surprised Mollie that her uncle and aunt allowed a Negro to call them by their first names and not address them as "Sir" or "Madam." During the conversation she refused to even make a furtive glance towards the young doctor. She decided to be civil if he asked her any questions, but otherwise, she ignored him as she felt somewhat intimidated by his presence.

Everyone was quiet for a moment and with her peripheral vision she saw Elijah looking at her. "Miss Williams, I hear you'll be living in these parts. I hope you like our little settlement and will learn to love it here too," stated Elijah.

"Thanks, Doctor. I hope to live her a very long time," replied Mollie slightly annoyed but faking a smile. There was one thing about Dr. Benson that she could not help noticing. Despite being a Negro he was a handsome man; however, she tried her best

126

to avoid encountering him at all costs and thankfully he did not appear to want any contact with her either. Dr. Benson was a very perceptive man and sensed that she wanted nothing to do with him. Regardless of her behavior he was very polite and continued his conversation with Joseph and Elsie.

"Two cups of coffee is my limit, Miss Elsie. I best be going as 4:30 comes mighty early in the morning, and I need to start plantin'," exclaimed Elijah.

"I appreciate your visit, Elijah. It's always good to see you. Sometimes, I think you're here to secretly check on our health," chuckled Elsie.

"Oh, Miss Elsie, you're giving me away," stated Elijah with a big smile on his face and about to laugh too.

"You're welcome to visit anytime ya like," said Uncle Joseph. "We've a few lambs about to be born this week, and I kinda wanted you to be here."

"Just tell me the day and if I am through a plantin' I'll be here."

Dr. Benson bade the family farewell and left the house. Othello neighed in the excitement of seeing his owner ready to take him home. He mounted Othello and said, "Giddy up, Othello. Time to go home." They rode away on to their farm in the cool night air. Mollie peered out the window feeling relieved that the young doctor was finally gone. She sure hoped he was not coming back too soon, but then remembered the lambs were about to be born any day now. "Maybe this next visit will be his last for a long while," she thought to herself.

Early the next morning, Mollie arose before her uncle and aunt and decided to make herself useful. She walked out to the barn to milk the cows. Both of the cows were Holsteins and were a little apprehensive about allowing a perfect stranger to touch their udders. Gently, she petted the older cow named Betty and reassured her that she was a kind young woman. Then, as she was milking Betty, Sallie, the younger cow and Betty's daughter, came over to Mollie contentedly knowing it was safe to be near her.

After milking the cows and taking the milk inside for Aunt Elsie, she gathered hay to feed the cows, horses, and sheep. The early morning was still cool and was very comfortable weather for her to do the chores. Soon, she smelled the bacon and eggs cooking and the smells rising into the air. The scent made her mouth water as she was slightly tired but very hungry and ready to eat almost anything. Feeding the animals and the dust lightly blowing in the air also made her throat dry and she was extremely thirsty.

Aunt Elsie went to the front door and called for Mollie and Uncle Joseph to come sit down to breakfast. When everyone came in and sat down Uncle Joseph asked God to bless the food. While they were eating Mollie expressed an interest in buying some land herself and making her own living. She also mentioned that perhaps someday in the near future she might find a suitable husband.

"I'm sorry to tell ya this, but there ain't many tracts of land left in these parts. If ya want your own you may have to go west," stated Uncle Joseph.

"He's right, my dear niece, but of course thar's the old Jenkins place next to ours and it already has a large house and barn on it," exclaimed Aunt Elsie with some hesitation as she remembered Mollie's reaction towards Elijah the night before.

When they finished eating, they took their coffee on out to the front porch so that they could talk some more. Once outside they started a conversation again. Mollie agreed that it was in her best interest and the most practical solution to buy the old Jenkins place and at a good price buy some sheep from her uncle and aunt to begin a living. She figured that if she ever needed any help her Uncle Joseph was nearby and prayed that she never needed any medical services from young Dr. Benson. Now things were beginning to look up for her and she felt the happiest she had been in months.

"I think I'll go unpack the rest of my things. Aunt Rebecca sent you something special and I need to give it to you, since I forgot to give it to you at the train station. Also, I wanna sit down and compose letters to Mother and Granny," cried Mollie. Aunt Elsie followed her to her room to receive her sister's gift. Mollie reached into her trunk and pulled out a small bundle wrapped with twine. Her aunt untied the package to find a beautiful lap quilt made in the log cabin pattern that Aunt Rebecca stitched and quilted with golden thread.

"It's absolutely beautiful! I must write Becky and thank her fer her thoughtfulness," replied Aunt Elsie. Aunt Elsie left Mollie alone so that she could unpack the rest of her belongings. Mollie took out her photograph album and looked at the photos of her family members. When she came to the photograph of her father a few tears rolled down her cheeks. Although she was a young girl when he died she still missed him terribly.

As soon as she composed herself once again Mollie began to write letters to her mother and grandmother. She made certain to include everything about her visit with Aunt Rebecca and the long train trip to Kansas. Nevertheless, there was no need to mention that her new neighbor was a Negro. It was not necessary to upset her mother anymore.

After addressing the envelopes Mollie asked Uncle Joseph to take her to the post office. Many weeks had passed since her mother and Granny had heard from her, and she wanted to mail her letters right away. Uncle Joseph decided it was a good idea as this was also a perfect opportunity to inquire about purchasing the old Jenkins place. Mr. and Mrs. Jenkins's former attorney Alfred Winkler held the deed to the property and had a small office above the post office.

The hopeful pair drove away and went into town leaving Aunt Elsie behind. Aunt Elsie was eager to begin baking bread and pies for lunch and supper. Besides, her hired man Jethro Mullins was outside working on the farm if she needed any help or protection.

On the way to town they passed Dr. Benson's home. He was out in his fields plowing and seeding for his early fall corn crop. Uncle Joseph shouted to get his attention and Dr. Benson waved back in answer to his call. Mollie kept facing the road refusing to acknowledge his presence. One reason that Mollie had such an aversion to Negroes is something that happened to her before her father died. A male slave had run into her and knocked her down without stopping as he was escaping from his master, a neighbor of theirs. As she fell she collapsed to the ground and received a concussion from striking her head on a rock. Her family already thought of Negroes as being inferior to Whites, and this instance fueled even more their dislike for them. Mollie especially grew afraid of male Negroes who were taller than she was. Seeing Dr. Benson brought back the memory of falling down and hitting her head against a rock. He was, after all, taller and strapping like the runaway slave.

Just outside of Fort Leavenworth was a serene smaller community called Summerdale. Uncle Joseph and Aunt Elsie went into the mercantile there to buy their basic staples and then ventured on to the post office next door. Fort Leavenworth was a little too fast paced for them now that they were in their sixties. Summerdale reminded them a little bit of Pine Mountain Township except the land was flatter and there were fewer trees.

About a half hour later Uncle Joseph and Mollie arrived in Summerdale. What few main roads there were, numerous people from various ethnic backgrounds walked along the boardwalk that stretched in front of all of the buildings. The boardwalks reminded Mollie of her home in Virginia and a few tears streamed down her cheeks thinking of living with her mother.

Whites, Negroes, and Indians alike roamed up and down these dirt main roads. Mollie had never seen or would have ever in her wildest dreams imagined such a sight as this. Her mother reared her not to stare at strangers and tried to survey the various groups quickly.

They stopped and parked outside of the post office. On the side of the building to the right was a set of stairs leading up to Alfred Winkler's law office. Together they climbed the steps and entered the second floor of the building. Mr. Winkler's secretary greeted them and asked them to state the nature of their business. The secretary got up from her desk and walked into his office. After a moment, she returned and announced, "Mr. Winkler will see you now."

"Thank you, Ma'am."

When they entered the office, Mr. Winkler quickly stood up and said, "How nice to see you Joseph. Who's this pretty young lady with you?"

"This, Alfred, is my young niece all the way from Virginia," replied Uncle Joseph. "She is planning to start a life of her own."

"You're a mighty brave young woman, Miss Williams," exclaimed Alfred. "Now that we've put aside all the formalities let's get down to business. My secretary tells me that you're interested in buyin' some property here. May I ask you what tract you are interested in?"

"I want to live near Uncle Joseph and Aunt Elsie, so I guess I am interested in the old Jenkins place." Alfred gave her a look of surprise and said, "Are you sure that's the farm you want? I mean the price is right, but a nice young woman like you don't want to live there."

"I've made up my mind, and it's the ideal place for me to settle," stated Mollie.

"All righty, Miss Williams, but I hope you know what you are a doin'," replied Alfred with a look of disbelief on his face.

"I do," answered Mollie. Alfred asked them to stay seated while he went to get the deed for Mollie to sign. Five minutes later, he returned with the deed and his secretary.

Mollie loosened the drawstring of her purse and drew out $500 for the land. "If you will sign here at the bottom my secretary and I will sign after you as witnesses as well as your uncle. Next week, I'll have a new deed written up for you to sign and then everything will be finalized," stated Alfred.

"We're much obliged for everything," cried both Uncle Joseph and Mollie in unison.

"It was my pleasure!"

They both arose from their chairs and proceeded to leave the building. Immediately, they went downstairs to the post office. Inside, a kind, middle-aged woman wearing an emerald green dress and auburn hair tied back in a bun asked to help them. Mollie handed the woman her letters to her mother and Granny and at the same time took out money from her purse to pay the postage. The woman smiled at them and bade them farewell as they exited.

Soon after that, they walked across the street to the mercantile to purchase salt, baking soda, and coffee. Just as they walked in Mollie noticed a Negro woman standing behind the counter. Uncle Joseph explained to her that the owners hired Miss Cleo Harris to look after the store for them since they were now approaching eighty years old. Miss Cleo had traveled to Kansas just after the Civil War upon being emancipated from a plantation in North Carolina. She appeared to be about sixty years old.

"Good af'noon, Mr. Williams. Can I help ye?" stated Miss Cleo.

"I need a pound a coffee, a pound a baking soda, and a pound a salt," replied Uncle Joseph. Miss Cleo smiled at Mollie and then went to measure the groceries using metal scoops. Mollie and Uncle Joseph decided to look around at the various wares scattered all over the store. Now that she was about to move into her own home she carefully studied the merchandise and pondered about what she needed as she became settled. Before she made any practical decisions, Miss Cleo returned to the front counter and announced that their items were measured out and placed in brown bags. They returned to the counter, paid for the groceries, told Miss Cleo goodbye, and went on their way.

Not long after that they climbed back into Uncle Joseph's wagon and proceeded on back to the farm. Along the way just outside of town Uncle Joseph and Mollie were talking intensely and not paying much attention to the road. Suddenly, the wagon drove over a large rock causing the front left wheel to split and break off. The wagon shook so hard it caused Uncle Joseph to fall off and land on his left leg shattering his ankle. He cried out in pain and asked Mollie to get some help. She hesitated at first but knew that she must seek out Dr. Benson who had the nearest farm to the accident.

Mollie ran down the main road as quickly as possible trying to avoid falling herself. After about ten minutes she found Dr. Benson out in his wheat field. Dr. Benson remembered that she had gone into town with her uncle and wondered why she was all alone and panting heavily.

"Miss Williams, what's wrong and where's your uncle"

"Uncle Joseph's been in an accident, and he thinks he's injured his ankle," exclaimed Mollie.

"Climb onto my wagon and wait for me to go in the house and get my doctor's bag," replied Elijah. Elijah walked quickly into his house and returned after a minute.

"Let's go."

On the way there Mollie remained quiet not wishing to start a conversation unnecessarily. She felt a little uncomfortable having to sit so close to him up on the wagon and Elijah knew it. Elijah also sensed her reluctance to talk and did not pursue it any further. Just moments after that, they found the site of the accident and saw that Uncle Joseph was still sitting near an elm tree on the side of

135

the road crying out in pain. Elijah politely helped Mollie dismount the wagon and together they hurried over to help him.

"I am so glad to see you, Elijah. Thanks for a comin' so soon," stated Uncle Joseph.

"When I saw Miss Williams alone I knew somethin' had to be wrong," replied Elijah.

"Mollie, I thank you too for remainin' calm in a getting' help fer me."

"Anything for you, Uncle Joseph."

Elijah made a splint to set the bone, and then he took out some bandaging to wrap it. This impressed Mollie somewhat that a Negro showed so much care and concern for a white man. She almost felt ashamed for the harsh feelings she had towards him. "Perhaps, he's not as bad as I thought," Mollie muttered to herself. Yet, time would tell whether she could completely vanquish any ill feelings about him. After all, he so much reminded her of the Negro who injured her long before her father's death.

"Joseph, we can repair your wagon later. Right now we need to get you home so that you can rest," stated Elijah. "We'll hitch your horses to the back of my wagon and take them home."

Mollie untied her uncle's horses and led them over to Elijah. Elijah asked Joseph to hop on one foot and then helped him climb into the back of the wagon. Mollie stood behind them in case they needed assistance. Then she strolled back to Uncle Joseph's wagon to get their groceries while Elijah tied the horses to the back of his wagon. Soon after that the three of them rode down the road to the Williams farm. She sat in the back with her uncle in case he needed anything. Uncle Joseph's two black horses glistened in the sun.

Not long after that they arrived at the Williams farm. Aunt Elsie was outside hanging clothes to dry on the line. Mr. Mullins was in the barn sharpening the various farm tools. Mollie climbed down from the wagon to go locate Mr. Mullins and Elijah walked over to Aunt Elsie to let her know what had transpired. She then rushed into the house hobbling with her cane to prepare the bed for her husband. Meanwhile, Mollie returned with Mr. Mullins who made haste and helped Elijah raise Joseph off the back of the wagon. Uncle Joseph continued to cry out in pain.

In a few short moments they carried him into his bedroom and stretched him out across it. Aunt Elsie spread a log cabin quilt over Joseph. Elijah handed Aunt Elsie a small bottle of morphine to give to her husband in the event that his pain became too intense. Although his pain was acute he was a lot like his mother in that he could endure severe pain. Even though he was calling out in pain he still was not ready to take any medication for it; however, Aunt Elsie insisted that he take some so that he may begin to get some rest.

Just before leaving Elijah said, "Elsie, be sure and send Mr. Mullins over if there's any changes. I'll come back tomorrow and check on him."

"Thank you, Elijah and may God bless you eternally fer yer kindness," stated Aunt Elsie. Elijah and Mr. Mullins left together so that they could repair the wagon.

Chapter 10

Weeks later, Jacob Gehring was in Mueller's mercantile purchasing staples for his grandmother Nancy. "Jacob, there's a letter here from Mollie to yer grandmother," cried Mrs. Mueller.

"Grandma'll be so excited as we ain't heard from her in over a month," replied Jacob. Excitedly, he paid her for the groceries and retrieved Mollie's letter. Before Jacob left Maggie Mueller called to him again, "Here's a letter fer yer Granny Williams that I found on the floor under the counter. Sorry about that." Jacob took the letter and then left the store.

Later on Jacob arrived home and found Nancy out on the front porch crying. "Grandma, what's the matter?" Joshua was there with her hitching up the team to her wagon. "It's yer Aunt Eveline. She's in bed and not expected to make it through the night. Yer cousin Joshua was just about to go into town and fetch yew to take us over thar."

At the moment, Jacob did not feel it was appropriate to give Nancy her letter until they came back home, so he put the letter in his pocket and the three of them climbed into the wagon. All the way to Robert and Eveline's home the trio remained silent except for a few sobs here and there from Nancy. As soon as they arrived, they noticed Granny Williams's phaeton parked in front. David, Jr. saw them from the window and ran out to join them.

"Nancy, Eveline's been calling for you," cried David. David and Jacob helped her down from the wagon, and then David

139

grabbed her arm and led her inside. Robert was out in the barn by himself. Everyone wondered why he was not sitting at Eveline's side but did not go looking for him. Some thought perhaps his way of dealing with her illness was to be alone.

Eveline had an inoperable tumor in her brain. After years of suffering, she was finally succumbing to it. Dr. Kinsler was by her side when Nancy entered her daughter's bedroom. Nancy tried to hide her sadness so that Eveline would not worry. Eveline smiled and in a stammering and weak voice said, "Mother, y-y-you are h-h-here."

"Don't talk, my darling. You need ta save yer strength so that ya can get better," stated Nancy who bent over and gave Eveline a kiss on her forehead. Tears streamed down her cheeks anyway, because she knew her oldest was dying. A small oil lamp burned on the table beside her bed. Her Bible was opened to the Twenty-third Psalm, her favorite verse. Granny Williams was sitting on another chair on the other side of the bed. She was thinking in her mind that it was so unfair for her granddaughter to die before she did.

Meanwhile, Robert was out in the barn burning papers in a metal milking pail. One of the papers he was burning was a witnessed addendum to her will turning over her property solely to her oldest child, Joshua. Jacob and Joshua brought the horses into the barn which startled Robert. "Whatcha doing, Father?" cried Joshua who was rather alarmed that his father would burn a fire inside with straw everywhere.

"I'm just a burnin' some old letters yer mother told me to destroy," cried Robert.

Knowing about Robert and Mollie's affair raised suspicions in Jacob's mind, and he did not trust him in the least. Robert was still afraid of Jacob but tried to not show it in front of Joshua.

David, Jr. rushed out to the barn and called out for Joshua, "Joshua! Joshua! Your mother is a askin' for you." Joshua exited the barn hurriedly and went back inside with his uncle. He dashed into his mother's room. Very weakly she asked him to come to her bedside.

"My darling Joshua, you've got nothin' to fear. You'll have everthing you need," cried Eveline grasping his hand as tightly as she could. Sadly, he then felt her lose her grip and then she breathed her last breath. Everyone, including Dr. Kinsler, began to weep for her. Dr. Kinsler pulled the quilt over her face to cover the entire body. The twins and Isaiah were in awe that their mother was completely covered and no longer breathing. They did not cry at first, because they were still in shock.

Five minutes later, Robert came into the house and entered the bedroom. No one glanced at him despite being upset that he was not by her side when she died. Then Robert said forcefully, "I want everbody to git home now. Joshua and I'll see to the burial. That's the way Eveline wanted it." They knew there was no point in trying to argue with him and carried out his wishes in disbelief and anger.

Nancy and Jacob drove over to Carrie's home where she and Polly were making jams. All of their children were outside playing several games together shouting loudly and laughing. Hiram was at the livery in town and Abraham was out in the fields irrigating his crops. Polly heard the wagon approach and went outside to investigate. She was pleased to see that it was her mother.

"Mother, I'm happy to see you. What brings you here this time a day and why're your eyes so red? Jacob?" exclaimed Polly. Nancy began to cry again.

"What's the matter, Mother?"

"It's yer sister Eveline. She died about a half hour ago."

"Oh, Mother, why didn't somebody tell me? Carrie! Get out here right now. Quick!" shouted Polly.

"Polly, what's wrong with you a shoutin' so loudly?" exclaimed Carrie. "Oh, greetings, Mother." Both Polly and Nancy were crying.

"Eveline passed away over a half hour ago. She didn't call for ya too, because she didn't want to worry ya. I'm sorry, but she died before I could even send someone fer ya," stated Nancy.

"At least we can help prepare fer the funeral," exclaimed Polly.

"That's where you're wrong, my dear girls. Robert made us leave and said he was doin' everthing himself. Ya know what a horrible and dangerous man he is. I'd a shot him if'n I'd had my rifle," replied Nancy.

"It just don't seem right to not have a funeral fer our oldest sister," said Carrie.

"We got to send a telegraph to Mollie and tell her not to come home," cried Polly.

"Grandma, I totally forgot to give this to you. It's a letter from Mollie," stated Jacob. He handed her the letter as well as the one for Granny Williams. She clutched the letter, closed her eyes, and held it tightly against her heart smiling. After a minute passed she sat down on Carrie's steps and opened the envelope. As she stuck her finger under the flap she received a paper cut. Fortunately, none of her blood spilled out of her finger. Nancy opened the letter which read:

May 1875

Dearest Mother,

I hope this letter finds you well. It's been weeks since we made contact, but I'm well. Aunt Rebecca and Uncle Increase were wonderful to me and I'll never forget them.

The trip to Kansas was long, but I enjoyed the scenery thoroughly. I miss all of you terrible, but I'm ready to start my new life here. I'll write you every week.

With all my love,
Mollie

When she finished reading the letter, Nancy refolded the letter, placed it back in the envelope, and put it in her apron pocket. "It's time yew returned to town to send Mollie a telegraph about

143

Eveline's death, Jacob. Remember to tell her to not worry about a comin' home since we ain't having a funeral," stated Nancy.

"I will, Grandma," replied Jacob. Jacob climbed into the wagon and went straight to town. He naturally intended to stop by the livery to tell his father the latest. Nancy went inside the house so that she and the daughters could console each other. No one felt like putting up preserves for the rest of the day.

Back at the Sutherland farm Robert and Joshua busily dug a grave in which to place Eveline on a hill behind the house. Robert had already been to the barn to uncover her casket that he stored in a tool shed. Because Joshua could not bear to look at his mother, Robert placed her body in the casket and sealed it shut with long square nails. As soon as they finished removing enough dirt, together they lowered the casket into the ground. The entire time Joshua wept and almost dropped the coffin a few times. Robert was too consumed with greed to really notice anyone's feelings other than his own.

"Joshua, go in the house and look after the younguns. I can finish up here," stated Robert. Too saddened to leave his mother's grave, Joshua reluctantly climbed back down the hill and went into the house. Once he was out of sight, Robert began to refill the grave with dirt and whistled cheerfully. He pondered about the control he now had over the water rights once he legally gained control of Eveline's land. This made him feel wonderful inside. After about a half hour he had completely refilled the hole and patted it evenly with his shovel. Then he hammered a wooden cross he had fashioned from two pieces of an old fence post into the head of her grave. Finally, he felt that she was at peace.

Robert returned to the house where he found Joshua and the younger children sitting in the parlor. "Joshua, I want ya to go over to yer grandmother's house and tell her that Eveline's buried. If she ain't home make sure and leave her a note," demanded Robert.

"Yes, Father. I'll do as ya say," replied Joshua still saddened.

"Take yer sister and brothers with ya. The walk'll do yall some good," stated Robert. All of them left their father alone and strolled on to their grandmother's house.

Back in town, Hiram went with his son to send the telegraph. Hiram left his hired man in charge and wished to go home immediately to console his wife. While Jacob went into the post office to send the telegraph Hiram waited in the wagon. After a few minutes, Jacob returned to his father and together they rode back to the Gehring farm. Along the way they talked about how poor Eveline's children would endure without her. They both felt Robert was not fit to rear his own young children alone. Luckily, their older brother Joshua lived at home and saw that they were well cared for and never neglected. In their opinion, Robert despised all small children including his own. Many times they had seen how unfairly he treated his young children but were reassured that Joshua was still there for them.

"Ve vill have to make sure that Perry, Millie, and Isaiah are alvays safe," stated Hiram.

145

"I can stop to visit them ever morning after my chores is done," replied Jacob.

"Good idea, son. I know zat Eveline vould approve," stated Hiram.

Moments later, Hiram and Jacob arrived at the Gehring farm. The Gehring and Thomas children were busily running around in circles and playing games in front of the house. All of the women were in the kitchen preparing for supper. Everyone had forgotten about lunch because they were too occupied with grieving over Eveline's death. Also, the children enjoyed playing together so much they did not appear to mind.

In the distance, Hiram and Jacob heard the bells jingling from another wagon approaching. David, Jr. and Granny Williams were arriving for supper in David's buckboard. Granny wore a black bonnet to match her black dress. David, Jr. was wearing his black suit and a black stovepipe hat to match. As soon as the buckboard stopped Granny yelled out, "Land sakes, David, did ya have to drive so rough?"

"Sorry, Mother. I thought you'd wanted to get here before dark?" exclaimed David, Jr. Hiram and Jacob quietly laughed together. Normally, Granny never complained about anything, but the death of Eveline was ever so strong in her thoughts. In her beliefs, a grandchild should *never* die before the grandparent.

"Good afternoon, Granny and David," cried Hiram and Jacob simultaneously.

146

"Nice to see you too, boys. Could you please help an old lady down?" stated Granny rather impatiently. After all of the formalities, Hiram led Granny into his house while the two other men parked their wagons near the barn. Grandpa and Grandma Greene were both home in bed with severe colds and flu-like symptoms. Nancy's widowed brother Charles Greene lived with them now and took care of them in addition to managing their dairy farm.

Shortly thereafter, the ladies called all the men and children to the kitchen to eat supper. After the blessing, all of the young children took their plates outside and sat on the boardwalk to eat. Hattie Thomas tripped and fell causing her plate to shatter as it hit against the ground. She began to cry, but her older sister Peggy consoled her and told her it was all right. "Is everthing all right out thar?" shouted Nancy.

"We're okay, Grandma," replied Peggy. She then shared her food with Hattie.

"Somethin' sure smells good," stated Robert. Peggy became startled as her back was facing him. Robert had come to the Gehring farm as part of his plan to make the Williams family believe his demeanor had changed for the better. He realized that Eveline's portion gave him control of the water rights. "Go inside and tell Hiram and Abraham I need tuh have a word with them, Peggy," exclaimed Robert.

"Yes, sir, Uncle Robert," replied Peggy.

147

Peggy went inside to get her father and Uncle Hiram. Both men seemed a little unnerved that Robert dared to show his presence at a time like this. They went outside and found him standing and talking kindly to all of the children. His behavior was rather suspicious, because he usually ignored all children. "All right, Robert, vat do you vant here?" exclaimed Hiram.

"I'm here to apologize to everbody fer the way I acted over my wife's death. Yes, I know I reacted in haste, but I was a grievin' for her and allowed all my frustrations to build up inside," answered Robert. Hiram and Abraham did not believe a single word he uttered but allowed him to continue explaining.

"May I go inside and apologize to everbody?"

"No, I think it's best fer you to leave right now. Ya need to allow the womenfolk time to get over their sadness and disappointment. Try a comin' back in a few days," stated Abraham. Robert left them.

Now that supper was ending everyone bade farewell and went their separate ways. Nancy, Granny, and Jacob decided to stay overnight and help Carrie with the dishes. Carrie was now the oldest girl and Nancy felt that at a time like this she needed her mother. Granny was just too tired to go home and elected to stay with Carrie and help her in any way.

"I'll come for you in the morning, Mother," stated David, Jr.

"That won't be necessary, Son. I plan to be here a few more days. Nancy said she and Jacob can take me home when I'm ready," replied Granny. David went on his way as the last of the visitors to leave.

Early the next morning Robert and Joshua went to see Eveline's attorney, Lorenzo Dow Mueller, as it was time to probate Eveline's will. Mr. Mueller began to read the will. Robert smiled as he waited to hear his name mentioned. When Mr. Mueller finished reading the will he glared at Joshua in anger. "Is that all? Ain't you forgetting me? Ain't my name in that damned document anywhere? What happened to the first will?" stated Robert forcefully and confused.

"I'm sorry, but Mrs. Sutherland sent for me one day last week to draw up a new one. At the time you were over in Washington County on business," exclaimed Mr. Mueller.

Robert looked over at Joshua and said, "You knew your mother was a goin' to leave everthing to ya, didn't ya? How could ya do this to me?"

"Father, I knew nothin' about it. I was with you that day, remember?" stated Joshua.

"Oh, yes, I do remember now. Somebody else must've persuaded her to change the will. Whoever did it is going to be very sorry he was ever born." Robert knew exactly whom to blame. The only person who could have possibly told Eveline was none other than his sworn enemy, Jacob Gehring. Already, he was thinking of ways to seek his revenge. "Thank you for your time, Mr. Mueller. We gotta go home now," stated Robert.

Just as they left Robert turned to Joshua and said, "Don't think I'll let yer mother get away with givin' you all her possessions. I was her husband, and I deserve to have everthing. Have I ever shown you anythin' more than love?"

"No, Father, I do believe you love me," stated Joshua. "I just think Mother woulda wanted me to honor her wishes." Suddenly, Robert's anger began to escalate. Then he angrily replied, "You'll sign the property over to me or else!"

"Father, I really do wanna do what Mother wanted."

"Either you'll give it to me, or I'll kill you. I killed your father, and I ain't afraid to kill you too." Joshua started to become frightencd. He always heard his father's death was a hunting accident. Also, Robert had shown so much care and concern throughout the years that he never doubted him for a minute. Finally, he decided to tell Robert that he would comply with his wishes, but secretly he wanted to think of a plan to stop him. "Father, I'll sign the property over to ya once the will's been filed in the courthouse." Robert smiled at him and they rode off to his mother Susan's to pick up the younger children.

Along the way, Joshua began to plot in his mind a hunting trip he wished to take with Robert the following day just before daybreak. He knew Robert enjoyed drinking whisky whenever he took trips deep into the woods, because that was where he usually hid his jugs from the family.

"Father, I'd like for us to go a huntin' tomorrow just before dawn, and I'll bring a note a statin' that I plan to give you

Mother's land," cried Joshua. Joshua knew that this got his attention and diverted any attention away from what seemed like a farce. Robert grew very excited inside but tried not to show it on the outside.

Very early the next morning long before daylight Joshua and Robert loaded their wagon in order to get started on time. The smaller children had spent the night with Susan since Joshua had suggested the hunting trip. After the sack of sandwiches was placed in front it was time to depart. In Robert's mind two things were going to be accomplished. He was getting control of Eveline's land and he had another chance to taste some of the whiskey he had hidden more than a month before.

An hour later, they made camp deep in the forest at Robert's favorite spot where he usually stayed as much as a few days at a time. Not too many yards from that site was a cliff that stretched over Wood's River. Unknown to Joshua was that this was the exact location where his father, Ephraim Thomas, was killed.

Suddenly, Robert reached his hand inside of a hollowed out oak log lying near the campsite. He pulled out a large stoneware jug filled to the brim with whisky. Immediately, he uncorked it and began to take five swallows before belching loudly. Joshua chuckled quietly to himself. Then Robert began to take even more swallows causing him to begin to lose control of his senses.

Joshua decided to go over to the wagon and pull out the rifles from the back. He knew that since Robert began imbibing

151

heavily he would soon doze off for a while. Now was the perfect chance to carry out his plan; however, he first went to locate some of the better deer hunting spots so that this trip was not a total loss. Close to 100 feet ahead of him he saw one of the prettiest bucks he had ever seen. Just as he was raising his rifle to shoot it he heard a gunshot in the distance behind which caused the buck to dart away quickly. Hurriedly, he ran back to the campsite to see what was amiss.

Upon arrival, Joshua found Robert lying on the ground clasping the jug in his right hand and a bloody gunshot wound near his heart. Right away, he rushed over by Robert to listen to his chest. There was no breathing sound at all and rigor mortis had set in. Joshua glanced around everywhere and found no sign of anyone. Although he himself had considered pointing a gun at Robert, he only intended to scare or maim him and not kill him. How would he ever explain this to anyone? Thankfully, no one knew that Robert had threatened him in order to get control of the land.

After a few moments, Joshua collected his thoughts and bent down once again to lift the body now covered in blood. He carried it over to the back of the wagon and placed it there. Next, he covered Robert's body with a blanket he found under a spare wagon wheel. The only thing he knew to do was to go home and inform his Uncle Hiram and Uncle Abraham what had happened.

Hours later, the family gathered together at Nancy's home. Even Robert's mother Susan was there with Isaiah, Perry, and

Millie. Susan was not an ignorant woman. She knew precisely what types of feelings the family and community had for him; however, this was her first born child and despite his many faults she loved him just as a mother should. "I know that Robert ain't been a model citizen of our community, but could I please request a funeral and proper burial fer him and his children's sake?" exclaimed Susan.

Everyone looked at each other and said nothing for several moments. Then Hiram and Abraham stepped aside and chuckled quietly to each other in unison, "We better have a funeral for him. Everyone in this county will wanna come just to make sure he really *is* dead." Finally, Hiram spoke out, "Mrs. Sutherland, Abraham and I vill take care of everyzing."

Susan walked over to Hiram with tears in her eyes and embraced him and said, "Bless you, Hiram. I'll never forget this."

Early the next morning, Nancy and her two daughters Carrie and Polly began to cook for the guests attending the funeral. Hiram and Abraham busily set up the barn to accommodate the plethora of people. Earlier before breakfast they had cleaned Robert's body and placed it in a suitable coffin that their neighbor Joshua Timmons had fashioned out of oak. Now, the only thing left to do was to wait for Reverend Fletcher to arrive so that they were able to start the funeral at 10:00 am.

It was now 9:45 am and droves of people began entering the barn. Susan, Joshua, and Robert's three young children sat on a bench in the front row. Behind them sat Nancy, her two daughters

153

with their husbands, and Granny Williams. All of the other benches were occupied by various family members, some of Robert's colleagues, and several townspeople.

As soon as Reverend Fletcher stood in front of the crowd he paused a few moments to gather his thoughts and pray silently that God would give him the right words to say. Being a man of God he harbored no hatred towards Robert, but he also disliked the kind of man he represented. It was going to be extremely difficult to be objective. In spite of this, he trusted God and went on.

When the funeral was over and the men had buried Robert, everyone reconvened at Nancy's farm for lunch. Susan was very pleased what everyone had done and approved of Reverend Fletcher's short but tactful eulogy. The entire family felt that his words were a blessing to them. Joshua was only twenty-one and made a promise that he would single-handedly rear his three younger siblings at the family home. This was indeed another blessing to the family and everyone was at ease. Besides, he was secretly courting a pretty former classmate.

Jacob went over to his Granny Williams when most of the guests left and began talking with her about Mollie. They were the only two people to know about Mollie's secret affair with Robert. "Granny, I do believe that Mollie oughta be pleased to hear that Robert's dead."

"Yes, perhaps, she'll wanna come home now. You be sure and send her a wire tomorrow."

"Yes'm. I will."

"Good. I 'preciate it, Jacob." Granny embraced Jacob tightly, and they both knew now that things were finally going to be all right.

The very next day, Jacob took his Granny in her black phaeton carriage into town to send a wire to Mollie. Granny had not been in town in several weeks and looked forward to the outing and spending time with one of her favorite great-grandchildren. Along the way he asked her to tell him about her early years growing up in Germany near the border of Denmark. She eagerly told him about her life there and the transition to America where she had to learn English at the age of fifteen. "Granny, won't it hard havin' to learn English?"

"It was at first, especially since my parents spoke very few words which gave me little practice."

"Then how did you learn to speak and write so well?"

"I learned by readin' newspapers in English, talkin' with neighbors, and practicin' with your great-grandfather when we courted and durin' the first few years of our marriage. Poor David never could converse with my parents because he didn't have time to learn much German. He did learn a few naughty words though," chuckled Granny. Both were engaged in the conversation so deeply they almost forgot the time and almost rode past town.

While Jacob went into the post office to send the telegraph, Granny sat on a bench outside of the mercantile. Moments later Jacob rejoined her and helped her back into the carriage. It was a beautiful day with few clouds in the sky and the air temperature

155

was favorable with a cool gentle breeze blowing through the air. Granny wished they had packed a picnic lunch because they were in no hurry to return to Nancy's. They talked more about Phoebe's early years and the ship's passage across the Atlantic, which totally fascinated Jacob.

Chapter 11

Just after lunch Mollie asked Uncle Joseph and Aunt Elsie if they needed anything from the general store in Summerdale. They both shook their heads in unison. Uncle Joseph was still in some pain despite the fact that his ankle was healing. He smiled back at Mollie as she left the house.

Today was the day that Mollie finalized the purchase of the Jenkins place. Mr. Winkler had been out of town and that is why it took longer than normal. She was eager to go by his office to pick up her deed. Also, it was her turn to collect the mail from the postmistress. On the way, she noticed that Dr. Benson's phaeton carriage was gone, as it was usually parked in front of his home. "I wonder where the good doctor's today?" thought Mollie to herself as she had begun to have more respect for him after everything he did for her aunt and uncle. Normally, he was out in his fields or working with his animals, but at the moment she had to make herself focus on the prospect of owning her own home.

As she parked the wagon by the post office she noticed that Dr. Benson was likely in the post office, because his phaeton was also parked there. She went inside to get the mail from the postmistress, who at the moment was reading a newspaper. Dr. Benson tipped his hat in acknowledgement of Mollie's presence and said, "How are you this morning, Miss Williams?"

"I'm well," replied Mollie. The postmistress looked up and handed Mollie her mail and a telegraph. Puzzled, Mollie unfolded the wire to see what it was about. After reading it she let out a loud sigh of relief.

"Is everything all right, Miss Williams," asked Dr. Benson.

"Yes, everything's more than all right. I received some slightly good news from back home in Virginia." Relieved, Mollie left the post office and proceeded on by foot over to the general store for a few supplies.

While she was perusing items on the various shelves she heard footsteps coming in her direction. She looked over to see Dr. Benson holding her mail. "Miss Williams, you left your mail on the counter over at the post office, and I'm returnin' it to you."

"Oh, thanks, Dr. Benson! I forgot all about it after readin' the good news," exclaimed Mollie. Then Mollie and the good doctor looked away from each other once again and went about their own business. Next, she went up to the counter and paid for her items. "On to the lawyer's office," thought Mollie to herself.

Mr. Winkler was out of his office when Mollie entered. His secretary, Mrs. Winkler, remembered her and handed her the deed. "Please tell your husband thanks for all he's done. I'm lookin' forward to keeping house." Mrs. Winkler assured her that she intended to and sent her on her way. Mollie strolled back to her wagon and started on the way home.

On the trip back to her aunt and uncle's farm she pondered over the telegraph she received. Robert was now dead and there was no reason for her to stay in Kansas any longer. She was not in any danger; however, she had just purchased some land and did not want to appear to be a failure to her family. Jacob and Granny Williams would understand why she came home but not anyone else, and she was not yet ready to reveal her secret affair with Robert to anyone. Thus, she was partly relieved and partly disappointed at the same time.

Aunt Elsie was in the front of the house feeding the chickens when Mollie pulled up in the wagon. Uncle Joseph was sitting on the porch getting some fresh air and had his sore ankle propped up on a stool. Mr. Mullins grabbed the horses' reins, unhitched them, and led them into the paddock. Mollie kissed her uncle on the cheek and then handed him the mail. Then Aunt Elsie cried out, "We're havin' sandwiches and soup for lunch today. I hope you don't mind."

"That sounds just wonderful, Aunt Elsie. Can I help you with anythin'?" replied Mollie.

"The soup's simmerin' on the stove as we speak and the sandwiches are on the kitchen table," stated Aunt Elsie. Mollie followed Aunt Elsie into the kitchen and found a serving tray on which to place bowls of soup. They all decided to have lunch out on the porch and enjoy the pleasant breezy day. Aunt Elsie followed behind Mollie with the tray of sandwiches. The lemonade was already placed on the table on the front porch.

After lunch Mollie announced she had some important news to share with them. "I received a wire from Jacob a tellin' me that my brother-in-law Robert's dead from a huntin' accident."

"That's so sad for those poor young children to lose a mother and a father in less than a month," replied Uncle Joseph.

Momentarily, Mollie was tempted to tell them about her affair, but she resisted the urge. Someday soon she wanted to discuss the subject only after she had settled in her own new home. "Yes, it is. I just hope that Joshua can find a way to keep the family together," exclaimed Mollie.

"Now that you got a home of yer own when do ya want to start a movin' in? We ain't trying to get rid of you, Dear, but we just wanna know when to send Mr. Mullins over to help ya," exclaimed Aunt Elsie who was about to laugh about mentioning trying to get rid of her.

"I think I'll try to go over there first thing tomorrow mornin' after breakfast and start dustin', sweepin', and moppin'," stated Mollie. Mollie went back inside the house into her bedroom and began to pack things together to make moving out easier the next afternoon. Aunt Elsie left Uncle Joseph out on the porch and offered to help Mollie pack her belongings.

Early the next morning after breakfast, Mr. Mullins brought the buckboard around the front of the house so that Mollie was able to drive to her new home and clean it out. He had already loaded the back with cleaning supplies after feeding the livestock.

160

"Miss Williams, if you need any help I'd be happy to assist you," stated Mr. Mullins gleefully.

"Thanks very much, but I think I can manage. Being alone oughta allow me to think about how I plan to set up my housekeeping,' and I hope you'll understand," replied Mollie.

"Anythang you say, Miss," answered Mr. Mullins.

Mollie left Mr. Mullins standing in front of the house, waved goodbye, and proceeded to her new farm. Aunt Elsie and Uncle Joseph were still inside but promised to check on her around lunch time.

Fifteen minutes later, Mollie entered the lane that led to her farmhouse. She never really had examined the house and barn up close. Mollie was taken aback at the size of the Jenkins homestead, especially since it stood on land in the middle of the prairie. It dwarfed her aunt and uncle's house and even Dr. Benson's home. "Mr. and Mrs. Jenkins musta had an intense hatred for Negroes," she thought to herself, "to give up such a large dwellin'. These people were surely of substance."

The Jenkins homestead was a two-story building completely overlaid with painted white clapboards and stone chimneys on either side of the house. All of the windows were multi-paned, but several of them were broken out and the dust storms had dirtied and weathered the clapboard. Although she had a lot of hard work ahead of her, she realized this house had a lot of potential.

Mollie went inside and took a tour. Downstairs was a kitchen, a parlor, and a medium-sized bedroom in the back. Upstairs there were four bedrooms. "I think if I rented out at least two of the rooms I'll surely make it." She decided that she needed to ask her aunt and uncle and even Dr. Benson to recommend tenants, but all of this had to wait, because she needed to clean the entire building from top to bottom.

Without delay, she raised all of the windows downstairs and then went upstairs to raise all of those. On the way up she took her corn broom to sweep the floors. Suddenly, Mollie heard the sound of an approaching wagon. She peered out and saw that Aunt Elsie was driving alone. "I thought she said she was a comin' over after lunch?" exclaimed Mollie in a low whisper.

Abruptly, Aunt Elsie came to a sudden stop that almost caused her to fall off her wagon. Hurriedly, she climbed down and entered the house loudly and shouted out, "Mollie, I'm here to help ya!" Aunt Elsie looked everywhere for her before ascending the stairs where she heard Mollie sweeping the floors. "Here, dear, let me sweep and you warsh the windows."

Mollie handed her the broom and then pulled a cloth out of a crate on the floor and after that carried an oaken bucket filled with soapy water over to the front bedroom windows. Next, she carried another bucket filled with clear water over to the windows for rinsing.

After an hour both women descended the stairs to clean the rooms downstairs. The floors appeared to have about an inch of dust covering them. Aunt Elsie took a bandana out of her apron pocket, covered her mouth and nose, and tied the ends behind her head. As soon as she started swishing the broom back and forth dust flew everywhere. "Lucky for us the windows are open and we got our bonnets on," stated Mollie with a smile on her face.

"Your Uncle Joseph said that you can go to the mercantile and get some glass panes for the winders. We'll be happy to pay fer them. Last year was a great year fer sheep's wool," exclaimed Aunt Elsie.

"Don't worry. As quickly as I can get more money I'll pay ya back."

"Do whatever you want, but we can manage just fine 'til you do," stated Aunt Elsie.

Hours later, they completed cleaning up the whole inside of the house. Aunt Elsie went out to her wagon and then returned with a basket full of food for their lunch. She had packed two ham sandwiches for each of them, a cream can full of milk, and an apple pie for dessert.

After lunch Aunt Elsie said, "Mollie, my dear, I'm a goin' to leave now and return with Mr. Mullins to brang your things. He's a takin' apart your bed to bring over as well as some extra furniture we've got stored out in the barn."

"Much appreciated, Auntie. I'll take the spare buckboard and follow you home. I can help Mr. Mullins load both wagons and then help set up things here." Mollie was indeed stronger than many young women near her age. All the years of hard labor helping her mother on the family farm really helped.

She was looking forward to setting up her own household and perhaps someday finding a proper husband. Although her experiences with Robert had somewhat soured any intentions to fall in love again, she did not want to live alone for the rest of her life. Therefore, she decided that she must never seek a man but wait for one to come into her life someday.

When they arrived back at the Williams homestead Uncle Joseph was still sitting outside on the porch, as Dr. Benson was there giving him a checkup for his bad ankle. Both men were talking loudly and laughing out loud like the best of friends. "Good afternoon, ladies. I understand you two have been a cleanin' an old house," stated Dr. Benson.

"They look like they've been a playin' in the dirt and with sum spiders," chortled Uncle Joseph. Aunt Elsie frowned, but Mollie and Dr. Benson both grinned.

"I hear that you're ready to move in, Miss Williams," exclaimed Dr. Benson.

"That's correct. I'm a movin' in today. My aunt and uncle are a lettin' me have some of their older furniture stored out in the barn. Aunt Rebecca and Uncle Increase gave me enough extra money, so I can buy a few more things," stated Mollie. She went on, "Mr. Mullins's going back with me to unload and carry things in the house."

"You'll do no such thing. I'll help Mr. Mullins set up your new home!" cried Dr. Benson with a stern look on his face.

"Bless you, Dr. Benson," shouted Aunt Elsie.

"It'll be my pleasure to help my friends and neighbors," replied Dr. Benson. Dr. Benson left them and walked over to the barn to assist Mr. Mullins who had already begun moving furniture outside ready to load them on the wagons. Mr. Mullins was pleased to see that another man was assisting him, because although Mollie assured everyone she was strong enough, he worried about her getting injured. He was also secretly pleased that there was soon to be less clutter in the barn.

Later the two men partly exhausted from all the lifting, accompanied by Mollie, returned to the Jenkins place. Mollie rode with Mr. Mullins and Dr. Benson drove on alone. Along the way, she hummed out loud some of her favorite hymns which pleased Mr. Mullins and Dr. Benson whenever he was within earshot of Mollie.

Mr. Jenkins had originally painted the barn with red paint. Years of neglect had allowed the wind and rain to erode most of the paint. Seeing the barn as they approached the farm reminded her of the one back home in Virginia. She knew now that she was going to enjoy living in Kansas even if it meant remaining alone for the rest of her life.

"Miss Williams, we're here," exclaimed Mr. Mullins as they were about to come to a stop in front of the house. Dr. Benson helped Mollie down from the wagon while Mr. Mullins untied the ropes holding the furniture in place. While the men moved furniture off the wagon, Mollie went to open the front door.

Hours later after all the furniture had been put into place, Mollie prepared supper for both men in her new kitchen. Mr. Mullins had gone to the Williams place and brought back the food supplies prior to the last load.

"Tomorrow, we'll go and buy you some livestock and a good supply of groceries to last you awhile," exclaimed Mr. Mullins.

"There's something I've been a meanin' to ask you about, Miss Williams. When Mr. Mullins mentioned the livestock it brought it to mind," stated Dr. Benson.

"All right, Dr. Benson. Go ahead. Whatcha wanna ask me?" questioned Mollie.

"Since you have a pasture fenced off that adjoins my property, I wanna offer you the option of rentin' to me. When the Jenkins family lived here I offered many times to rent their unused acreage, but they always declined. I'll offer you a very fair price," replied Dr. Benson.

"We can talk more about it after supper, Doctor," stated Mollie.

All through supper Dr. Benson wondered what her decision was going to be. From the moment he first met her he ascertained that she was only casually tolerant of Negroes. He had a strong feeling that he wasted his time even suggesting it to her. On the

166

other hand, her tract was some of the best pasture land in the whole county.

"Miss, you sure do know how to make a good beef roast and biscuits," exclaimed Mr. Mullins.

"Thank you! It was my pleasure, Sir," replied Mollie.

"Well, I must be a goin' now. Your aunt and uncle is expecting me back right away, because we've got a lotta harvestin' to do bright and early tomorrow mornin'," stated Mr. Mullins.

"Goodbye and thanks again for all your help," said Mollie. Mollie looked over at Dr. Benson who appeared slightly nervous. She remembered how kind he was to help tend to Uncle Joseph in her presence and figured he was already doing these things before she arrived there. It did not really matter to her what he used her pasture for, because she could really use the extra money. Also, she figured with his help and Uncle Joseph's help they might recommend a suitable boarder.

"Dr. Benson, I've made my decision. Because you're a good friend to my aunt and uncle and help them in any way, I'll gladly rent you my field. I'll be completely honest with you that although I normally don't do business with Negroes, I can sure use the money."

She could tell that he did not expect her to agree to it. "I fully appreciate your kindness, and I'll have the rent money in your hand the first day of ever month," cried Dr. Benson. "Now, I gotta

167

go home. If you want me to help you and Mr. Mullins with your own livestock just stop by my place on your way."

"That's very kind of you to say. I'm sure we can use your help," stated Mollie.

"Until tomorrow…"exclaimed Dr. Benson.

"Good night, Doctor," said Mollie.

Thirty minutes after Dr. Benson left, Mollie decided it was time to retire for the night. The insect chirping seemed louder now that she was alone and except for her home it was extra dark all over as there was no moon out tonight.

Mollie bolted the front door and then blew out the oil lamps in the kitchen and parlor. The remaining lit lamp stood on a table in her downstairs bedroom and cast shadows up and down the hall and on the stairs.

"Maybe this weekend I can purchase some bedroom furniture for the upstairs rooms," thought Mollie to herself. "I hope I can find a boarder soon, because it's gonna be awful lonely out here by myself."

All night long, Mollie had difficulty sleeping since she was in a strange room in a strange house. Every few seconds she heard creaking noises, especially after the wind blew. At first, it made her nervous but then she remembered that the house was just settling because of being empty so long. "Mr. Mullins will help me make the necessary repairs," she thought to herself. Finally, about midnight she fell asleep.

Chapter 12

Many weeks had passed since Mollie moved into her new home. Dr. Benson had guided about two dozen thoroughbred Arabian horses onto her fenced pasture to graze. Every morning about 5:30 am he came over to feed the horses bales of hay and for an extra treat some alfalfa in the afternoons. Sadly, she still did not have any boarders.

One early morning Mollie heard a small wagon approaching and looked out the kitchen window. Driving the black phaeton carriage was an elegantly dressed man about sixty years old with a full head of graying hair. He was likely six feet four inches tall. Sitting beside him was a fashionably dressed woman about the same age wearing gold rimmed spectacles, and she also had graying hair. Then Mollie remembered who they must be.

Mr. Winkler, her attorney, had attended a school board meeting and met the middle-aged couple who were applying for the teacher's position. They were coming from out of state and needed a place to stay. The man's wife offered to help clean and cook wherever they could find a place in exchange for room and board.

As soon as the wagon slowed down, the man climbed down and walked onto the porch leaving his wife behind. He looked rather stern and walked with a slight limp that was likely a war injury. Regardless, he quickly made his way to the door and knocked loudly. Mollie opened the door.

"May I help you, Sir?"

"Yes, my name's Edgar Jones, and I'm here about renting a room. You see, I've just accepted a position at the Summerdale School," exclaimed the man.

"Oh, I've been expectin' you. Mr. Winkler told me you were a comin'."

"Miss Williams, may I be honest and ask you a simple question?" stated Mr. Jones.

"You may."

"Aren't you a little young to be a living alone out here on the prairie? My wife and I presumed that you were a lot older."

Getting slightly annoyed with Mr. Jones's attitude, Mollie said, "If you and Mrs. Jones wish to find another living arrangement, I'll not stand in your way."

"On the contrary, Miss Williams, my wife and I'll remain here on a trial basis. I'll pay you the first month's rent as agreed. My wife, Dora will gladly help you cook and clean in addition to our rent. She really hates to sit and do nothing all day," exclaimed Mr. Jones with a serious look on his face.

Then he went on to say, "If we find we like it here then we'll make this our permanent home." Next, he paid Mollie the rent and returned to his phaeton. He and his wife drove away returning to town to pick up a few supplies and to retrieve their personal belongings from the hotel.

Mollie thought long and hard while the Joneses were gone. She was beginning to have second thoughts about renting to them, as they did not seem to have much of a personality. At least Edgar Jones did not, because he very rudely failed to introduce his wife to her.

While she paused to think about what could be a mistake, Dr. Benson arrived right on time on horseback to check on his horses. Earlier in the day he had fed them and her animals, but now he was leading them out of the paddock where they drank from the water troughs. As his horse galloped past Mollie, Dr. Benson waved and smiled at her. She always waved back and smiled too, out of politeness. When he was no longer close she went back inside to work on making lunch for herself and her new tenants.

A half hour before lunch was ready, Mr. and Mrs. Jones returned with all of their personal belongings. Mr. Jones helped his wife down and together they unloaded the back of the phaeton. Then, Mrs. Jones went to the front door and knocked.

Not long after, Mollie answered the door and said, "Now that you and Mr. Jones live here you no longer need to knock on the door. Here is a spare key to the house."

"Miss Williams, I appreciate what you're doin' for us. It'd please me even more if you called me Dora," cried Mrs. Jones.

"Then Dora it is. You must call me Mollie," stated Mollie.

Dora Jones felt more at ease now that she finally had the chance to greet her landlady. Unlike her husband, it did not bother her in the least that Mollie was barely an adult. She was completely intrigued by Mollie's honesty and even temperament. At the same time, she was perplexed that such a beautiful young woman was unattached, but she minded her own business.

Before going back into the kitchen Mollie led Mrs. Jones up to her room. She had asked Mr. Mullins to polish furniture, paint the walls, and varnish the floors. He also nailed any loose boards on the outside of the home. The tenant room was to look so inviting that the tenant may never want to leave. Having her own room refurbished and refurnished had to wait until more money came in. Just as Mr. Jones ascended the stairs and entered the room, Mollie said goodbye and returned to the kitchen to check on the meal.

"Edgar, that beef stew Mollie is a cookin' smells heavenly. I think we found the perfect place to stay."

"I think she's too young! As soon as we have been here a few days, I want to look for more suitable quarters. Besides, that rancher next door to her is a Negro, and I hate coloreds. You know I don't care one thing about them."

Dora stayed quiet and began to put their clothes in the bureau and wardrobe. Then she and Edgar poured water from the pitcher into the bowl to wash up before lunch. The whole time Edgar frowned and refused to look at his wife.

"Lunch's ready," called Mollie from the bottom of the stairwell.

"We're on our way!" replied Dora. Edgar descended the stairs first with his wife following behind him. He clearly showed no chivalry towards women and always believed they should have a lower station in life than men.

When they entered the kitchen, Edgar sat down before both ladies. Dora smiled at Mollie and then waited for her hostess to seat herself at the head of the table before she sat down. Mollie asked the blessing for the food.

While they were eating, Dora several times complimented Mollie on the wonderful meal she prepared. "The beef stew, green beans, squash, and rolls are some of the best I've ever tasted," stated Dora. Mollie thanked her and then waited to see if Edgar intended to make any comments. He continually ate his food silently, but Mollie ascertained that he was enjoying his food.

"I'd like to announce to you that our neighbor, Dr. Benson will be a joinin' us for supper tonight. He plans to stop by after he finishes up with his horses and then washes up," exclaimed Mollie.

The Joneses did not realize that Mollie had a lot of contact with Dr. Benson. Edgar looked up from his plate in disgust and said under his breath, "Blasted colored doctor!" Dora, however, continued to smile boldly, because she was happy to just be in a nice home for a while.

Finally, after lunch was finished, Dora assisted Mollie in clearing off the table and washing up the dishes. As he got up from the table he said, "I need to go to the school and get a few things. My first day will be tomorrow. The minister's wife is teaching the children until I am ready to begin my new position." Then he went upstairs to prepare to leave.

Moments later, Edgar hobbled out the front door and went on his way. As soon as he was out of sight, Dora had a look of relief upon her countenance. She was the happiest she had been since they arrived that morning.

"Mollie, if you need for me to do anything just name it. I'm here to serve you," cried Dora.

"You just don't know how much I appreciate your help and kindness. I know that at least you and I can become good friends. Also, I'll no longer be alone at night," replied Mollie. "All of the rooms do need to be dusted and mopped, and I'll gladly help you," stated Mollie.

"I really oughtn't be saying this, especially since I don't know you well, but I feel that I can confide in you," said Dora.

"Go ahead, I'm a listenin'," replied Mollie seeming to not be alarmed to what Dora was about to say.

"There's no doubt in my mind that you realize I've got a troubled marriage," exclaimed Dora.

"Yes, I do, but what happens between married couples ain't none of my business," cried Mollie. "But please go on…"

"My husband and I met about ten year ago, and then we married just nine year ago. It was at the start of The War that my first husband was killed."

"Dora, you were married before? I hadn't the slightest idea."

"It's true, and I've got an adult son who fortunately survived the War. He lives over there in Minnesota where he operates a livery stable. Only since last year did I have enough courage to admit to my current husband that I even have a child," exclaimed Dora, "And that's when the problems began."

"Why would your husband have a problem with you being a widow with a grown up son? I don't understand what the problem is," replied Mollie.

"When I show you a photograph of my son you'll understand," stated Dora.

She went upstairs to her bedroom to retrieve the photograph leaving Mollie behind downstairs feeling bewildered. After a few minutes, she returned with an ornately carved wooden frame containing a tintype photo of a man about forty years old. As soon as Mollie laid her eyes on the photo she understood completely what the problem was. In the photo was a mulatto man who one could tell was her own begotten son. Obviously, Mr. Jones had a sheer distaste for Negroes, and it bothered him that his wife had been married to a Negro.

"Now, I know you understand my dilemma lookin' at the expression on your face. My first husband was a prominent Scottish merchant in Boston. We were on a trip to Tennessee when we encountered a runaway slave. The runaway slave broke into our room and tied us both to chairs. He stabbed my husband in the heart, and he died instantly.

Then, before he left, he left one of my arms tied up and raped me. I wanted so badly to lose that baby, but my Christian upbringing prevented me from a doin' so. I moved in with my mother back in Boston and I stayed hidden away until my baby was born. Thankfully, my baby looked more like me and I fell in love with him immediately."

"What happened to the slave? Did they ever catch him?" asked Mollie

"As far as I know he ain't never been caught. If I ever see him I'll forgive him, because it poisons the body to hold a grudge," stated Dora. "Many years later, after I met Edgar, my son was old enough to live alone, and I had no need to mention him."

"From what you told me and the way your husband is actin' I assume that your son ain't welcome around Mr. Jones."

"Ephraim, that's my son's name, ain't never met Edgar. Thankfully, Ephraim's stayed in touch with me all these years. There were times that he came to see me while Edgar was at school. I want Edgar to meet my son, but I fear it'll never happen."

All of a sudden, both women ran out of things to say and they also realized they needed to continue with the day's chores. Mollie went outside to tend to her horses and other livestock. She and Dora had gotten so deep into conversing that she forgot to gather the eggs. Dora stayed inside dusting, sweeping, and mopping the floors.

Time passed and the sound of a horse's harness jingled in the distance. It was Edgar Jones returning from town with several books stacked in the back. He wore his normal solemn unemotional look on his face whenever he was not angry. Edgar spied Dr. Benson giving his horses their afternoon alfalfa and his phlegmatic look changed over to a scowl. "How am I ever going to sit through supper being at the same table as that blasted Negro? Miss Williams's got a lot of nerve and better not place him beside me is all I can say."

Edgar Jones had grown up in Mississippi with his grandparents who were wealthy, cruel slave owners. They beat their slaves regularly as their own form of amusement. Their grandson also whipped them as a teenager. Therefore, he learned from an early age to treat slaves and free Negroes as refuse in his eyes. Dr. Benson despite his super intellect, charm, and perseverance meant absolutely nothing to him.

Dora came outside to assist her husband with whatever he needed to bring inside. As was his custom, he made no effort to converse with her when she helped. No words of gratitude ever crossed his lips. She was accustomed to his behavior and did not allow his contrariness to affect her.

Mollie crossed the front yard carrying an egg basket full of brown eggs. Her uncle Joseph gave it to her, as it was a basket that his grandfather Williams made and used as a young man in New York. For being an antique basket, it was made of very durable materials. She walked into the house and went directly to the kitchen to begin preparing for supper.

"Make sure and not place that colored beside me at supper tonight," shouted Edgar as he ascended the stairs up to his bedroom to prepare his lessons for tomorrow. Mollie made no comment and continued to wash the vegetables. Dora entered the kitchen and began to mix up dough for the biscuits.

Hours had passed and it was almost time to sit down to supper. All of a sudden, they heard a horse neighing. It was Dr. Benson arriving on his pure white stallion, Othello. He patted him on the head gently and then tied Othello to the iron hitching post and walked to the front door. After he knocked, Mollie answered the door, greeted him with hospitality, and led him to the kitchen.

"Here are some roses from my garden for you, Miss Williams," cried Dr. Benson.

"Thanks, Dr. Benson. I'll put them in some water and place them on the table," stated Mollie enthusiastically.

"By the way, you can call me Elijah. After all, we're good neighbors," said Elijah who smiled back at her.

She told him to sit down beside her place and wait for the others to join them. He wore a charcoal gray suit with tie and black leather boots. Dora had already gone upstairs to get her husband ready for supper.

While Mollie was taking the biscuits out of the oven, Dora and Edgar entered the kitchen ready to sit down. Elijah stood up and waited for Dora and Mollie to sit down. To keep Edgar from having to sit near Elijah, Mollie put both men on either end of the long table, and the women sat between them. Edgar rudely sat down before anyone else.

Mollie asked Elijah to say the blessing. All during the prayer Mollie remembered what she and Dora talked about earlier.

Personally, she felt she could never fall in love with a Negro even though Elijah was kind and close to her age. No! He was not even an option. She figured that since she lived in a close proximity of a Negro no man would even think about courting her. All during the meal everyone remained quiet.

After supper, Edgar excused himself from the table and insisted that Dora go with him. Dora gave Mollie a look that made her know she was sorry for not helping to clean up. Together they went up the stairs and intended to remain up there for the rest of the night.

"Elijah, I wish to apologize to you for my tenants' behavior tonight. Mr. Jones is a little difficult to get along with. Normally, I think I'd expect Dora to help me clean up as that's her job now. But as you can see her husband made her follow him upstairs. So, I'm sorry to bid you farewell as I've got these dishes to clean up."

"Have no fear, Miss Williams. I'll help you clean your kitchen." Elijah took off his suit jacket and then rolled up his shirt sleeves. Mollie could not help but notice him uncovering his strong, muscular arms as he started to wash the dishes. She boiled some hot water, and then moments later poured it into the sink. This pleased her very much that Elijah committed this selfless gesture.

Once everything was cleaned up it was time for Elijah to leave. "Elijah, if you ever wanna stop by for breakfast some mornin's feel free to do so."

"Why thank you, Miss Williams. I do appreciate that. And again I thank you for the lovely meal."

"Good night, Elijah. And please call me Mollie."

"Good night and sweet dreams, Miss Mollie."

Now that everything was taken care of Mollie was a little more relaxed. She blew out all of the candles and oil lamps. When she passed the stairwell to get to her bedroom she overheard the Joneses snoring. "I'm glad some people have no problem a fallin' asleep right away," she said quietly to herself.

On his way home Elijah thought out loud, "You know, being Miss Mollie's beau ain't such a bad thing. She's a smart, good natured and beautiful young woman. I think I'll try to court her." Othello neighed loudly as if he thought Elijah was talking to him.

Chapter 13

It had now been a month since the Joneses had moved in. Naturally, Edgar was just as cantankerous as ever but chose to have his meals served in his room while he graded papers. Dora faithfully served him like a maid, but she never complained a bit. She felt that it was her duty as his wife to do his bidding.

Early one morning after breakfast, Elijah brought three dozen purple pansy plants in the back of his buckboard. It was getting nearer to the end of fall and he thought she would appreciate any attempts to adorn the front of her home. Mollie was outside feeding the chickens and noticed Elijah arriving. She stopped what she was doing and walked over to him. When she reached him he was busily unloading the flowers from the back of the wagon. Mollie was pleased to see the flowers but wondered why he brought them.

"Miss Mollie, I brought you some posies to plant in front of your house to look perty for the winter," said Elijah.

"That's very kind of you! I really didn't expect this, because you planted my tulip bulbs for me two weeks ago."

Without even being asked Elijah had been doing a lot of the outside chores that required a man's touch such as repairing the outside of the old buildings. Edgar Jones only paid for his room and handled duties relating to the school. Poor Dora mostly took care of any housework, waited on Edgar, and was too fatigued to do much of anything else.

It was a rather windy day, and they had to be careful that the plants did not blow away. Elijah kept the loose plants inside crates to keep them stable. He told Mollie to go back inside and tend to her other duties, and he would solely plant the pansies. "I'll bring you some fresh lemonade," cried Mollie.

Elijah grew fonder and fonder of Mollie every day. Although at first when they met he felt that she resented him, he no longer felt that way now. Mollie always treated him with even more kindness, especially after he showed compassion, in her presence, towards her Uncle Joseph when he was injured; however, at the moment he ascertained that she did not have the same feelings for a man that he had for a woman. He knew that if God wanted him to have Mollie as his wife that it would happen. Elijah just needed to be patient.

After he had planted one dozen of the pansies, Mollie brought him a tall cut-glass tumbler full of sweet lemonade. "That's mighty refreshing, Miss Mollie. It tastes like what my mother used to make. I thank you kindly."

"You're most welcome, Elijah. The front of the house'll look so pretty this winter." She smiled at him and then went back inside to start lunch. Today was the day for baking extra loaves of bread to send over to her Aunt Elsie. Thus she needed to get busy again. Later on, she and Elijah were invited over to the Williams farm for supper, and she planned to bring a few dried apple pies.

Elijah intended to stop by for Mollie on the way. Edgar and Dora were staying home as Edgar was not interested in meeting his landlady's family.

When Elijah finished planting the rest of the flowers he went inside to tell Mollie that everything was done. "I'll stop by here about 5:30 to take us over to Joseph and Elsie's."

"I'm a lookin' forward to it!" stated Mollie happily. Elijah went outside to go home and Mollie went back to her cooking. Dora came into the kitchen and helped Mollie with some of the baking. She seemed happy especially since her husband was away at school. Since only Mollie and Dora were having lunch today they only planned to eat soup.

Shortly thereafter, time passed and Mollie started to get ready for when Elijah stopped by. As she was washing off she heard Edgar and Dora arguing with each other. Mollie became alarmed, so she hurriedly put on her dress and went upstairs. On the way up the stairs she heard glass crashing onto the floor. She was sore afraid that Dora was going to be seriously injured that she unlocked the door with her key and rushed inside. Edgar had a butcher's knife in his hand trying to scare Dora.

Mollie quickly grabbed Dora to take her downstairs. But, just as she came near Dora, Edgar swung the knife, trying to stab Dora, and stabbed Mollie in the back instead. Immediately, Mollie dropped to the floor.

"Edgar! What've you done?" cried Dora. Instead of seeing what he could do to help, Edgar ran outside towards parts unknown. Dora was in a state of panic and did not know what to do, at first. Elijah would not be there for another half hour and poor Mollie would surely bleed to death. She came to her senses and ran to the barn to mount one of the horses. There was no time to put a saddle on the horse's back, so she rode off to get Elijah. She hated to leave Mollie alone but had no choice. Dora traveled across the adjoining pastures to save time. Thankfully, there was still enough daylight so that she was able to see where she was going.

After just a few moments, she found Elijah's house. She climbed off the horse and knocked on the door repeatedly without stopping until Elijah came to the door. Her hands were sore after that.

"Anything the matter, Mrs. Jones?" stated Elijah.

"Dr. Benson, come quickly. Mollie's been stabbed in the back and needs your help. My husband did it and he's run away," cried Dora almost out of breath.

"Ride over to the Williams's farm and have Joseph and Elsie go back to Miss Mollie's with you. Make sure you tell Mr. Mullins to go for the sheriff. I'm sorry, but your husband has got to be arrested. I'll go straight over to tend to Miss Mollie. Hurry! There ain't time to lose!"

Dora rode off to the Williams farm while Elijah grabbed his doctor's bag. Quickly, he ran to the barn and mounted Othello. He made Othello gallop as quickly as he could move.

When Elijah arrived he almost ran Othello up the steps he was so anxious. The door was ajar and he charged right in. Elijah looked all over for her downstairs and could not find her. He grew worried but went upstairs to check just in case she was in one of the other bedrooms. Something told him to try Edgar and Dora's room. There were drops of blood on the floor near the doorway, so he knew it had to be the right room.

As he entered the room he found her almost lifeless body on the floor behind the door. He scooped her on the bed face down. Next, he looked around the room to find something to press down on the wound to help stop the bleeding. Elijah ascertained that she had already lost a lot of blood and was barely alive. Over by the fireplace he found a flatiron, picked it up, and placed it over the wound on her back. Then he started a fire in the fireplace in order to heat up the fire poker. While he waited for the fire poker to heat up he checked on Mollie's condition. She still lay unconscious. Moments later, he took the fire poker out of the fire and pressed the tip on her now exposed wound. He pressed down continually until he cauterized it. To be sure the wound stayed closed he also stitched it.

In the distance, he heard harness bells jingling. Dora, Elsie, and Joseph were on their way to help out in any way possible. Then within minutes, Elijah heard the hustle and bustle downstairs of people. Elsie ascended the stairs to check on Mollie.

"Shhh! Elsie. Miss Mollie needs her rest. We'll have to whisper. Come with me out to the hall," stated Elijah. Elsie and

Elijah left the room briefly to discuss Mollie's condition. Both had grave expressions on their faces. Elijah did not relish the fact that he had to tell Elsie that there was still a large chance that she would not survive her injury. Things were not looking well at all for her.

"Miss Mollie lost a lot of blood and was hardly breathing when I found her lying on the floor. Her breathing's still very weak, so I'll have to stay here with her until I am sure she'll pull through. She's in a lot of pain, so I gave her a shot of morphine to help her rest better. Elsie, I'm sorry to say this but there's a great chance that Mollie won't survive." Tears rolled down Elijah's cheeks, so Elsie knew he genuinely cared more for her than just as his patient.

"I 'preciate everythin' you've done for my niece. Joseph and I are forever indebted to you. We gotta trust God in what His will shall be."

Elijah went back into the bedroom to sit beside Mollie while Elsie went downstairs to the kitchen to make fresh coffee. The breads and pies intended for tonight's supper were still partially warm. Elsie decided to take some coffee and some dried apple pie upstairs for Elijah. Dora was in the kitchen too helping to clean up where Mollie had been baking and offered to make some fresh coffee.

Dora knew that since her husband was now a wanted man that she had no income to pay her room and board. Nevertheless, at the moment she was more concerned about her landlady's physical condition.

"Mrs. Williams, I'll be happy to carry the coffee and pie up to Dr. Benson," exclaimed Dora.

"You're very kind to do that. While you're upstairs I'll let my husband know exactly what's a happenin' with my dear Mollie," said Elsie. Aunt Elsie went into the parlor where Uncle Joseph was reclining his sore ankle on an old overstuffed red velvet sofa. Although it had been over a month since he injured it, he still felt some pain. He rested his leg as often as needed and now required the use of a cane. Elsie sat down beside him.

"Joseph, I must tell you what Elijah told me about our dear Mollie."

"And what's that Elsie dear?"

"Mollie's condition's very serious I'm afraid to say. Elijah say there's little hope that she'll make it," said Elsie who then began to weep. Joseph put his arms around her and held her tightly and together they cried.

Then Uncle Joseph spoke up and said, "You realize we hafta wire her mother tomorrow and let her know her condition's grave."

"I'm so afraid poor Nancy's heart'll fail her over this. But I know she has to know. I'll have Mr. Mullins take me to town."

Meanwhile, Elijah sat on a sturdy oak handcrafted side chair beside the bed. Mollie breathed very slowly and still remained unconscious. He was in great fear that she may never

187

regain consciousness. As she slept he made a bold move and held her right hand. Elijah tried his best not to discuss her possible failing condition in front of her, because he personally believed that the unconscious patient still heard what people said. He instructed everyone to discuss anything negative about her outside of the room. Once in a while he took a bite from his pie and sipped some of the strong coffee. The doctor was determined to remain by her side until he saw some improvement, if that were God's will.

Later on, Elsie came back upstairs to sit with Elijah. "Elijah, is there anything else we can git for you?"

"Everything's fine for now, Elsie. Oh, there's something I need. I'll need somcone to look after my farm and horses here in the pasture."

"Don't worry. Mr. Mullins'll take care of everythin'. I'm sure we can probably hire Mrs. Jones to do some odd jobs for us too. Remember that her husband's left."

That evening when everyone else went to bed, Elsie stayed up holding her colt revolver. She wanted to be ready in case Edgar Jones dared to show his face while the house was quiet. Suddenly, Elsie heard the horses neighing outside. Elsie opened the bottom right drawer of Mollie's desk and found some candles. Then, she pulled one out and lit it from the oil lamp. Next, she quietly opened the back door and crept outside. Over near the barn she heard that someone was disturbing the livestock because the cows were mooing and the chickens were clucking. Slowly, she walked over to the barn with some apprehension. "What if that's Edgar Jones a waitin' to kill me?" thought Elsie to herself.

When she finally made it to the barn the noises stopped, but she still detected a presence. Once she poked her head inside, she discovered that it was none other than Mr. Mullins. "Mr. Mullins, what're you a doin' here outside in the dark?"

"I was afraid that Mr. Jones might come back and hurt one of you while you slept," answered Mr. Mullins.

"You're a very kind and considerate man. We're all thankful to have you here with us."

"Don't worry, ma'am. I'll sleep out here in the barn and if there's the least little strange noise I oughta wake up. Good night ma'am."

Josiah Mullins was around six feet six inches tall and had a very muscular physique. His skin was tanned from the sun and slightly dry and leathery to the touch. Years before, he was widowed and had two young daughters to rear alone. Those two daughters were now all grown up and married with their own families and lived in Minneapolis. Josiah had worked for the Williams family for fifteen years and could be trusted wholeheartedly. In those fifteen years neither of his daughters visited him, so he thoroughly enjoyed interacting with the Williams family and Dr. Benson.

Early the next morning Elijah rushed downstairs to the kitchen where Elsie and Dora were cooking breakfast to give everyone the latest news. His face appeared a little more eager than the night before.

"Elsie, Miss Mollie had a difficult night last night. There were a few times I thought we were goin' to lose her. Her heart almost stopped after midnight last night. Hours after that, she cried out loud but in a very weakly restrained voice. Then this mornin' she opened her eyes for the first time."

"So, Elijah, do you think our Mollie is a goin' to recover than?"

"It's still too early to tell. I must go back up and sit with her again."

"I'll bring your breakfast up to you," stated Dora.

"That's very kind of you, Mrs. Jones. I look forward to it," replied Elijah.

Elijah ascended the stairs once again and entered the bedroom. As he walked over to the bed, Mollie opened her eyes and in a weak voice said, "Where were you, Eli?" She was unable to muster enough strength to finish his name.

"Your aunt and uncle wanted to know how you were feeling this morning. Elsie's preparing breakfast and Dora is bringing some up directly." When Elijah sat down to the right of her once again she grabbed his hand, smiled, and closed her eyes once more. Before she drifted off to sleep she said, "Eli." Elijah continued to hold her hand tightly even while she slept. He knew that she appreciated his presence.

Not long after that Dora knocked on the door. Elijah told her to enter quietly and she brought a very delicious looking tray of food. She brought scrambled eggs, crispy beef bacon, buttered toast, and a glass of milk. For Mollie she brought more water and a bowl of chicken soup should Mollie have enough strength to swallow it. Elijah mouthed the words, "Thank you" to Dora for her kindness.

Suddenly, there was a very loud knock at the front door. Elsie arose from the kitchen table perplexed as to who was knocking on the door so early in the morning. The person knocked several times impatiently.

"I'm a comin'," shouted Elsie.

Just as she opened the door she saw the deputy sheriff standing there looking overworked and overwhelmed. "Ma'am, I'm here to inform you that we've captured our suspect. We found Edgar Jones hidin' in an old mine shaft two mile north of town. Your niece's horse is safe and sound in town at the jail," stated the deputy. "He had a pistol pointed at me, so I naturally had to shoot him. Mr. Jones is not dead but injured." After he told Elsie that Edgar Jones most likely had to be hanged he returned to town.

Elsie went back to the parlor to inform Joseph that Edgar had been captured. He was relieved to know that if Mollie survived she had no reason to worry about being harmed by him again. Shortly thereafter, Elsie returned upstairs to tell Elijah everything that transpired. Elijah, too, was pleased to hear that Edgar was locked away forever.

"Elijah, you can go home now. If there's any change I'll send Mr. Mullins for you."

"No, thanks, Miss Elsie. I'm not leaving Mollie's side. If I get tired I can rest on the floor at the foot of the bed," stated Elijah emphatically. "I plan to stay until she can climb outta this bed on her own."

She ascertained once again that Elijah displayed a deep concern for Mollie. At the present time, however, she was unaware that Elijah was beginning to fall in love with her beloved niece. Regardless, she knew that Mollie was in good hands as long as she was under the constant care of Dr. Elijah Benson, likely the best doctor in all of Kansas.

Afterwards, Dora came to the door once again to remind the Williams's of an important detail that they forgot. In a whisper she said, "Mrs. Williams, I think we ougtha let the poor dear's mother know what's happened to her. If you wish I'll gladly ride into town and send the wire."

"Oh, thank you, Dora! We would all appreciate it."

With that Dora went back downstairs to the kitchen to fetch her bonnet. Then she remembered another important detail. "I forgot to ask Mrs. Williams where Mollie's mother lives. How silly of me!" she said to herself in a low tone.

Joseph heard her prowling around in the kitchen and hobbled with his cane to see what she was doing. "Dora, if you go into town could you please get me some more stationery? I need to write my mother a letter. It's just been too many months since I wrote her last. She may think I died," chuckled Joseph.

"Your mother's still a livin'? She must be a wonderful woman, because you're such a kind man," cried Dora.

"Mother's 101 years old and will be 102 next spring, if she makes it," said Joseph.

"Amazing! Before I forget where does Mollie's mother live? I'm a goin' to send her a telegram while I'm in town."

"Nancy Williams, my sister-in-law lives in a settlement in Virginia called Pine Mountain," replied Joseph.

"Thank you, Mr. Williams. I will be on my way then," stated Dora. She then went outside the back door where her husband's black phaeton carriage was parked. When Edgar left he neglected to ride away in it but instead took one of Mollie's field horses, which was faster for his escape anyway.

All of a sudden, dark clouds formed in the sky. Some drizzle dripped from the sky, but it did not stop Dora from going into town. Minutes later just outside of town she noticed that she heard thunder. It made her rather nervous, because her father had been struck by lightning and died minutes later. "I sure as hope I can make it into the post office before it gets worse," said Dora with a look of worry on her face.

She was thankful to make it to the mercantile without consequence. Miss Cleo was on the front porch sweeping dirt onto the street. "Good day, Mrs. Jones, go on inside and hep yourself to look round. I'll be right in," she shouted.

"Take your time. I've got plenty of time," answered Dora. Dora climbed the steps of the store and went inside. Miss Cleo followed right behind her as she had already finished the sweeping.

Dora went over to the section of the mercantile where she found books, pencils, quills, and writing papers. She picked out what she needed and approached the counter. Miss Cleo took her money, put the paper in a bag, and sent Dora on her way.

The post office was empty except for the post mistress. She was busy stamping post marks on the envelopes and at first did not notice Dora standing waiting for service. While she waited she recalled that she needed to send her son a wire as well to inform him about Edgar.

"Good day, Mrs. Jones. Is there anythin' I can do fer you?" stated the postmistress.

"I need to send a wire to Mrs. Nancy Williams over in Pine Mountain Township in Virginia," replied Dora.

"Is there anythin' in particular that you wanna say?" exclaimed the postmistress.

"Yes, I need to inform Nancy Williams that her daughter Mollie's been seriously injured and is a clingin' to dear life."

"The poor young woman! She's such a sweet and kind person. I'll keep her in my prayers. I'll have this message ready in a couple of minutes. Is there anythin' else I can help you with?"

"As soon as you finish with that wire I need to send one to my son in Minnesota." Dora paid her the correct amounts for both telegrams and then proceeded to leave and drive home. The rain came down harder and the thunder grew louder making Dora feel more worried and it startled her horse. Silently, she said a short prayer for protection and then began to feel better.

Two weeks passed and Mollie was finally able to sit up in bed. She had noticed in the meantime that Elijah was readily at her side during the entire healing process. Whenever she looked up at him she smiled in approval and he always smiled back. She was so accustomed to seeing him every day that her fondness for him grew and grew. Mollie was not sure what was happening to her, but she was beginning to have emotions that she recalled feeling not so long ago. Then it hit her. The feelings she remembered were similar to those she had when she fell in love with Robert.

Mollie evaluated the situation as she lay quietly. Was it even possible that she could ever fall in love with a Negro? Next, she pondered as to how something like this might develop. First, Elijah was always at her bedside during the entire ordeal. Second, although she lay unconscious at times she remembered hearing Elijah plead with her to fight for her life as she drifted in and out of consciousness. Finally, he held her hand tightly as he used his other hand to place wet cloths on her head to help her feel better. All of these actions of a self-sacrificing human being convinced her that this was not impossible. No man would spend two weeks of his life with a woman unless he also cared about her.

"Elijah, I've something important to ask you, and I want you to be truthful."

"Ask away, Miss Mollie."

"I wonder if you could be a fallin' in love with me."

Elijah made no hesitation in answering her right away, "Absolutely, Miss Mollie. I've indeed fallen in love with you."

Mollie looked at him at first with a serious expression on her face making Elijah doubt her reciprocation of love. But then her almost stoic expression changed to a look of sheer delight. "Elijah, these past few weeks you've taken excellent care of me. Thus, I must confess that I'm in love with you too."

One would have thought that someone had just told Elijah that he was inheriting the entire world and all of its riches. He was so ecstatic at this news that he climbed out of his chair and jumped for joy. No longer did he need to live alone. Now he looked forward to possibly spending the rest of his life with a very special woman.

"Miss Mollie, I must ask you quite seriously. I wanna go ask your aunt and uncle for permission to court you. Even if they approve our relationship, I gotta warn you that even out here in the West people will not take kindly to a Negro courtin' a white woman."

"My dear Elijah. I don't care what other people think. I love you so much that I want us to grow old together." Elijah told Mollie that he was coming right back because he had a very important task. He went downstairs where Aunt Elsie and Uncle Joseph were sitting in the kitchen.

"Joseph and Miss Elsie, I've something very important to ask you both. As you know, I've been spending the last couple of weeks taking care of Miss Mollie. Well, I gotta confess that I've fallen in love with her and she with me." He stopped talking because he was a little apprehensive about asking for their permission.

"What is it that you want to ask us?" said Elsie and Joseph in unison.

"I...I... I want to request your permission to court Mollie and eventually marry her."

"No, I'm sorry. That ain't gonna happen. You both are a askin' for trouble. Besides, it's against the law for a Negro to marry a white man or woman," cried Joseph.

"Mollie and I are deeply in love with each other and that's all that matters."

"I'm sorry, Elijah, but I think it's best for all concerned that you drop this and go on home. Mollie's well enough to no longer need you here," said Joseph.

Elijah could not believe what he was hearing. The two very people he thought were his closest friends did not care about his happiness. Were these the same people who helped him settle here not so many years ago? What was even worse was the fact that Elsie said nothing which indicated to him that she supported his decision. Confused and saddened, he went upstairs to get his doctor's bag and to bid Mollie farewell.

"But Elijah, I'll talk to them and get them to change their minds."

"Absolutely not, Miss Mollie! You mustn't go against your aunt and uncle. Perhaps, someday they'll change their minds, but for now I'll go back home and tell Mr. Mullins he no longer needs to care for my farm."

Afterwards, he went downstairs leaving Mollie alone with tears streaming down her cheeks. She was heartbroken thinking about losing her second love. No man had meant this much to her since the time she truly loved Robert. As she heard him gallop away on his white stallion Othello she wondered if maybe she was only imagining these feelings. Her eyes grew heavy, so she fell asleep once more.

Elsie went upstairs to check on Mollie. She discovered her to be in a deep sleep. While she was sleeping Elsie heard Mollie talking in her sleep. Mollie was saying, "Elijah, please don't leave me. I love you forever." This was something she did not expect and wondered if perhaps Joseph was being unreasonable. Then she came to her senses remembering hearing about a slave hanging for just allowing a white woman to ride on the same horse as he rode her to safety. Undeniably, Joseph did make the right decision for Mollie's own good and Elijah's.

Chapter 14

Now it was October and Mollie was completely healed. Edgar Jones had been hanged for his crimes against the Williams family. His wife Dora decided to remain in Mollie's home and be her trusted servant and friend. Dora's son Ephraim was beginning to send her an allowance every month for her personal expenses so that she could survive in the plains. Ephraim Blair was a successful horse rancher in Minnesota who easily afforded to send his mother money even with a wife and five children.

Elijah Benson continued to stay busy raising his thoroughbred Arabian stallions. When he finished feeding and watering them and herding them into their stables each day he returned home. Rarely, did he have much contact with Mollie or Joseph and Elsie. Sometimes he encountered them in town and of course was always cordial towards them. Still, they tended to avoid striking up any intense conversations. Elsie always hoped that someday Elijah would forgive them for ceasing his attempts for courtship.

Nowadays, Mollie was a lot more withdrawn and seemingly unhappy most of the time. She and Dora were still good friends, but Mollie tended to request that she be left alone most days. Clearly, one could see that she was heartbroken and did not know what else to do. Even when she cooked now the food did not taste quite right and Dora usually offered to do it.

Early one morning Dora offered to go into town to get the mail and do the shopping. Mollie needed more coffee, tea, sugar, and dried beans. On the way into town a few flurries fell out of the sky and the winds felt rather frigid. Dora felt like she was going to be chilled to the bone before she ever made it into town. As she passed by his farm, she found Dr. Benson in the front of his house repairing wagon wheels. She waved as she drove on. Elijah tipped his hat and then went about his work.

Later on once she was inside the post office the postmistress handed her a letter from her son Ephraim. Without any hesitation she opened the letter to find a photograph tucked inside. "What a sweet photo of the entire family!" cried Dora enthusiastically. Next, she bade the postmistress goodbye and went outside to sit on one of the cold benches on the post office porch.

She looked at the photo once more before she unfolded the letter. Inside the letter was her usual twenty dollars allowance. After putting the money inside her apron pocket she began to read her son's letter. Ephraim stated what he always said in his letters that he wanted her to come live with him on his ranch. Whenever Dora replied to his letters she said that she appreciated his kind offer but wanted to remain independent a little while longer. She promised him that when she became the slightest feeble she would agree to come reside with him. Still, there was one thing in this letter that surprised her immensely. Her dear Ephraim wished to come visit her early next spring along with his wife and five children. She became so excited that when she got up she almost forgot to go to the mercantile for the supplies.

Over at the mercantile Miss Cleo was sweeping leaves off the porch that had blown on it the night before. She whistled as she worked. "Good morning, Miss Cleo. Despite the coldness it's a beautiful day," stated Dora.

"Greetings, Miss Dora. You seem extra happy today."

"I'm very happy. My son and his family are a comin' to see me next spring," declared Dora.

"Well, go on inside and I'll be in, in just a minute. I gotta get rid of them leaves," exclaimed Miss Cleo.

Dora went inside and looked around at the various bolts of cloth. She found an emerald green gingham bolt that particularly pleased her. "This would make a very pretty dress for when my Ephraim comes." For the longest time she clutched the ends of the cloth in her hand admiring it.

"That's a pretty pattern you're a holdin' there," stated Miss Cleo as she entered the building.

"Yes, it sure is. I plan to make a new dress to wear for when my son comes to visit me."

"Miss Dora, you've got months yet to go."

"It never hurts to plan ahead."

Miss Cleo gathered together Dora's supplies and then measured them into brown sacks. Next, she cut off enough fabric so that Dora had more than enough to sew her dress. Finally, Dora paid her for the groceries and the material and proceeded out the door with her packages.

The snow flurries had stopped, and it was a little less windy. Dora could hardly wait to tell Mollie about her wonderful news. Despite the cold temperatures, her excitement warmed her on the inside.

As she arrived home, she found Mollie outside in the front yard tending to her sheep. Mollie planned to shear her sheep the following spring to make thread for blankets and clothes. At the moment, she was feeding them and examining the quality of their wool like she always did before preparing the midday meal.

Mollie left the sheep's pen and walked over by Dora to help her take the supplies into the kitchen. She smiled at Dora but made no sounds. Together they put the coffee, tea, sugar, and dried beans into their proper crocks. When they finished they began preparing lunch.

Just as he always did, Elijah arrived on time riding Othello to tend to his Arabians. Elijah had left his brown leather work gloves out by the paddock the previous day. Mollie looked outside the kitchen window and saw him inside the paddock pouring oats into the feed troughs. She went out the front door, picked up the gloves from the table on the front porch, and carried them in the direction of the paddock.

Right when Mollie drew closer to Elijah she stepped into a hole and lost her footing. Elijah quickly rushed to her side and held her up. Instinctively, they embraced each other tightly and then kissed each other on the lips. Elijah pulled away quickly and said, "I'm so sorry, Miss Mollie. Some strange feeling came over me and I couldn't help myself."

"Don't apologize, Elijah. I had that same strange feeling and didn't want you to stop." After saying that they held each other again and kissed for what seemed like an eternity.

"Elijah, I love you so much, and I've missed you."

"I, I, I thought you no longer wanted me around other than caring for my horses. I've missed you too," stated Elijah.

"No matter what my aunt and uncle say I want us to court, even if we got to keep it as a secret."

"My dearest Mollie, I do love you too." He kissed her on the cheek and then said, "Yes, we *will* try to make this work." For a few minutes they held hands and smiled at each other.

Mollie kissed him on the cheek as she prepared to return to the house. She remembered she needed to help Dora cook lunch. "Elijah, you're welcome to have lunch with us. We're a roastin' a chicken."

"If you want me there, then I'll be there. By the way, thanks for bringin' me my gloves. I wondered where they had ended up"

She left him alone and returned to the house feeling the happiest she had felt in many weeks. Elijah began to hum his favorite song as he finished up his work. He, too, was exhilarated after several weeks of his own unhappiness.

Dora came outside looking for Mollie, because she had been gone longer than she expected. Once she found her she noticed that Mollie seemed more at ease and more animated. "Why Miss Mollie, you look very pleased about something. What has happened to you?"

"Elijah and I are beginning to court each other," stated Mollie happily.

"But what about your aunt and uncle? Won't they put a stop to it?"

"We're going to court each other secretly, and you gotta promise to help us by not revealin' this to anybody. Do ya promise?"

"My dear friend, all I want is to see ya happy again. I do promise."

Mollie smiled at Dora and grasped her right hand firmly giving it a squeeze of gratitude. Together they returned to the kitchen to finish preparing for lunch.

Elijah went home instead of stopping for lunch. Regardless, after their conversation earlier she had no doubts that Elijah still loved her and most likely had a previous engagement. Nonetheless, she expected to see more of him in the coming months.

****

It was now a week before Mollie's first Thanksgiving in Kansas. She had bought a white tom turkey the beginning of November and each day onward fed him to fatten him up. Now that it was getting closer to Thanksgiving the temperatures were even colder and snow from previous snowstorms remained scattered on the fields. Because of this the poor tom had to stay in the barn at night to keep from freezing to death. When the time came for the tom to be killed Mollie made arrangements for Elijah to do it. Memories of watching her father kill the turkey still haunted her.

Elijah once again stopped by for lunch each day. Sometimes he brought some rye bread that he baked himself. Mollie and Dora both often commented that Elijah's homemade rye bread tasted better than their own mothers' bread. He always humbly thanked them for their kind words and once told them it was because of carefully watching his mother bake breads when he was a child.

Today, Elijah was bringing some of his delicious bread to serve with Mollie's beef roast and intended to arrive soon. Together Mollie and Dora prepared turnips, potatoes, and squash (all vegetables stored in the root cellar). Uncle Joseph and Aunt Elsie were joining them but had no idea that Elijah was a frequent visitor. No doubt that it would surprise them immensely.

About 11:30, after Mollie's mantle clock struck, Joseph and Elsie drove up the lane with their buckboard which slightly slid due to the ice on the road. Elsie was not worried, because they had driven through worse blizzards when they first moved to Kansas.

"I wonder what Elijah's white horse is a doin' tethered to the porch?" asked Elsie.

"Perhaps, he's checkin' to see if the ladies need wood or anythin' else before he goes back home," replied Joseph.

Joseph and Elsie walked in the front door with knocking and announced, "We're here!" They took off their coats and gloves and head coverings and proceeded on to the kitchen. To their surprise they found Elijah standing by the table placing plates and eating utensils on it.

Elsie walked over to Mollie and pulled her by the left arm motioning for her to follow her to the back door. "We'll be right back. I need for Mollie to help me with somethin' out back." Mollie thought it was strange for them to go outside without coats, but she did not protest. She ascertained that her aunt was curious about Elijah's presence.

"What's Elijah doin' here? I thought your uncle and me made it clar that you weren't to go a courtin' with him."

"Don't worry, Aunt Elsie. He wanted to go home as usual after a tendin' his horses, but it was so cold outside and we'd all this extra food... if you don't mind can we go back inside now? It's freezin' out here!"

"Yes, my dear. We'll talk more later." They went back inside to find the men already sitting at the table and Dora placing the beef roast in the middle of the table. Mollie hoped that she did not have to discuss Elijah with Elsie again and wished that she would forget all about it.

"Shall we pray? Bless this food, O Lord, so that it may nourish our bodies, Amen," prayed Uncle Joseph aloud. Then,

Dora carved the roast serving first the men, the women next and herself last.

"We were surprised to see ya here today, Elijah. You haven't been by our farm in months," exclaimed Elsie.

"Things have been kinda hectic around here with takin' care of my Arabians and runnin' my own farm. I just may have to hire a man to help me," stated Elijah. He surmised that Elsie was insinuating that they were courting against their wishes and added, "Miss Elsie, I'm way too busy now to focus on any romance with any woman."

Elsie and Joseph looked at each other with expressions of relief. Mollie and Elijah avoided direct eye contact to keep from arousing suspicion. Dora spoke up to change the subject, "My son Ephraim's a comin' to see me next spring once all dangers of snow are gone. It's been quite a few year since I seen him last."

"That's wonderful news, Mrs. Jones. I can only imagine how excited you must be," stated Joseph. "The only child Elsie and I ever had died when she was but five year old. She drowned in a nearby pond." That was startling news to Mollie, as she never knew her aunt and uncle ever had a child.

"He's anxious to meet all of you. I don't know for sure if he's a comin' alone or bringin' the whole family like he said in his letter," exclaimed Dora.

After lunch Elijah left and went back to the pasture to tend to his horses. Dora told Mollie to go ahead and sit with her family in the parlor while she cleared the table, put away the food, and cleaned the kitchen. She promised to bring them a fresh pot of coffee as soon as she finished in the kitchen.

In the parlor Mollie said, "Dr. Benson's remained busy and hardly has time to help us with the wood choppin'. But, we do owe him a debt of gratitude for all the wood he supplied for us before the end of October."

"Mollie, we know you once loved Elijah, but we shore hope you realize it was for yer own good that we broke off yer courtship. You'd be askin' for nuttin but trouble. Here on the prairie people still frown on Whites mixin' with Indians or Negroes, and if you two got married you'd never go back to Virginia. Elijah would either be jailed or hanged there," stated Elsie.

"Your aunt's right, dear niece. We're just a tryin' to protect you both. In time you'll find a suitable husband as there's many eligible men livin' in this county. You and Elijah oughta do just fine as good neighbors. Of course, you may consider movin' to help you forget Elijah," exclaimed Joseph.

Uncle Joseph's suggestions were rather appalling to her, and although some of Aunt Elsie's statements were true, she had no intention of giving up her chance to be Elijah's wife. He was an intelligent man and likely knew exactly how they could live harmoniously as man and wife. After all, he did save her life. Therefore, she said in a convincing tone to them, "You both know what's best for me." As she said that Dora entered the parlor carrying a tray with a coffee pot piping hot, sugar bowl, creamer, and four cups and saucers. After serving the family Dora poured her own coffee and sat down to visit with them.

Very early the next morning Mollie arose extra early before the time she usually heard Dora getting out of bed. She intended to take a little trip before breakfast and before Elijah came over to feed the horses. Mollie put on her prettiest dress, a green one she got in Tennessee with the matching hat, boots, gloves, and long emerald green mantle. Then she went out to the barn and mounted one of the wagon horses and rode off in the direction of Elijah's farm. It was raining outside, but she did not care because she needed to see him right away.

When Mollie arrived in front of Elijah's home he was just then coming out the front door getting ready to leave. "Why Mollie, what brings you here this early in the mornin'?" She stepped upon the front porch.

"There's something' I've been meanin' to tell you for a very long time that I've neglected and been ashamed to tell you. After you hear what I got to say you may not wanna marry me next spring."

Elijah looked puzzled and worried. "Maybe all the discussions she's had with Joseph and Elsie has caused her to change her mind," thought Elijah to himself. "Go ahead, my dear. I'm a listenin'."

Mollie was rather heartbroken at the thoughts of losing her true love forever. Elijah treated her the way a woman should be treated with kindness, gentleness, patience, and sheer love.

Obviously, she appeared apprehensive and Elijah sensed it immediately. He grasped her hand to comfort her and then she began.

"You've probably wondered why a young woman like me moved so far away from her aged mother who needed *me* the most."

"The thought crossed my mind, but I never wished to pry into affairs that don't concern me," exclaimed Elijah.

"On my sixteenth birthday I'd gone into the woods where my grandparents had a cabin, so I'd be alone. This was somethin' that I routinely did several times a week. Then the next thing I knew my brother-in-law Robert had joined me. He began talkin' with me each day after that and convinced me that he'd fallen in love with me and then I began to fall in love with him. Things went well at first and later on greed built up inside of him and he struck me several times. Twice he beat me so hard that I lost two children I was a carryin' by him. Many times he threatened to kill me if I told anybody. Later on, I realized that he only wanted me for my portion of my late father's land. Robert terrified me so much that it was necessary for me to relocate to Kansas near Uncle Joseph and Aunt Elsie. Before I came here I sold my land to another brother-in-law. So you see, I'm an impure woman and no one includin' you'll ever want me again."

She sobbed loudly and rested her face against Elijah's chest while at the same time wrapping her arms around his waist. Elijah lifted her head and embraced her tightly.

"If I ever see Robert in Kansas he'll never see Virginia again," stated Elijah.

"Robert died in a huntin' accident, so you won't have to worry about him a comin' here," replied Mollie who was still almost choking on tears.

"Dearest Mollie, I love you with all my heart, and I still want to make you my own wife. What's past is past. These last few months I've witnessed myself what kind of woman you really are. There never lived a gentler, kinder, more compassionate human being."

Again Mollie rested her drenched face against Elijah's blue plaid work shirt. He held her tightly, lifted her whole body into his arms, and carried her over to the sofa in his parlor. As soon as she lay flat she fell asleep with a smile on her face. Somehow Elijah knew that things were going to be all right and Mollie's sadness would dissipate.

Elijah left Mollie a note informing her that he had to tend his horses and that he planned to return in time to prepare their breakfast and not to panic if she discovered him missing. As soon as Elijah arrived at Mollie's homestead he told Dora to venture over to his place and they could eat breakfast there together. Dora was eager to help in any way.

Meanwhile, back at the Benson farm, Mollie awoke to find herself all alone. At first, she assumed that Elijah probably was laboring somewhere outside, but she arose from the sofa to look for him. Just as she was about to go outside and explore the

211

barnyard she discovered a folded note on a cherry candle stand by the door. She unfolded the note and read it learning that Elijah went to feed the horses but planned to return in time to prepare their morning meal.

Suddenly, Mollie heard a wagon approaching jingling its harness bells. She looked outside to find that Dora had arrived which surprised her somewhat. After Dora climbed down from her wagon she knocked at the door and Mollie led her into the parlor.

"I've come to have breakfast with you and Dr. Benson. He caught me just in time before I started cookin' for us. That's very kind of him, don't ya think?" stated Dora.

"It most certainly is. Elijah's been accompanyin' us for breakfast for so long I thought it was a welcome change," cried Mollie.

"Ain't you the least bit afraid of your aunt and uncle finding out? I mean, I know we talked about this before now, but I'm still afraid they'll shun you if somehow this secret is found out."

"They won't find out until we're already married. My heart's aflutter for him and I'll not pursue anybody else. It's still illegal for us to marry here, so I don't know what we'll do. God's will always prevails," stated Mollie.

About a half hour later, the two women heard Elijah's horse Othello galloping on the practically frozen ground. He dismounted his horse and then led him into the barn. Within minutes, he walked towards the house in anticipation of eating with his two good friends.

Once inside the kitchen he started a fire in the stove. A few cinders flew to the floor as the wood burned. Next, he sliced off several pieces of bacon and dropped them into an iron skillet greased with butter. Then into another iron skillet he cracked half a dozen eggs. Elijah wanted to do all of the cooking, so he instructed the women to stay put in the parlor. Both Dora and Mollie were captivated by the delicious smells permeating the air in the whole house. They could hardly wait to devour every bit of it. When it was time to finally eat, Elijah called the half-starved ladies to the kitchen table bedecked with blue willow plates, cut-glass tumblers, silver flatware, and cloth napkins. Mollie was utterly impressed with the display which made the rest of the kitchen look rather drab. It seemed odd that a single man had such fine things in his kitchen. Although Elijah was a successful farmer and rancher in his own right, he still needed a woman's touch in decorating of the home, in her opinion. Finally, everyone sat down to their morning feast, said a blessing, and then ate.

Chapter 15

The day before Thanksgiving when Mollie was in the post office she received a letter from Aunt Rebecca Patton. Enclosed in the letter was $500 with an attached note giving her instructions to deposit the money into the bank. "I didn't wire them that I needed more money! Of course, I can always use it." She read the letter and stopped at a section that excited her. Mollie was overjoyed to discover that Aunt Rebecca and Uncle Increase planned a trip to see her in early spring. "How wonderful it'll be see both of them again! Now, I'll need to get really busy and spruce up my home for their visit. I'm sure Elijah won't mind helping out." After finishing the letter she put it back in the envelope and placed it in her right pinafore pocket. Then she proceeded onto the bank to deposit the money. Now, she had a total of $1200 in the bank to survive for many months to come. Everyone had been so good to her. Thus, tomorrow she truly had an extra good reason to give thanks.

On her way home she stopped by Elijah's home to remind him about tomorrow. When she came to a halt she climbed out of her buckboard and began to search for him. She went into the barn first and located him over by the cows where he was feeding them. Elijah grabbed her right hand, kissed it, and then pulled her closer to him. They embraced tightly and then kissed each other directly on the lips. Next, he motioned for her to follow him to the front porch where they sat down on his wicker set. "Mollie, I've been thinkin' a lot about us getting married someday."

"I look forward to that day, but I'm afraid it won't happen too soon." Her composure then changed and she appeared distraught.

"Wait a minute, my love. I do have a plan. The other day when you were here, and I was at your place I had a long conversation with Dora. Did you know she has a mulatto son?"

"Yes, I did know. She showed me a photograph of him with his family."

Elijah went on, "Dora tells me that her son lives in Minnesota where it's legal for Whites to marry Negroes, Asians, or Indians."

"What're you a tryin' to tell me, my dear Elijah?"

"What I'm tryin' to say is we can go to Minnesota next April by train and get hitched."

Mollie jumped up from her chair almost falling over and kissed Elijah on the cheek. Then Elijah said, "You do realize we'll have some opposition from your family here and people in the community, don't you?"

"I don't care, Eli. I love you and want to spend the rest of my life with you. Nothing can keep us apart." Soon after that she started to leave and walked over to her buckboard. "Don't forget to bring the bread, rolls, and pies tomorrow. Remember Uncle Joseph and Aunt Elsie will be there too."

"Don't worry, my love. I'll not forget. Now don't you fret about them. I'll behave myself around them." He once again reached out to grasp her right hand and kissed it tenderly. "Until tomorrow, my love."

Thanksgiving morning, Dora and Mollie arose earlier than usual to prepare the afternoon meal. Mollie went down into the root cellar to get a salted ham hanging up on one of the support beams. Then she returned to the kitchen where she found a large galvanized tub and filled it with water. She intended to soak the ham and scrub it to remove the excess salt. While she did that Dora peeled potatoes for the mashed potatoes and potato salad. Any moment they expected Uncle Joseph and Aunt Elsie, because Aunt Elsie promised to help. Mollie grew so fond of the tom turkey that she let him live.

Not long after that they heard the harnesses of many horses. Mollie looked out the window to see that Aunt Elsie, Uncle Joseph, and Elijah arrived at the same time which she thought appeared rather awkward. Elijah wore a black suit, black boots, and a black hat and to her looked rather debonair. She continued about her work and allowed Dora to show everyone in.

"Aunt Elsie's here, Mollie. I'm ready to help you!" shouted Aunt Elsie.

Uncle Joseph entered the parlor to catch up on some reading while Elijah carried in a large basket of baked goods covered with a red and white gingham cloth. Aunt Elsie also carried in a large basket of foods and led Elijah into the kitchen with her. They smiled at each other but spoke few words.

"That's fine, Elijah. You can put your basket right there on the table and then go join Uncle Joseph in the parlor. I'll call ya if I need you," cried Mollie.

"Anything you say, Miss Mollie," stated Elijah who then left the kitchen to go to the parlor. Joseph sat on a wingback chair reading a farmer's almanac. He looked up at Elijah and said, "Good day," and then continued reading. Although Joseph and Elsie became his friends long before Mollie arrived in Kansas, he did not bear a grudge against her now that they were only casually friendly towards him.

Dinner was now ready and everyone sat down at the kitchen table. Uncle Joseph, being the oldest, said the blessing. Since Elijah was a skilled doctor he had the honor of carving the ham. Once finished they passed their plates and Elijah served them some ham.

During dinner no one made much conversation. Mollie decided to speak up, "I got a letter yesterday from Aunt Rebecca. She and Uncle Increase are a visitin' Kansas next spring. Ain't that wonderful news?"

"It's been years since I seen my sister. We'll have a wonderful time catching up on old times. I think I'll make a quilt for her," exclaimed Aunt Elsie.

"If you need some help sprucin' up the place I'll be happy to help you, Miss Mollie," exclaimed Elijah.

217

"We can help ya too," insisted Aunt Elsie.

Once again everyone returned to eating their Thanksgiving dinner. Dora arose from the table to place more wood into the fireplace, because it began to grow a little colder inside. While she was near the window she noticed that snow was falling down thickly. "My, my. I think we're gonna have a blizzard directly," said Dora aloud.

Mollie, Elijah, and Aunt Elsie joined her by the window. The wind speed increased and blew against the kitchen door. "Elijah, would you please secure the door for me? I think we may all be spendin' the rest of today together," cried Mollie.

"Yes, Miss Mollie, and as soon as I do that I suggest we put my horses and your aunt and uncle's horses in the barn," replied Elijah.

"Not a problem. What about the stallions out in the pasture?" stated Mollie.

"I'll help Elijah with those," exclaimed Uncle Joseph. "Just being a good neighbor."

"Thanks, Joseph. I appreciate your kindness," said Elijah.

Together Elijah, Mollie, and Uncle Joseph went outside to put the horses out front into the barn. Then the three of them climbed onto workhorses and galloped away to the pasture. The three of them led the stallions towards Elijah's place and on into the stables. Meanwhile, the snowstorm grew stronger and stronger. Mollie's horse reacted nervously and almost threw her off, but

Elijah came to her rescue. Uncle Joseph observed Elijah's quick reaction and smiled in approval.

About an hour later, without hesitating, the party traveled back in the direction of Mollie's abode. Suddenly, Uncle Joseph's horse stepped into a deep prairie dog hole and lost its footing. He and the horse both tumbled to the ground and as they fell, the horse landed onto both legs. Instantly, the bones in his legs crushed as well as his pelvis.

"Uncle Joseph!" shouted Mollie whose voice was muffled by the heavily falling snow. "Speak to me. Are you all right?" He was unable to speak to her because the fall caused him to get a concussion and made him unconscious. Mollie began to weep while Elijah literally jumped off his horse to examine him.

"Mollie, we've got to get him to your house immediately. But I'm afraid I have some sad news. It appears that all the bones below his waist have been broken. If he ever wakes up he's gonna be in the worst pain a body could ever withstand."

"You're a doctor, Eli. Ain't there something we can do?"

"I'm afraid not even the best surgeon in the world can help him now. Let's not waste time arguing. We gotta get him to your place now." Before they left, Elijah took out his pistol and shot Uncle Joseph's horse, because it broke its ankle. "We'll bury the horse once this storm passes."

Elijah lifted Uncle Joseph and placed him face-down across the saddle of his horse. He and Mollie walked and pulled the reins of Mollie's horse heading towards Mollie's home.

The wind blew fiercely, and they had to keep the horses calm despite their constant neighing in fright. This was certainly one of the worst blizzards that Elijah had ever seen since homesteading on the plains. Although Mollie's farm was normally only fifteen minutes away by buckboard the storm delayed them by thirty minutes more.

At the same time, Dora and Aunt Elsie became worried. "They've been gone over an hour, Dora! I'm afraid something's gone wrong!" exclaimed Aunt Elsie.

"Don't worry, Ma'am. I'm sure everything will be all right. Perhaps, they're a takin' it slow so's they don't get hurt some way," replied Dora.

"I hope you're right," answered Aunt Elsie doubtfully.

Finally, Elijah and Mollie just barely made out the dark shadowy form of a barn in the near distance. "We're almost there, my love," cried Elijah.

"Praise be! I thought we'd never make it back. Aunt Elsie must be worried, and I don't know what we're gonna tell her," stated Mollie with a bit of sadness in her voice. Once again she began to weep.

"There, there, my dear Mollie. Your Uncle Joseph always enjoyed helpin' others. If he dies it won't be in vain," stated Elijah who surmised that it was highly unlikely that Uncle Joseph would survive the very next day.

Slowly but surely they made their way to the front of the home. Once on the porch Mollie quickly unlatched the door and

Elijah carried Uncle Joseph into the parlor setting him on the sofa. "Go put the horses in the barn," stated Elijah.

"Land sakes! What's all that racket?" cried Aunt Elsie. She rushed into the parlor to find her beloved husband asleep on the sofa. "What's going on? Why's Joseph asleep? Where's Mollie?"

"I'm afraid I've got some dreadful news to share with you. When we went to put all the horses in the barn everything was just fine. It was on our way back that things took a turn for the worse. Joseph's horse lost its footing when it stepped into a prairie dog hole. The horse broke its ankle and tumbled down on him breaking all his bones below the waist. I'm sorry, but I'm sore afraid he's not gonna survive by morning. He's bleeding internally. Mollie's a puttin' our horses away now."

Aunt Elsie bent over to kiss her ailing husband on the cheek. At the same time tears streamed down her cheeks. "I love you, Joseph." Then she sat down on the chair beside the sofa, leaned her head over on the arm of it, and cried hysterically. Elijah tried to comfort her, but she pushed him away and asked him to leave them alone together.

Moments later Mollie returned from outside and joined Aunt Elsie in the parlor. She walked over to Uncle Joseph and found him breathing slowly like someone struggling to breathe. Aunt Elsie rose up from her chair and embraced Mollie tightly.

All of a sudden, Uncle Joseph in a weak voice called out, "Mollie… Elsie." His eyes remained closed, but he desperately tried to tell them something.

"Uncle Joseph? Can you hear me?" In a much weakened voice he replied, "I'm sorry, Mollie. You marry Lijah. He good man. I'm sorry. Elsie, he good man." Uncle Joseph closed his eyes for the very last time.

"Elijah, come quick!" shouted Aunt Elsie. Elijah immediately dashed into the parlor and motioned over towards Uncle Joseph. He leaned his ear upon his chest to listen to his heart. There was no sound. Then he took out his stethoscope from his doctor's bag and still there was no sound. "I'm so sorry. Joseph Williams's dead."

Aunt Elsie began to build up some anger inside and cried, "Elijah…" But then she remembered that Joseph volunteered to help them with the horses, and it was no one's fault. Immediately, she finished her thought, "I wanna ask for your forgiveness, Elijah. I wanted to lash out at you for my husband's death, but I realize now that he was a helpful man and chose his fate."

"Your apology's accepted, but I can't help but feel guilty over this incident," exclaimed Elijah.

"Please don't," said Mollie. Mollie left the room for about two minutes and then returned with a bed sheet. She completely covered Joseph's body and once again left the room. Aunt Elsie left followed by Elijah who closed the door to make certain that the cats were unable to get into the room. The three of them walked into the kitchen where they found Dora washing the dishes.

"If nobody minds I'll put on a pot of coffee. Elijah, how about cuttin' us some slices of your apple pie? It looks heavenly," stated Aunt Elsie trying to be brave and hiding her sadness. While she made coffee and Elijah sliced the pie, Mollie placed clean blue willow dessert plates on the kitchen table.

As soon as Dora finished washing the dinner dishes, the four of them sat down at the table to make plans for Joseph's burial. Aunt Elsie made it perfectly clear that she wanted a small, private funeral with just the four of them in attendance. "Joseph and I've lived in these here parts and are well-known throughout the community, but there's nobody I'd consider my good friends except for you three."

Dora, Mollie, and Elijah smiled back at her and then stood up to hold her hands and embrace her. "We love you, too," exclaimed the three in unison.

"You've all been so kind to us since you've lived here. I don't know what I'd do without you," cried Aunt Elsie.

"Auntie, don't ever worry about being all alone. You've got us now to look after you completely, and if you don't mind me asking, I'd like to invite you to move in with me here," replied Mollie.

"That's a very generous offer, but I believe I'll just stay in my own home at least until spring. We'll see."

Afterwards, the four of them went into a discussion about what to do with Joseph's body. Aunt Elsie decided that as soon as the storm subsided they must remove the corpse and take it to her farm. Elijah decided when he got to Aunt Elsie's farm to dig the grave and fashion a marker out of wood and burn Joseph's name

223

into it. Thankfully, the ground was not too hard, because they were just beginning to get the worst of storms. Elsie said not to put the birth and death dates on the marker. She planned, however, to write his date of death in her Bible as soon as she returned home.

It was time for bed, so Aunt Elsie and Mollie went to Mollie's bedroom to sleep and Elijah went upstairs into one of the spare bedrooms. Dora stayed downstairs in the kitchen to clean up before retiring herself.

Very early the next morning Mollie went to the barn to feed the animals and milk the cows. She was thankful that the snowstorm had finally stopped. Although the barn was only two hundred feet away, it took her a few extra minutes to get there because of the knee deep snow. Elijah was already out of the house and over at his dwelling caring for his own livestock. Aunt Elsie and Dora were busily preparing breakfast for the entire household.

Once inside the barn, Mollie heard a strange sound in one of the cow's stalls. She strolled quickly to find out what was amiss. Mollie smiled when she discovered that her cow, Sapphire, had given birth to twin calves. Normally, she expected the cows to give birth in the spring, but this was definitely a pleasant surprise. She could hardly wait to tell everyone about it at breakfast.

Next, she went to get an extra pail to skim off the cream in order to make fresh butter using her wooden churn. This was a special churn that Aunt Elsie had brought with her to the frontier from Virginia. Granny Williams had stenciled red flowers on the outside when she still lived in New York, but years of wear had practically rubbed them off completely. Now there were just the outlines of the flowers and small spots of red in the middle.

After milking the cows and making some butter it was time to return to the house. The tables were set and everyone else was ready to sit down but waited for Mollie's return. As she walked back she almost dropped the pails of milk and butter when she stepped onto some ice under the snow.

"Phew! Lucky thing I kept my balance. We need the milk and butter for breakfast."

Elijah looked out the window and saw Mollie approaching. He ran outside to meet her and carry the pails for her. Together they walked into the back door of the kitchen to get ready for breakfast. "Guess what everyone?" asked Mollie.

"Yes, my dear? What is it?" replied Aunt Elsie.

"My favorite cow, Sapphire gave birth to twins! Ain't that wonderful?"

"That *is* good news!" stated Elijah smiling. "After last night we needed somethin' to cheer us up."

Finally, they all sat down and Elijah asked God to bless the meal. During the meal they remained quiet as they remembered Joseph and his life's work.

Shortly thereafter when breakfast was finished and the women had cleaned the kitchen, Elijah carried Joseph's body out to the buckboard; however, since the snow was still so deep, he climbed upon one of the workhorses and galloped away in the direction of Aunt Elsie's farm, because she had a sledge stored inside her barn. He needed to check on her livestock as well and feed them.

When Elijah arrived at the Williams farm, he found Mr. Mullins just coming out of the barn. "Good day, Dr. Benson. Turrible storm we had last night," shouted Mr. Mullins.

"It sure was. Poor Mr. Williams suffered an accident and died last night," exclaimed Elijah.

"Oh, I'm so sorry to hear that. He was the best man I ever worked for in me life, and I've been a workin' since I were fourteen. Why that's forty years now," replied Mr. Mullins with a bit of remorse. He began to think this might be his last month of work now that Joseph was dead. "If there's anythin' and I mean anythin' I can do fer the family, please let me know."

"There's one thing. Can you help me to dig Mr. Williams's grave? I've already made a marker for him early this morning, but I was waitin' to get some help to dig the grave."

"Say no more. I'll go with ya to bring the body back here to store in the barn. You go on and I'll foller after ya in the sledge."

"Thanks, Mr. Mullins. Your kindness won't go unrewarded."

Meanwhile, back at Mollie's farm, Mollie was preparing to write up a message to send a telegraph to Granny Williams. Aunt Elsie and Dora were in the kitchen already preparing for the midday meal. Mollie stated that she had her heart set on chicken and dumplings, so Aunt Elsie was determined to cook it according

226

to her mother's method, which was the way Mollie preferred it over anyone else's recipe.

Not long after, Elijah returned and stopped out front. He tethered the horse to the porch and went inside the house. Minutes after he arrived, Mr. Mullins appeared in the sledge drawn by Joseph's two pure black stallions that always shimmered in the sunlight. He climbed down from the sledge as soon as it stopped and approached the front door. Elijah saw him and invited him inside and on into the parlor.

Mollie walked into the parlor and said, "If you gentlemen don't mind I need to take the sledge into town, because I'm sending Granny Williams word of Uncle Joseph's death. Elijah, would you take me to town?"

"It'll be my pleasure. We may be late because of the snow, but we can hurry if we leave now."

"All righty. I'll go get my coat and bonnet, and I'll meet ya outside."

She first returned to the kitchen to tell Aunt Elsie that she was departing soon. "We may be late a comin' back for lunch. I just wanna be sure Granny knows right away."

"Don't worry, my dear. I'll keep a plate warm fer both of ya," stated Aunt Elsie.

"Thanks, Auntie. I'll see ya soon." She embraced her aunt and then went to get her coat, bonnet, and gloves. After that she went out from where Elijah had the sledge pointed towards town.

Along the way into town Mollie admired the snow topped fields. On one farm she noticed several children outside playing various games in the snow. She waved to them, but they were too engaged in their frolicking to notice. Elijah held her left hand firmly with his right hand while he steered the sledge with his left. He reached over and kissed her on her left cheek. She in turn smiled at him and reached over to kiss his right cheek.

Once they approached town they made their way over to the post office. The postmistress lived in a small house behind the post office, so of course she was almost always there.

"Good morning. I wish to send a telegraph to my grandmother in Pine Mountain Township in Virginia," stated Mollie.

"That'll be just fine, Miss Williams. Good morning to you, Dr. Benson," exclaimed the postmistress.

"Greetings to you too," said Elijah.

Mollie handed the note to the postmistress to transcribe over to a telegraph. She examined it carefully and then said, "I'm so sorry to hear of your loss. Your Uncle Joseph was truly a good man. When he first came to Kansas he really helped a lot of people in need. Yes, he was truly a good man." The postmistress processed the information and sent off the telegraph. Next, Mollie and Elijah bade her goodbye and went over to the mercantile to purchase a few supplies.

As usual, Miss Cleo was inside whistling some of her favorite songs. When she heard the bell jingle as Mollie and Elijah entered, she looked up and surmised that they both appeared to be upset about something by the solemn expressions on their faces. "Miss Williams, can I help ya with somethin'? You look kinda sad."

"Uncle Joseph died last night after a fall," stated Mollie.

"Dear me. I'm so sorry to hear that. Mr. Williams is the one who convinced the owners to let me run the place. 'She's as honest as they come' is how he put it to them. I'll never forget as long as I live what he did for me," replied Miss Cleo.

"Anyways, we need more coffee and some dried beans. Seems like we use so much of it," chuckled Mollie.

Elijah went to another counter and admired the wedding bands and various cameos. Although Miss Cleo was busily measuring out the coffee and dried beans she noticed exactly what he was looking at. She smiled again and then said, "Anything I can help you with there, Dr. Benson?"

"Oh, no thanks! Just thinkin' about next spring when I take a little trip up North," said Dr. Benson with a slight grin on his face.

Miss Cleo handed the dry goods over to Mollie. Elijah walked over to her and said, "Mollie, if you don't mind could you please take those things to the sledge and wait for me? I've got somethin' I need to ask Miss Cleo."

"All righty, but don't be long."

As soon as she was outside and out of sight he asked Miss Cleo to meet him over by the cameos. "I'll take your most expensive one in the case."

"My, my, Dr. Benson. That'll cost you twenty dollars. I didn't know you were a courtin' someone," exclaimed Miss Cleo.

Elijah smiled at her and said, "I just might be."

Miss Cleo found a small box and placed the cameo inside it. Then she wrapped it in brown paper and fastened it with string. "Whoever gits this pin must be one special lady."

"Oh, she is. She really is." Then he told her farewell and left the store to rejoin Mollie. He climbed into the sledge and they drove away.

Later, when they returned home and had eaten lunch it was time to transfer Uncle Joseph's body to his home. The ground was still frozen, so Mr. Mullins and Elijah placed the body in the tool shed out in the barn. "If it warms up tomorrow or Sunday, we can bury him then," stated Elijah.

While the women were in the kitchen washing dishes and preparing for supper the men stayed outside tending to the outdoor chores. Then Elijah and Mr. Mullins went back to each other's farms to tend to the livestock. Snow began to fall once again but not enough to prevent them from working.

Hours later, Elijah returned driving the sledge filled with extra firewood. The snow was tapering off and made it easier for him to see the path to Mollie's home. Once he stopped in front of the house he smelled the wonderful scents of baked bread and beef stew. Elijah went around to the back of the house and stacked firewood beside the back door of the kitchen. After he finished the task he opened the door and carried some wood inside to put in the fireplaces.

"Elijah, would you please go call Mr. Mullins to come inside? We're ready to eat supper," exclaimed Aunt Elsie. He went outside but could not find Mr. Mullins within sight, so he went over to the barn.

"Oh, there you are. Miss Elsie says it's time to eat supper," stated Elijah standing near the cows' stalls where Mr. Mullins was sitting to be alone.

After supper when it was time for everyone to go to bed Elijah called Mollie aside. "What is it Elijah? Is somethin' bothering you? Because, if it is, I wanna know."

"Mollie, we've been courting for quite some time now, haven't we?"

"Yes, we have," said Mollie.

"To show you how much I have enjoyed these last several weeks with you I've got a gift for you." Elijah handed her the small box wrapped in brown paper and tied with string. She opened the package carefully and revealed what was inside. It contained one of the most beautiful cameos she had seen in her entire life. Tears streamed down both cheeks because she ascertained that a gift like this was very costly and meant what she already knew and that was Elijah loved her very deeply. "Thank you, Elijah. It's absolutely gorgeous. I shall wear it tomorrow."

Elijah and Mollie embraced each other and then kissed each other's cheek. "Good night, Elijah, my love."

"Good night, my dearest Mollie."

Chapter 16

Winter had passed and no one could have been more
relieved than Dora, Aunt Elsie, Mollie, and Elijah. For in the
spring Mollie and Elijah were planning a trip to Minnesota to
exchange vows. Aunt Elsie looked forward to seeing her sister
Rebecca once again, and finally, Dora's son Ephraim was visiting
in March.

Mollie's sheep were ready to be sheared and Elijah
intended to help. Aunt Elsie and Dora offered to wash and card the
wool and later make thread, because Mollie wanted to utilize
Elijah's loom to weave coverlets for the next fall and winter.

Early one morning at the end of March Mollie and Elijah
were herding the sheep into the barn to shear them. Normally, they
used the paddock, but Elijah's stallions were grazing in it. The
long winter made it difficult for Mr. Mullins to have the
opportunity to build the extra paddock on Elijah's farm.
Fortunately, Aunt Elsie had canned enough foods to last them well
into the spring, because trips to the mercantile were tedious
through the deep snow that blanketed the countryside for many
weeks on end. Truly, all of the repairs and extra chores had to wait
and put everything behind.

These sheep came from a Scottish farmer living in a
settlement south of Summerdale. Thus, they were still young
enough to produce more than an adequate supply of wool for many

years to come. Four ewes each gave birth to twins, so Mollie now had eight beautiful cottony white lambs to raise.

In just a week's time Aunt Rebecca's train would be arriving. Uncle Increase was not near death, but he felt that he must not travel a long distance and needed to manage the business as he trusted no one to run it for him. Aunt Elsie wanted to spruce up the house and requested that Mollie help her.

Ephraim, Dora's son, was arriving just days after Aunt Rebecca. Dora made an extra effort to mop all of the floors and dust each room. When Mollie was finished with her sheep and working at her aunt's homestead and the others had completed their tasks, Dora decided to make a special supper for everyone who labored.

By the time suppertime arrived everyone was exhausted. Aunt Elsie said the blessing and all of them ate a spectacular meal of pork roast, boiled potatoes, boiled squash, and biscuits. While they were eating they heard the horses neighing and the approaching sound of harness bells.

"Goodness! I wonder who that could be at this hour," exclaimed Mollie. Mollie rose up from her chair and walked to the front door. There standing in a most regal blue velvet dress was none other than Aunt Rebecca!

"Aunt Rebecca! You're here early. We weren't expectin' you until next week."

"I know, dearie. I know. I just thought dear Elsie could use me help before next week. Poor thang's a widow now," replied Aunt Rebecca.

"Well, come on in. Oh, I see you brought Vincent with you."

"Why yes, I did. I'm rather use to bein' comfortable. Vincent, brang my bags inside, please."

"Of course, Madam," stated Vincent.

Immediately, Mollie showed Aunt Rebecca to one of her spare rooms upstairs. The room was, of course, very simplistic compared with what Aunt Rebecca was accustomed to. There was a pine rope bed with a log cabin patterned quilt laying on it. Mollie directed her attention to the wardrobe and chest of drawers. At the foot of the bed was a flat-topped trunk. Beside the bed stood a walnut candle stand with an oil lamp sitting on it. Aunt Rebecca had a look of contentment despite the more rugged surroundings.

"Would you like somethin' to eat?" asked Mollie.

"Why no, my dear. Vincent and I stopped to eat at a restaurant in Summerdale," replied Aunt Rebecca. "If you don't mind please ask Elsie to come up here?"

"Anythin' you say, Aunt Rebecca." Mollie quickly but carefully descended the stairs to get Aunt Elsie. When she entered the kitchen she found everyone else cleaning up the supper dishes and sweeping the floor. Elijah was playing his guitar to entertain the ladies as they worked.

"Aunt Elsie, Aunt Rebecca needs to see you upstairs immediately," stated Mollie. "I'll finish up the dishes for you."

"I thank you. Probably Rebecca wants me to help her unpack a few things. I'll be back shortly," exclaimed Aunt Elsie. She ascended the stairs and joined her sister.

Inside her room Aunt Rebecca was busily laying out her night clothes and taking out her Bible to read before going to bed. Vincent was in the adjoining room also preparing for bed but awaiting further instructions from his employer.

"Oh, there you are, Sister," stated Rebecca enthusiastically. "I called ya up cheer because there's something I wanna propose to you, and I need an answer right away."

"Go on, Becky. I'm a listenin' to ya."

"Actually, thar's two things I wish to propose. First, would ya like to come live with me in Chattanooga? You'd be much closer to Mama and Papa."

"That, I don't know. I hate to leave poor Mollie alone. If I leave she won't have any family here at all. How can I do that to her?"

"Elsie, that brings me to my second proposition. If you agree to come live with me I'll buy out your farm, and you can leave it to Mollie. What do you think about that, Sis?"

"The thought's crossed my mind many a time since Joseph died. I couldn't think of a better person to take charge. Our good friend and neighbor Elijah Benson helps us out, and I think he'd help her run the farm."

"Now, that's thinkin' in a postive way. You're soundin' more like Mama everday!"

Together they placed the remainder of Rebecca's clothes in the wardrobe and the chest of drawers. Then Rebecca said, "We can talk more about this tomorrow once we're all rested."

Rebecca and Elsie both exited the room. Elsie went downstairs while Rebecca went to Vincent's room to tell him to take the rest of the night off. He was expected to sit with the family and enjoy breakfast with them in the morning which was something he never engaged in back in Tennessee. Although he was in her employ, Rebecca decided to allow him *some* liberties while they were in Kansas.

Vincent was born in London, England to Ethiopian immigrants who hoped for a better life. He entered the United States twenty years earlier when he was forty-five years old. His wife of twenty-four years died of heart failure and his twenty-four year old son came to America with him to start a new life. When they first came to the United States they settled in Philadelphia where Negroes were treated better than in the South. While he was in Philadelphia after a few years of low-paying jobs, he discovered an advertisement for a butler in Tennessee. Steady work was difficult to obtain for Negroes other than menial positions; however, the butler position promised to offer a more than generous salary. Vincent's son Daniel met and married a native of Nigeria and therefore remained in Philadelphia to rear five daughters.

Early the next morning, Vincent arose earlier than usual as he intended to go for a walk, because his physician required it for his aging health. He quietly descended the stairs after getting dressed and went outside. As he walked down the lane, he noticed the wind speed began to increase which stirred around some of the dust. He had read about dust storms, but this was the first time he had ever experienced one. Immediately, he ran back to the house to warn the women. Elijah had left for his farm earlier and Mr. Mullins was back at the Williams farm.

Mollie and the others were still fast asleep unaware of the impending doom. He ran up the stairs and knocked on his mistress's door loudly.

"Yes? Who's it at this hour?" cried Rebecca.

"It is I, Vincent, your butler. I've something to tell you. Please hurry as it is urgent," exclaimed Vincent.

Aunt Rebecca climbed out of bed and put on her robe at the foot of her bed and then opened the door. She ascertained by the expression on Vincent's face that this was a very serious matter.

"Now tell me, Vincent. What's wrong and please answer slowly."

"I just came from outside, and I think a dust storm of some kind is forming. We must warn the others," answered Vincent.

"I'll wake up Elsie. You go wake up Mollie and Dora."

Quickly, Vincent ran to Dora's door and told her to get up and meet everyone downstairs. Next, he hurriedly climbed down the stairs and on to the direction of Mollie's door. At the same time the horses, cows, sheep, and all the other farm animals made loud noises of distress. Just as Vincent was about to knock on Mollie's door she opened it still in her nightgown and jumped.

"Oh my, Vincent. You startled me! I didn't expect to find somebody on the other side of my door."

"Sorry Miss, but I came to warn you about the dust storm brewing outside," stated Vincent.

"I wondered why I heard all those animal noises outside. Come, let's go outside and make sure all of the animals are safe in their pens."

"Yes, Madam."

Together Mollie and Vincent went outside to secure the barn and the chicken coops. Then they gathered up all the dogs and cats and led them into the barn. The cats had to be carried. Just as they left the barn Elijah arrived mounted on Othello.

"Can I help?" exclaimed Elijah.

"Yes, dear. We need to go inside and place sheets and towels under all of the openings leadin' to the outside," cried Mollie.

Vincent thought it was rather odd for a white woman to speak so lovingly to a Negro, but he had the tactfulness to make no comment. He rushed back into the house with Mollie while Elijah led Othello into the barn with the other animals. Then after about five minutes Elijah rejoined them inside the house. Already the dust began to blow everywhere coating anything in its path.

"Elijah, praises to God that you're also here to help us," shouted Aunt Elsie. Mollie, Elijah, and Vincent began to roll up all area rugs and put them near the walls. Next, they placed and stuffed towels and sheets under doorways and then draped sheets to cover fireplace openings. Thankfully, the former owners had the good sense to install closeable shutters on all the windows in case of dust storms. Elijah and Vincent secured all of the shutters in plenty of time to save the windows.

"I'm sorry you had to come see us in the middle of a storm, Aunt Rebecca," stated Mollie.

"No need to apologize, my dear. It coulda happened at any time," replied Aunt Rebecca assuredly.

During the storm they continued to hear animal noises and the sounds of boards hitting the sides of the house as well as the roof and outside walls creaking. Despite the natural disaster they all ate breakfast and prayed that God would see them through it.

Two hours later when the winds had died down Mollie, Elijah, and Vincent went outside to explore the farm. They immediately noticed boards scattered across the barnyard. Mollie looked heartbroken at the site of her barn with its missing boards and a few dead chickens.

"I see this old barn should've been repaired a very long time ago. With luck we'll have time to repair it before the next storm," stated Elijah. Elijah and Vincent went on into the barn to search for hammers and nails. Meanwhile, Mollie opened the shutters on the ground floor and then went inside to open the shutters from the upper floor. Aunt Elsie and Aunt Rebecca removed all sheets and towels and placed them near the laundry tubs.

"Aunt Elsie and Aunt Rebecca, could you please go outside while Dora and I sweep? Seems like no matter how hard you try to keep the dust out you still got some to sweep away," stated Mollie.

"Sure thang, dear. Rebecca and I'll go over to my place and check on thangs with Mr. Mullins," said Aunt Elsie. They put on their bonnets and walked towards the barn to hitch the team to Rebecca's rented wagon. Vincent graciously prepared the horses and wagon for them. Elijah rode away to inspect his own farm.

"Do you want me to drive you to the Williams farm, Madam?" stated Vincent.

"That ain't necessary. This'll give us two sisters a chance to be alone and talk more, but thanks anyways," cried Aunt Rebecca.

On the way to the farm Rebecca asked Elsie about coming to live with her and Increase. Elsie hesitated a little before she said, "Rebecca, I've decided I'll come to live with you. After roughin' it all my life I wouldn't mind livin' the rest of my life in luxury. But at the same time I wouldn't mind doin' my fair share round the place."

"Elsie, we're goin' to enjoy ourselves. It'll be like old times when we was girls livin' at Mama and Papa's. I still cain't believe poor Joseph's gone," stated Rebecca.

"It gets harder and harder each day, but I'll make it. God has a plan in everthang we do in our lives," replied Elsie with a few tears trickling down her cheeks. On they went to Aunt Elsie's farm.

Meanwhile, Elijah was at his farm assessing any damage there might be. Unfortunately, he found his house to be full of dust, because most of the windows had shattered. In spite of that, none of the stallions suffered any injuries as the sturdy barn kept them completely safe. Elijah's barn had a few loose planks but nothing major as far as any damage was concerned. He was very thankful that there were no casualties in this strong dust storm unlike storms he had seen in the years he had lived on the plains.

Mollie, Dora, and Vincent rode over in Mollie's buckboard to see if Elijah wanted help with the cleaning. Vincent walked over to the barn to help Elijah reattach some loose planks. Then Mollie and Dora went inside Elijah's house to sweep away glass and dust out the front and back doors. After they finished sweeping they took some oaken buckets out to the water pump to obtain water to scrub off the counters and furniture that were completely covered with dust. Finally, Elijah and Vincent nailed some boards across the exposed windows to protect the house from the elements.

A few hours later when the work was complete the men and women gathered back at Mollie's place to eat lunch. Although Aunt Rebecca had servants to wait on her every need, she still remembered how to prepare delicious meals and offered to make lunch for everyone. The other women insisted on helping her, but she refused and asked them to wait with the men in the parlor and stay out of her way in the kitchen. They welcomed any opportunity to have a break from cooking.

As everyone else waited in the parlor together, they smelled the wonderful aroma of beef stew and fresh bread wafting throughout the air. "I see Rebecca hasn't forgotten how to cook after all," commented Elsie.

"Oh yes, Madam sometimes helps the cook back home. Every Sunday after church she makes some of the best custard you ever tasted in your life," stated Vincent.

"When we were young girls a growin' up together our Grandma Greene, Papa's maw, taught us how to make custard. Rebecca was the only one who always did it just right. Nancy and I always burned ours, so we vowed to never make any more of it," chuckled Elsie as she spoke.

"I always wondered why I ain't never had any custard before," replied Mollie with a grin.

An hour later, Rebecca called the group into the kitchen for lunch. The table was covered in the middle with beef stew, fresh baked rolls, corn on the cob, boiled squash, and boiled carrots. To quench their thirst Aunt Rebecca squeezed fresh lemons for lemonade. Everyone was pleased with the delectable display placed on Mollie's table.

After lunch Mollie asked Elijah to meet her outside by the barn. The aunts, Dora, and Vincent remained inside to clean up the kitchen and scrub away the rest of the dust that had settled in any of the cracks and crevices.

Elijah had no knowledge of what Mollie wanted to tell him, so he was slightly puzzled. "My dear Elijah, after havin' been over at your place earlier I've come to a decision."

"Yes, my love?"

"There's a spare bed in Vincent's room, so I want you to stay here permanently until we get hitched. Tomorrow, we can move your personal belongings from your house into either your barn or mine."

Elijah reached out his hand to grasp her hand and pulled her closer so that he could kiss and embrace her. At the same time Aunt Rebecca and Vincent were on the front porch sweeping and witnessed everything.

"I wonder if Elsie knows what's a goin' on here. It don't look like your normal friendly embrace," thought Rebecca to herself.

Vincent said nothing out loud but thought to himself, "All I can say is they are going to have a lot of problems if they decide to wed."

"Stay here a moment, Vincent. I gotta have a word or two with my sister," exclaimed Rebecca.

Rebecca went inside slamming the door behind her and made her way to Elsie. "Elsie, where are you?"

"I'm upstairs, dear. You sound upset. Anythin' wrong?" cried Elsie from the top of the stairs.

"What's goin' on with our niece and that colored doctor?" shouted Rebecca.

"First of all, stop a shoutin' at me. Second, please lower your voice," pleaded Elsie.

"I won't lower my voice until you tell me what's a goin' on," stated Rebecca.

"Well, if you must know I'll tell you, but let's go in your room where we can be in private," answered Elsie somewhat disgruntled with her sister.

Rebecca ascended the stairs and they went into Rebecca's room. Elsie closed the door behind her and said, "Mollie and the doctor are plannin' to get married this spring in Minnesota. They fell in love back when Mollie almost died when she was stabbed by Dora's husband."

"And you approve of this?"

"Let me finish, grumpy. At first, Joseph and I didn't approve, but Elijah did such a wonderful job a helpin' us all and saving Mollie's life we consented. Poor Joseph consented on his deathbed."

"They're gonna have a whole heap of trouble from society. Mark my words. But if they love each other there ain't much we can do. Elsie, give me time to accept this, and I'll even ask for God's help," exclaimed Rebecca.

"Thank you. All I ask is you treat them both kindly now that ya know." cried Elsie who then grasped her sister's hand. They smiled at each other and then embraced.

245

****

Weeks had passed into April, and it was time for Elijah and Mollie to travel to Kansas City to board the train to Minneapolis. Both were very excited and nervous at the same time. Aunt Rebecca and Vincent were still staying at Mollie's with Elsie until they returned from their wedding tour in London where Elijah's older sister and her British-born husband were living. Dora was still awaiting the arrival of her son Ephraim who was nearly a month late.

Mollie and Elijah busily loaded the Saratoga trunk with all their clothes in the back of Aunt Elsie's buckboard. Mr. Mullins assisted Vincent in loading all the other cases. The two men also checked the wheels to make certain they were safe and placed the canvas on top of the wagon. Mr. Mullins offered to drive them to the train station.

Aunt Elsie rushed out to the wagon carrying a large picnic basket filled to the rim with ham and cheese sandwiches and a cherry pie. "This is fer all of you to eat on the way. I thought you might get hungry out on the road."

"Thank you, Auntie. That's very sweet and thoughtful of you," stated Mollie.

Dora, Aunt Rebecca, and Aunt Elsie told them goodbye and said they intended to pray for them to have a safe journey. "Elsie and I'll surely miss ya both while you're gone. We've got a big surprise a waitin' fer ya when ya return," stated Rebecca.

246

"We best get goin.' We don't wanna be late fer the train," said Mr. Mullins as he was climbing into the driver's seat. As soon as he was situated and ready to leave everyone said farewell again and the wagon pulled away. Aunt Elsie cried while Aunt Rebecca had her arm around her shoulders to comfort her.

The trip to the train station was long, tiring, and dusty. Mr. Mullins and Elijah took turns driving and resting so they could make it to the Kansas City train station by nightfall. Although their train did not depart until the following morning they wanted to get plenty of sleep to keep from oversleeping or being too tired the very next day. Mollie chose to rest when Elijah rested so that they could discuss their plans once they arrived in Minnesota.

Several hours later just before dusk they arrived near the train station in Kansas City. Nearby, they found the same hotel where Mollie, Uncle Joseph, and Aunt Elsie stayed when she first arrived in Kansas. She felt a little sad thinking about her Uncle Joseph and began to ponder about the idea that perhaps if she had not come to Kansas he might still be alive.

"Dearest, what's the matter? You look troubled?" exclaimed Elijah.

"This is the same hotel where we stayed when I first got here. I was thinkin' about poor Uncle Joseph and how he might still be alive if I'd never come here," said Mollie who then began to sob.

"Do you want us to find a different hotel?" stated Mr. Mullins.

"I'll be fine in a little bit. Really, I will," stated Mollie.

"Now don't you go on thinkin' like that anymore, my love. None of us know when it's our time to die," said Elijah as he reached over to hold her hand. Mollie smiled back at him to reassure her fiancé that she was going to be fine.

Mr. Mullins dropped off Mollie and Elijah in front of the hotel and then went to park the buckboard. Mollie went inside to book rooms for her and the men leaving Elijah on the steps with the smaller bags awaiting Mr. Mullins. The attendant announced that she had arrived just in time, because she rented the last two rooms. As she walked away she heard him tell the others behind her that all the rooms were now full.

Moments later Mr. Mullins returned ready for bed. The three of them went upstairs to their adjoining rooms to prepare for bed. Briefly, Mollie stepped into Elijah's room to embrace him and kiss him before she retired for the night. Then she bade both men good night and went into her own room.

Early the next morning the trio went downstairs to the restaurant to eat breakfast. They decided they needed a plan to keep Elijah from riding in the luggage car. Mollie put on one of the elegant emerald colored outfits with matching hat that Aunt Rebecca bought for her. When she bought the tickets she planned to tell the attendant that Elijah was her personal servant and she needed him to assist her at any given moment. She could think of no reason why the plan would not work. After all she was wearing a very expensive outfit and her story was believable.

Once breakfast was finished Mr. Mullins went to bring the wagon back to drive them over to the train station. Mollie and Elijah waited on the steps with their entire luggage awaiting Mr. Mullins's return. About five minutes later he returned, stepped down, and helped Elijah load the back of the buckboard. As soon as they packed everything away the men helped Mollie climb up into the wagon.

Just as they arrived at the train station it began to drizzle. Thankfully, Mollie remembered to pack her parasol. Again both men helped Mollie climb out of the wagon. While the men busily unloaded the back Mollie walked over to the ticket booth to buy two tickets to Minneapolis. She told the ticket agent that she was traveling with her personal servant and required him to sit next to her. Then she went on to say that she had had some irregular fainting spells and worried about traveling alone. The ticket agent looked at her outfit and surmised that she must be a very wealthy young woman.

"Normally, we don't allow coloreds to travel anywhere with the Whites, but seein' as you're a woman of substance and are afraid to travel with your faintin' spells I'll approve it," stated the agent.

"Bless you, kind sir!" exclaimed Mollie with a sound of relief in her voice.

Elijah and Mr. Mullins rejoined her carrying the Saratoga trunk with one hand each and the smaller bags with their other hands. Together they went to the train to give the luggage to a porter as soon as they found one. Along the way a few people attempted to give luggage to Elijah thinking he was also a porter, as he was dressed in his doctor's black suit and hat. Mr. Mullins spoke up and said, "Leave the poor man alone!"

When they finally found a porter and located the proper train they each bade farewell. "Take good care of my aunts, Mr. Mullins," stated Mollie.

"I sure will, Miss Williams. And you ain't got nothing to worry about. You two have a wonderful trip, and I wanna congratulate you," replied Mr. Mullins quietly. He hugged them both and waited for them to board the train.

While they waited in line to give their tickets to the conductor, a man behind them said to his wife, "Imagine that. A colored man's a comin' onto this car. I hope he don't sit near us." Mollie became angry, but Elijah whispered into her ear, "Calm down, my dear. We'll be in Minneapolis tomorrow and then on our wedding tour."

As soon as it was their turn to board the train Mr. Mullins waved goodbye and went on his way. Mollie gave their tickets to the conductor just as Elijah waved back to Mr. Mullins.

"Excuse me. Miss, but that colored man has got to ride in the baggage car," stated the conductor.

"Sir, I already went through this same conversation with the ticket agent. This man, Mr. Elijah Benson, is my personal servant who must attend to me in case I faint again."

The conductor examined the tickets again and discovered the ticket agent made a notation on Elijah's ticket allowing him to proceed onto the passenger car. "I'm sorry, Ma'am. I didn't see the note at first. Go on and board then." He frowned at Elijah as he passed him.

Mollie and Elijah found their seats just moments later. Various people exchanged looks with them but spoke in low whispers in reply. Sitting across from their seat was a middle-aged couple dressed modestly. They ascertained that the couple was likely poor farmers on a very special trip, because they appeared to be rather excited.

"Good mornin', folks. I'm Mollie, and this is my personal servant, Elijah. We're takin' a trip to Minneapolis to attend a wedding."

"What a coincidence. We're Charles and Hetty Miller, and we're also going to Minneapolis to attend our youngest daughter's weddin'," stated Charles Miller. "Our daughter is marryin' a doctor she met while she was in college there. He sent us money for our trip, otherwise we'd have missed the weddin'. All our children live at Summerdale near us."

"You're joking! I live in Summerdale too near my Aunt Elsie Williams," said Mollie.

"I know your Aunt Elsie. Once when we were a strugglin' to make ends meet she and her church group brought us enough food to last a month. Even when we got our finances straight she still checked on us. You've got a very special aunt," cried Hetty Miller.

Knowing that they all had so much in common they talked for hours and hours until it was time to lie down. The trip did not seem as long since all had such a wonderful time together.

Chapter 17

Early the next day the train pulled into Minneapolis. The Millers hated to see them go, but they all promised to meet for supper one day when both couples returned from Minneapolis.

"We hope you both have a very nice weddin'. You make a wonderful lookin' couple!" said Hetty rather quietly.

"But how'd you know?" exclaimed Mollie stunned.

"Anyone could tell by the way you two looked at each other and talked about each other that you're the ones gittin' hitched," said Charles Miller.

"And we approve. We originally came from Massachusetts and we're staunch abolitionists. You oughta be happy with whoever you wanna marry. Anyway, we see our daughter a comin' this way. See ya when you get back," said Hetty Miller.

"Thank you, Charles and Hetty. We look forward to it," stated Mollie as she left them. "Weren't they the kindest people you ever did meet?"

"Yes, my love. They certainly were. We need to go find us a hotel with two rooms. Tomorrow you're goin' to be Mrs. Elijah Benson!" exclaimed Elijah ecstatically.

Shortly thereafter, they collected all of their bags and the Saratoga trunk. Not far from the front of the train station were several cabriolets waiting. Mollie walked to the front of the station and approached one of the drivers.

"Sir, could you please come help us with our luggage? We'd also like to hire you for the rest of the day, if that's possible."

"But of course, Madam. Just show me where it is," stated the driver. The train station was busy and all of the porters were assisting other passengers and that is why Mollie sought the cabriolet driver. Together, they went to the back of the station to help Elijah with their baggage.

"Mollie, we need to send a wire to my sister to let her know where we are," stated Elijah. "Don't forget to let Miss Elsie know as well."

"Sure thing, my love, but we need a hotel first," replied Mollie.

The cabriolet driver picked up one end of the Saratoga trunk while Elijah lifted the other end. Mollie carried the two smaller bags which were not anywhere near as heavy. As they made their way to the front Mollie noticed there was a telegraph office in the front of the train station.

"Elijah, I'm goin' into the telegraph office. I'll only be a moment," declared Mollie. She went inside to send telegrams to Aunt Elsie, Elijah's sister Polly Okpodu, and to Granny Williams. Deep inside she knew her granny approved of her marriage no matter who she married. Granny Williams told her once many years prior about a family from Ethiopia living on a farm near hers in New York. They always managed well and never were at odds with any of their neighbors or fellow townspeople. Mollie never understood why Granny Williams had any tolerance of Negroes when everyone else in the family ignored them including her. After falling in love with Elijah she regretted ever having any animosity towards Negroes and vowed to support any cause that benefited them.

Afterwards, she left the office and walked over to the cabriolet where Elijah and the driver were waiting for her. The driver stepped down, opened the door, and helped Mollie climb inside. Soon they departed for the nearest hotel in downtown Minneapolis. Not long after the driver found a suitable hotel that likely had large suites so that Mollie and Elijah had separate rooms until their wedding the next day.

"Driver, Miss Williams and I'll go check into the hotel. Bring our luggage in," stated Elijah.

"Yes, Sir! Right away, Sir!" exclaimed the driver.

They proceeded into the hotel on to the front desk. "We need a suite containin' two bedrooms. We're getting' married tomorrow and want everything to be respectable until that time. Can you accommodate us?" said Elijah.

"There's one suite left, but it's only got one bedroom. The sittin' room is very nice though. We do have a single room across the hall from it," cried the clerk.

"I think the one suite will be just fine. Miss Williams can have the bed and I'll sleep on the sofa in the sittin' room. After all, one night will not inconvenience us," replied Elijah.

While Elijah and Mollie each signed the guest register the cabriolet driver returned with their luggage. A bellhop assisted him in carrying in the Saratoga trunk. Soon after that everyone climbed the stairs to the empty suite.

Upon entering the suite Mollie stated out loud, "This room's very elegant. It reminds me of one of Aunt Rebecca's bedrooms back in Tennessee. Oh, it's ever so lovely."

"I'm glad you like it, my darling," exclaimed Elijah. "Driver, please give us about a half hour to freshen up. We want you to take us to buy our wedding rings and then we wanna go eat an early supper at one of the finest restaurants in the city."

"Will do, Sir. I'll wait for you downstairs in the lobby," stated the driver. As he left, the bellhop asked them if they needed anything else. Elijah reached into his pocket and gave the bellhop a silver dollar.

"Thank you, Sir!" exclaimed the bellhop enthusiastically. He appeared rather astonished that a Negro could spare that much money. "If you need anythin' at all I'll personally attend to it."

"That'll be all. You can go now," said Elijah.

Later on, Mollie and Elijah exited their room wearing two of the fanciest outfits and descended the stairs to the front lobby. There they found the driver standing near the entrance holding a corsage.

"Miss Williams, this corsage is for you. Somebody delivered it to the front desk just moments ago, so I told the clerk I'd hold it for you."

"It's absolutely beautiful! Thank you! Whoever coulda sent this?" stated Mollie.

"I had it sent over, my dear. You needed a lovely flower to go with your lovely dress," replied Elijah. Mollie smiled at him and then kissed him on his right cheek. After that they left the hotel following the driver to the cabriolet parked out front. Passersby stared as Mollie and Elijah held hands on their way to the cab, but they did not care, because they were too much in love.

The driver helped Mollie climb in first and then Elijah went in after her. "Driver, I noticed a large mercantile on the way here halfway away from the train station. We want to buy our rings there," stated Elijah.

"Anythin' you say, Sir," stated the driver. Immediately, they drove away to the mercantile. It was about four-thirty and the mercantile likely closed at five o'clock, so Elijah asked him to hurry. Along the way they noticed that the streets were filled with wagons making them almost impassable. Elijah was afraid they might not make it.

Not long after that the mercantile was in sight. Mollie noticed that across the street was a beautiful white-painted church surrounded by a picket fence. "Elijah, if you don't mind pickin' out the rings by yourself I'll go inside that church and ask the minister if we can get married there. It's a lovely church!" exclaimed Mollie.

"All right, dearest Mollie, if you insist. I'd rather you see the rings first, but I'll manage," replied Elijah.

As soon as the carriage halted in front of the mercantile, Elijah helped Mollie down and walked her across the street. Then he hurried back to the store to look for wedding bands. Just as he entered, a woman about eighty years old wearing a black dress with a white apron and lacy white dust cap on her head exited a door in the back.

"I'll be right there, Sir," exclaimed the elderly woman. "It's almost closing time, and I didn't expect any more customers."

"Take your time, Ma'am. I'm in no great hurry," stated Elijah.

Just as the woman made it to the front she stared at Elijah for a few moments and then said, "I'm sorry, but I've never seen a colored man wearing such an expensive and fancy-looking outfit."

"That's quite all right. I get that all the time. You see, I own a large cattle and horse farm back in Kansas and I studied medicine in Europe," said Elijah.

"Once again, Sir, I'm terribly sorry. How can I help ya?"

"I wanna see your weddin' bands and money's not a problem," stated Elijah.

"Yes, I can see that. Now foller me over to the other counter."

Together they walked over to the counter in the middle of the store. Elijah peered at some of the most beautiful rings he had seen in quite some time. He and Mollie decided to be as practical as possible and not purchase something too ostentatious. After examining several rings he chose two simple gold bands of pure gold.

Meanwhile, Mollie sat down on one of the pews in the sanctuary waiting for a minister. While she sat she imagined how the ceremony looked and how excited she expected to be before, during, and after the ceremony. Soon after someone called out, "May I help you, Miss?"

Mollie was startled after being in deep thought and turned around to see who it was. Standing behind her was a middle-aged man with graying hair dressed in a typical black reverend's suit.

"Oh, yes, Reverend. I'm hopin' to be married here tomorrow, if the church's free."

"That won't be a problem. How does 11:00 a.m. sound to you?"

"I think that sounds perfect!"

"We have Sunday school rooms where you can change into your wedding gown and your fiancé can get into his wedding suit," stated the reverend.

"Thank you, Reverend... What's your name?"

"I'm Reverend Canute, and I'm pleased to make your acquaintance. By the way, do you have family in town to join you?"

"No, Sir. My fiancée and I are here alone. You see, we live in Kansas and this is the nearest state that will marry us," said Mollie.

"So, I see. You're marrying an Indian."

"Well, actually, I'm marryin' a Negro."

"Don't worry, Miss. I'll marry you both. Why, just last month I married a Negro woman to a white man. My wife can stand in as a witness to your wedding. Now what did you say your name is?"

"My name's Mollie Williams, and tomorrow you're going to make me the happiest woman ever," stated Mollie ecstatically.

Just as she was about to leave Elijah was crossing the street to rejoin her. Reverend Canute glanced over at him thinking how nobly dressed this Negro man appeared.

"This is my fiancé, Dr. Elijah Augustus Benson," cried Mollie.

Reverend Canute reached out his hand to shake Elijah's and said, "Pleased to meet you, Doctor. I'm Reverend Canute."

"The pleasure's all mine, Reverend."

"The Reverend's marryin' us tomorrow at 11:00 a.m. Does that agree with you, my dear?" said Mollie.

"That sounds wonderful! Well, we're gonna get some supper at a French restaurant we saw near the hotel. You're welcome to join us and discuss the ceremony and any expenses, if you like. It's our treat," exclaimed Elijah.

"Thank you both! That's very generous of you. I'll just go and tell my wife next door where I'll be."

"Why not bring her along? There's plenty of room in the cabriolet and we'd enjoy the company," said Mollie

"You're both so kind! It'll be my great pleasure to join you both in holy matrimony. I'll just be a minute," said Reverend Canute. Then he went into the parsonage to retrieve his wife. Meanwhile, Mollie and Elijah returned to the cabriolet and climbed in. Elijah asked the driver to go across the street and park in front of the church.

Immediately after they parked in front, the reverend came outside holding his wife's hand. She was dressed in a sapphire blue dress with a matching hat. Over her arms she had placed a dark blue shawl.

"This is my wife, Sarah Canute."

"Pleased to meet you," said Mollie and Elijah in unison.

"It's so generous of you to allow us to eat supper with you. Samuel was right. You two are a kind and amiable couple. May God continually bless you both," said Mrs. Canute.

Then, as soon as the Canutes climbed into the carriage the driver led them on their way. Along the way both couples talked about things such as what brought the Canutes to Minneapolis from Massachusetts and how Elijah and Mollie ended up in Kansas.

Minutes later, they arrived in front of a French restaurant. Elijah helped Mollie climb down and then Reverend Canute helped Sarah climb out. The driver secured the brake and then said to Elijah, "If you don't mind, Sir. I'm going down the street to get a bite to eat myself. I'll return in an hour."

"That'll be fine. We oughta be done about that time," replied Elijah.

The two couples then went inside of the restaurant. A man with a French accent wearing black dress pants, black shoes, a white dress shirt, a black tie, and an apron, escorted them to their table. He stared at Elijah but made no comments. Once everyone sat down Elijah announced, "Bring us your best bottle of champagne."

"Will do, Sir," stated the waiter.

Their table was adorned with a crisp, white linen cloth, sterling silver candleholders, and the sterling flatware rested near ivory napkins bundled by sterling holders. Both couples were pleased with the beautiful table as well as the elegance of the entire restaurant and the gentleman playing classical music on his violin.

"I've never been in a French restaurant before, Elijah," stated Mollie.

"Neither have we," cried Reverend Canute.

"While I studied medicine in France I ate at lots of places much like this one. I'd say the owner must be French," stated Elijah.

A man eavesdropping from a nearby table whispered to his wife, "Imagine that! A colored who studied medicine in Europe. I bet he thinks he's pretty clever."

"I'll say. But whoever heard of a colored doctor?" exclaimed his wife with a frown on her face.

Soon, the waiter returned with a bottle of champagne and four glasses. After he filled the glasses he said, "If you're ready I will take your orders."

Naturally, beneath the French menu items were English translations; however, the Canutes and Mollie asked Elijah to order for all of them in French. The waiter was so impressed by Elijah's almost perfect accent he asked, "What part of France do you come from?"

Elijah smiled and said, "Oh no, Sir. I only studied medicine at the University of Montpellier."

"You certainly could have fooled me, Sir," stated the waiter who then left to present orders to the chef in the kitchen.

While they waited for their food, Reverend Canute talked about the ceremony and what they needed for it. Mollie busily wrote down everything on a piece of paper that she had pulled out of her purse. She smiled the whole time excited about the very next day. Mrs. Canute did not reveal her plan to make a small wedding cake to show her appreciation for being taken to supper.

Almost twenty minutes later, the waiter returned with some of the most aromatic and captivating foods served on fine bone china decorated with small blue and yellow flowers. Both couples were very much pleased with what they saw.

"It all smells wonderful!" cried Mollie. "This'll most definitely satisfy our appetites."

The waiter left once again and only returned occasionally to see if they needed more coffee or water. None of the food was wasted, because everything was savored by the guests.

When an hour passed and everyone completed their meals the waiter returned with the bill. Elijah paid the bill and left him a most generous tip. The waiter was taken aback, because he had never been tipped that much before. "Thank you, Sir! You're most kind."

Elijah stood up from the table and the rest of the party followed. The four of them walked to the entrance and exited the restaurant. Their driver awaited them just outside as he had promised ready to help the ladies inside the cabriolet.

All the way back to the church, the reverend reiterated what a spectacular time he had with the wedding couple. His wife also expressed her gratitude for an enjoyable evening. Minutes later, the cabriolet stopped at the church and the Canutes climbed out. Then the driver returned the bridal pair to the hotel.

"Driver, if you'll return tomorrow at 9:00 a.m. in the mornin' and drive us to the church I'll make it worth your while. Here's your payment for today," exclaimed Elijah.

"A thousand thanks, kind Sir. I'll be here at 9:00 a.m. on the dot," remarked the driver excitedly. After he made certain that Mollie and Elijah had everything he departed for the night.

Mollie and Elijah approached the front desk to retrieve their key. The desk clerk remarked, "Is there anything else I can do for you?"

"No, thank you. We've all that we need," said Mollie. The clerk attended to the guests waiting behind Mollie and Elijah and then they ascended the stairs. They entered their room quietly and then Elijah closed the door.

"We have a lot to do tomorrow, so I think we oughta turn in now," said Elijah.

"I agree with you, my dear. I'm rather tired right now. Good night." Mollie embraced Elijah and then kissed him on the lips.

"Good night, my love. I can't wait to call you Mrs. Elijah Benson."

Straightaway, Mollie went into the bedchamber and closed the door behind her. Elijah undressed, put on his nightgown, blew out the lamps, and lay on the sofa. He had difficulty falling asleep at first thinking about the marriage ceremony. When he finally drifted off to sleep he had a dream. In the dream everyone was there at the church including Mollie's Uncle Joseph. Just after the minister said, "Is there any reason that these two cannot be married," Uncle Joseph walked up to Mollie and shouted, "She can't marry a Negro," and took her out of the church. Elijah began running after them and woke up.

Suddenly, Mollie came running out of her room. "Elijah, is everythin' all right? I heard you yellin'. I'm sure everyone upstairs did too."

"It was just a bad dream, my dear. No need to worry," exclaimed Elijah.

"Are you sure you don't wanna talk about it?" stated Mollie.

"I'm sure. Please go back to bed. We've got a full day ahead of us," replied Elijah. He stood up and kissed Mollie on the cheek to reassure her that he was fine. Then she went back into her room and lay down.

The following morning Mollie and Elijah arose early to wash up and have breakfast in the restaurant downstairs. It was terribly busy, so they had to wait longer than usual to eat. Once the waiter brought their food they were more than satisfied.

As soon as breakfast was finished the same cabriolet driver arrived at 7:30 a.m. Mollie wondered why he was already there and an hour and a half early at that. "What's he doin' here so early?" asked Mollie.

"I asked him to come early and take you to the church. Mrs. Canute had some things to discuss with you before the weddin'. He'll come back for me in plenty of time," replied Elijah.

"All right, but I feel kinda strange going so soon without you," cried Mollie.

"You'll be just fine. You've got nothin' to worry about. We *will* have our wedding! Now, go on with him," said Elijah assuredly. He held her hand long enough to politely kiss it and then sent her on her way.

When the driver helped her into the cab she noticed that there was a long, flat box bundled with string on the seat. "I wonder what's inside?" thought Mollie to herself. As soon as she sat down the driver climbed to his seat and drove on to the church.

Shortly thereafter, they arrived in front of the church where Mrs. Canute was awaiting her arrival. The driver once again climbed down from his place and then opened the door for Mollie. Mrs. Canute clasped her right hand and said, "Good morning, Miss Williams. I've got a surprise for you. Driver, please bring that box with you."

The driver brought that box along with another long box strapped onto the cabriolet. Then, he followed Mrs. Canute and Mollie into a room beside the sanctuary. He set the boxes down and then left to go after Elijah.

"Go ahead and open the boxes, Miss Williams. Open the heaviest one first," exclaimed Mrs. Canute.

Mollie untied the string and then lifted the lid of the heavier box. Inside she found the most exquisite white wedding dress she had ever seen. The dress looked just like one she had seen in a *Lady's Book* magazine. Next, she opened the lighter box and discovered a white veil with a wreath of orange blossoms on the crown. "Wherever did these boxes come from?" asked Mollie.

"It was Elijah. Yesterday when you weren't looking he slipped me a note asking me to go find you an elegant wedding dress and veil. One of our church members has a large mercantile with quite a selection of dresses, and he gladly obliged by letting me go in after hours," said Mrs. Canute.

267

Tears began to stream down her cheeks. She could not fathom how empty her life would be without Elijah. "This'll be the most perfect weddin'!" exclaimed Mollie loudly.

"There's another surprise for you, but it'll have to wait until after the ceremony," stated Mrs. Canute. "Now we've got to start getting you ready for the ceremony."

"You and the Reverend have been absolutely wonderful to us. We don't know how we're ever goin' to repay you," said Mollie.

"There's no need to worry about that, because we love to see young couples so happy. Now before we get you dressed is there anything you want to say to Elijah during the ceremony?" stated Mrs. Canute.

"I've got some things to say in front of witnesses that come from the heart. I don't need to write 'em down."

"Good, my dear. We've still got about two hours before we have to get you ready. I'm dying to know what you and Dr. Benson plan to do after the wedding."

"Elijah and I wanna go visit his older sister and her family in London. Her husband's also a physician and doin' very well. We intend to stay a week."

"The Reverend and I envy you going to London. We were married there when we were both on furlough from being missionaries in Africa. Why, we even caught a glimpse of Queen Victoria when she was in her gilded carriage."

"Excuse me, ladies, but I want to go over the ceremony with you again so that things run smoothly. Then when I am finished I'll go and wait for Dr. Benson in my office and go over it with him," stated Reverend Canute.

Once again time passed and it was a quarter after ten o'clock. "Oh my, Miss Williams! We've been so busy talking up a storm I didn't realize it was already after ten. We need to get you dressed," cried Mrs. Canute.

Mollie undressed and then put on a crisp ironed white slip. Then Mrs. Canute helped her put on her gown. Next, Mollie put on her best shiny black leather boots. Mrs. Canute hooked the boots for her using boot hooks. Finally, Mrs. Canute placed the veil upon her head. "Miss Williams, you look absolutely beautiful! You remind me of my own daughter not so many years ago. Now wait right here, and I'll get your wedding bouquet."

After a few minutes, Mrs. Canute returned with a lovely bunch of blue, yellow, and red wildflowers befitting for a lavish or simple ceremony. She ascertained by the expression on Mollie's face that she was extremely pleased. Meanwhile, they heard the voices of Elijah and Reverend Canute in the sanctuary.

"Well, Miss Williams. I'll leave you now and get ready to play the piano. Elijah has chosen a very nice song, and I need to practice for the procession. Your cue to enter the sanctuary is when I begin to play louder. You look lovely, my dear!" cried Mrs. Canute who left the room and then closed the door behind her.

269

Soon after that Mollie heard the sound of the music getting louder and then she exited the Sunday school room. She marched slowly synchronous with the beat. As she entered the sanctuary, she gazed upon the eager look on Elijah's face. Not long after that, she joined Elijah at his side and waited for Reverend Canute to begin the ceremony. Meanwhile, Mollie herself felt very nervous and ecstatic at the same time.

When the music stopped Reverend Canute began to say, "We gather here together to join our new friends Elijah and Mollie in holy matrimony. Before I begin, Mollie has something she wants to say to Elijah from the heart."

"My dearest Elijah, you completely saved me from a dyin'. I fell in love with you, because I saw in your eyes the great love you have for me and your own personal sacrifice of time until I recovered to stay by my bedside. Elijah, I'll love you forever!"

"Elijah will now make a formal statement from his heart," proclaimed Reverend Canute.

"Dearest Mollie, from the moment your aunt and uncle brought you to Kansas, and I first laid eyes upon you I knew you were the woman for me. Mollie, I'll love you until I die," exclaimed Elijah.

"We'll now continue with the ceremony. Elijah Augustus Benson, do you take Mollie to be your lawfully wedded wife to have and to hold until death do you part?"

"I will," said Elijah.

"Do you, Mary Phoebe Williams, take Elijah to be your lawfully wedded husband to have and to hold until death do you part?"

"I will," said Mollie.

"By the power invested in me by the state of Minnesota and the power of our Lord and Savior, I now pronounce you man and wife. Let no man put asunder what God has joined together. You may kiss the bride," stated Reverend Canute.

Elijah kissed Mollie passionately and embraced her tightly for several moments before Reverend Canute said happily, "You two can stop kissing now." All four of them laughed. Mrs. Canute walked over to the couple and said, "The Reverend and I have planned a small reception in your honor. While you wait for us to prepare it our son, a photographer will take your portrait."

"We thank you for all you've done for us in a strange city," exclaimed Mollie.

"I'll just go next door to the parsonage and fetch our son. It won't take him long to set up things here," stated Mrs. Canute. Reverend Canute left the sanctuary and went to help set up the reception for when his wife returned.

Shortly thereafter, Mrs. Canute returned with her son carrying his camera and she carried the rest of his equipment. "This is my son, Allen Canute. He's very happy to take your portrait."

"Very nice to meet ya, folks! This is the perfect time of day to take your photograph being that the sanctuary has lots of sunlight at the moment," exclaimed Allen Canute.

Allen led them into the sanctuary and Elijah carried the equipment that Allen could not carry. As soon as everything was placed on the floor, Allen busily put together the camera and the other equipment. He asked Elijah to open the front doors and any other doors that allowed as much light as possible inside.

"Before I take your portrait I'll need for you to change outfits. White dresses don't photograph well. I believe Dr. Benson has seen to it that you've got some appropriate clothes to change into. I'll wait for you to change." Mollie and Elijah left to go change in one of the Sunday school rooms. Elijah put on his black doctor's suit and Mollie put on her emerald green traveling dress.

Fifteen minutes later, they returned to the sanctuary and Mr. Canute was ready for them. "I want your photograph to turn out as perfect as possible," stated Allen with enthusiasm in his voice. "Dr. Benson and Mrs. Benson, I want you both to stand up on the platform in front of the stained glass windows. Mrs. Benson, I want you to stand on the right and Dr. Benson, you can stand beside her on the left."

Elijah put his left arm on the left side of Mollie's waist. Then they stood together for what seemed forever waiting for Allen Canute to take their portrait. As soon as he finished he said, "If you'll go on into the other room for the reception I'll bring you your portraits in about an hour."

Upon entering the Sunday school room Mollie was captivated by one of the most beautiful frosted cakes she had ever seen. Elijah, too, was fascinated with the cake and the other refreshments. Mrs. Canute served the red fruit punch in a sparkling cut-glass punch bowl.

"Is everyone ready to eat?" exclaimed Mrs. Canute. All four of them sat down at an ornately carved table covered with a crisp white starched linen tablecloth. On top of the table set four fine bone china plates decorated with blue and pink flowers and were surrounded by sterling silver flatware. "Absolutely beautiful!" stated Mollie. "Let's commence eating!"

After an hour when it was time for the bridal couple to return to the hotel, Allen Canute brought them a small wooden box large enough to contain four cabinet cards memorializing their wedding day. "Mother told me I had to wait for when you started to leave and not interrupt your party. I hope that's all right," cried Allen Canute.

"We weren't the least bit worried. Elijah and I were intrigued by the spread your parents put out here for us. There were no thoughts of portraits. Just our happiness," replied Mollie.

"Dearest, we must be goin' on our way. We wanna start the nuptial journey right away," stated Elijah.

"Goodbye all. We thank you for a wonderful time in your beloved city. Neither of us'll ever forget this," said Mollie.

Happily, Mollie and Elijah proceeded onto their hotel in hopes of beginning their new life together as husband and wife.

Nothing could keep them from their eternal bliss. They knew already that they faced opposition from society because of being an interracial couple. Despite this, they loved each other and that was all that ever counted.

Upon arrival at the hotel they went in the front door but were stopped by the desk clerk. "I've got a telegraph for you that just came in 'bout a half hour ago," exclaimed the clerk.

"I appreciate it," stated Elijah who took the envelope and handed the clerk a tip. "It's addressed to you, my dear Mollie."

Mollie opened the envelope and read the telegraph. As soon as she finished Elijah surmised by her worried look that something was amiss. "What's the matter, dear? You look extremely upset," cried Elijah.

"It's Mother. She's very ill. I don't have my details, but I gotta be with her. We hafta leave for Virginia right away."

Elijah thought for a moment about the problems they would face together in the South but then reassured her by saying, "We'll do whatever's necessary for you to see your mother."

Next, Mollie embraced Elijah and kissed him upon his lips. "Thank you, my dear husband. I love you so much!" She held onto him for several minutes before she realized that they must make immediate plans to travel to Virginia.

Chapter 18

Early in the morning Mollie and Elijah arose to find that it was raining heavily. Despite the inclement weather they were determined to go to the train station. They needed to stop by the post office and send a telegram to Aunt Elsie.

"Let's get something to take with us for breakfast. We can get an earlier start this way," said Elijah. Then they washed up and put on their best traveling clothes. Next, they packed together all their belongings and went downstairs to check out.

"I hope that your room met all your expectations, Mr. and Mrs. Benson," exclaimed the manager.

"That's Dr. and Mrs. Benson, and yes, we had real good accommodations," stated Mollie sternly.

Elijah smiled at Mollie and patted her on her shoulder. Next, he whispered in her ear, "It's nothing. We can't change how some people feel."

Shortly, they went into the hotel restaurant and sat down at the only empty table available. Someone had placed a cut-glass vase full of yellow daisies in the center of the table. Mollie thought it looked breathtaking.

"Elijah, if you don't mind can we sit *here* and eat breakfast?"

"Why, Darling? Is somethin' wrong?"

"No, of course not. I'd just rather sit and enjoy a nice meal together before we have to get on that train," stated Mollie before she grabbed his hand and held it under the table. Again Elijah smiled at her with his pearly whites, and she smiled back.

A woman in a black dress wearing an apron approached the table. With a look of distaste on her face she asked, "Can I help you?"

"Yes, we each want biscuits with gravy, sausage, eggs, and coffee," exclaimed Elijah.

"I'll be back with your order in about fifteen minutes," stated the woman attendant firmly.

"That woman's about as friendly as a mountain lion," said Mollie to Elijah slightly above a whisper.

"Shh, my dear. She might have heard you," exclaimed Elijah trying to calm her.

In fifteen minutes time the cantankerous woman returned with their plates of food. She almost dropped them on the table, left, and then returned a minute later with a coffee pot to fill up their cups. Under her breath she murmured to herself, "Wish that colored would hurry up and get outta here." Then she said aloud, "If you need anythin' else just ask," said the woman.

"Everthin' looks and smells wonderful!" stated Mollie.

The woman walked away hurriedly as if she were rushing away from a fire. Mollie and Elijah decided they did not need to ask her for anymore help.

As soon as they finished eating they got up from their table and exited the hotel. Once they were out of sight the server said, "Thank goodness they're gone. I hate coloreds."

"Me too!" said an elderly woman sitting at the table near her. "I felt so nervous the whole time he was in here."

****

On the way to the post office the rain stopped, and the sun began to partially show between the clouds. The streets were muddy but not impassable. Mollie was relieved that her outfit would not get drenched.

Just as the coach stopped in front of the post office it became stuck in the mud. The coach jolted when the driver attempted to move closer to the entrance. "Driver, stop here. We can walk on. I don't want my wife jerked anymore," stated Elijah sternly.

"I'm sorry, Sir! It won't happen again." The driver climbed down from his seat and assisted Elijah in helping Mollie step onto the walkway avoiding any contact with the mud. Together they lifted her onto the pavement. "Again, I'm most sorry, Sir."

"Don't mention it. Just wait for us until we come back and then take us on to the train station."

"Yes, Sir!" exclaimed the driver.

Elijah was rather irritated with the driver but Mollie remained calm. They entered the post office together and proceeded over to the front counter. "We're not open yet. Come back in an hour and I can help you. I just came in early to catch up on some of my paperwork," said the postmaster.

"I beg of you, Sir. We have to take the next train to St. Louis and we'll miss it if we have to come back. My mother's very ill and may even be a dyin'. I just gotta get a wire to Virginia and my folks in Kansas," pleaded Mollie about to cry.

"All right. All right. I'll make an exception. I do hate to see a grown woman cry. And I really can sympathize with you," stated the postmaster calmly.

Next Mollie filled out two pieces of paper. One message was to send to Jacob and the other was for Aunt Elsie. She handed them over to the man who said, "I'll send these immediately as soon as I open up. I promise."

"Bless you! We'll never forget you for this," stated Mollie overjoyed. Elijah and Mollie left the post office and met their awaiting coach. The driver had by then pulled the coach out of the mud and was ready to take them to the train station. Once he saw them he dismounted the coach and stood by the door to help them reenter it. Mollie and Elijah climbed in and they went on their way.

The train station was crowded as expected. They still hoped to be able to purchase tickets for the next train to St. Louis. When they were finally next in line they hoped to buy their passage without consequence. Mollie walked up to the ticket agent and withdrew money from her purse. "I wanna purchase two train tickets to Rural Retreat, Virginia."

"You can ride in the train but the colored man has got to ride in the freight car," said the agent.

Mollie thought for a moment and then decided to use the same plan as before. "This man's my personal servant. I haven't been well, and I need him to watch over me in case I have another faintin' spell along the way."

"If you say so, Madam. Don't complain to me or the conductor if passengers complain. Wait a minute!" He looked at Mollie's left hand and then at Elijah's left hand and noticed they wore matching wedding bands. "What kind of trick do you people think you're tryin' to pull? You two are married! I ain't letting him ride this train."

People standing behind them began to grumble and murmur to themselves, because they had to wait in line for a long time. They did not understand what Mollie and the agent discussed, but they were upset just the same.

Then Mollie began to cry and said, "Please, Sir. My husband and I planned to take our bridal tour to London, but I got word that my mother's seriously ill. I'm afraid if I don't try to go home now I'll miss my chance to see her alive." When she finished she continued to sob loudly.

"Things are going to be all right. I'll let him go in your car, but I'm warning you. I can't promise you won't face more problems, especially when you get to Tennessee. You know what it's like in the South."

"Yes, Sir. I do. We thank you! Now we can be on our way," said Mollie as she gave the money to the man, and then he gave her two tickets. As she and Elijah began to walk away several people in line stared out them with frowns on their faces for having to wait so long.

"Next in line, please."

Elijah and Mollie gave their bags to a porter and then hurried over to their train. The conductor gave them strange looks but allowed them admission. Other passengers were perplexed but said nothing more than whispers when Mollie and Elijah sat down together.

"I've never been to your part of Virginia before. Just after the War I did go to Richmond before I moved out West with my first wife," exclaimed Elijah. Things looked rather devastatin'."

Mollie laid her head on her husband's shoulder and rested until she fell asleep. Elijah knew it was a long trip and ascertained that things would not be much different in the South even with the war long over. He also knew that he and Mollie could not act as husband and wife as long as they stayed in Virginia.

****

After about two weeks of train travel and stopovers in between, they finally arrived at the train depot in Rural Retreat. Small children were running back and forth near the tracks even before the train came to a complete stop. One woman grabbed her young son by the nape of the neck and slapped him across the face. Mollie and Elijah quietly laughed together as they disembarked.

There waiting on the platform was Jacob Gehring and Granny Williams. She knew Jacob was coming, but it was a total surprise to see her dear grandmother still standing as straight as a thirty-year old in front of her. No one ever guessed that she was 102 years old now. She ran up to Mollie and embraced her tightly and then kissed her on her right cheek. Mollie, in turn, held her grandmother for several moments with tears streaming down her cheeks.

"I thought I'd never ever see you again," stated Granny.

"That's what I thought too," exclaimed Mollie.

Granny Williams smiled at Elijah and said, "So, this is the lucky man who stole yer heart, Mollie. I'll admit he's a very handsome young man."

"Yes, he is! You know he saved my life and that's when he captured my love," stated Mollie.

Elijah grinned at Granny Williams, tipped his hat to greet her, and then went back to the train to collect their baggage. Jacob followed him to help carry the Saratoga to the back of his wagon and then they went to get the rest of the bags. Next, he and Jacob helped the ladies climb onto the buckboard. Jacob and Elijah sat in the front and Mollie and Granny Williams sat on the back seat.

On the way back to Pine Mountain Township, Mollie spotted a restaurant along the main road. "Jacob, can we stop here? I know everyone's gotta be famished by now." She looked at her father's pocket watch and said, "It's not but 12:45, and we still got plenty of time to get back before dark."

"That's an excellent idea, and Mollie and I'll pay for it," stated Elijah.

Jacob and Granny Williams both smiled at them in agreement. They were both hungry as well. You could smell the delicious aromas of fresh baked bread, roast chicken, and beef stew coming from the restaurant. It made them feel even hungrier than they realized.

Shortly, Jacob slowed down the wagon and stopped near the front of the establishment. Several wagons were parked in front, but there was still enough room to get close enough for Granny Williams to have nearer access to the porch.

Both men jumped off first and then helped the ladies down. Together, they walked up the steps of the restaurant and entered. People were talking but suddenly stopped when they saw Elijah. The owner came up to them and said, "We don't serve his kind in here. He's gonna hafta sit outside and eat alone."

"Slavery ended eleven years ago, and my husband goes wherever I go," said Mollie. A woman gasped as she said this. "We're all hungry after our long train ride and wanna eat before we get back to Pine Mountain."

"I don't care what you say. Coloreds ain't got no business in my eatry. Ya'll gotta leave before I send for the sheriff," said the owner.

"Granny Williams, I'm truly sorry about this," cried Elijah.

"It's not your fault some of these people around here are so pigheaded. We can find somewhere better to eat along the way.

My granddaughter runs a restaurant north of Elk Creek just outside of Wythe County. She'll serve us somethin' good," replied Granny Williams.

"Which granddaughter are you a talkin' about, Granny? I didn't know any of our relatives had an eatin' place," cried Mollie.

"Your cousin Phoebe Morgan Wilson and her daughter Callie Ward run a hotel and restaurant. They just opened it last month," explained Granny Williams. "Do ya remember the old Ward homestead that belonged to Phoebe's in-laws?"

"Yeh, I do Granny."

"Phoebe, her husband Richard, Callie, and her husband Isom fixed it up nicely. They've got eight bedrooms upstairs. That place is absolutely beautiful! Just wait 'til you see the restaurant!"

More than an hour later they arrived in front of a magnificent looking three-story painted white manor house with green shutters and a picket fence completely surrounding it. Callie was on the porch watering the plants.

"Granny, it's so good to see ya! You look so radiant and beautiful!" stated Callie. Granny Williams was wearing a lilac colored dress with a matching hat and purse. Around her neck she wore a necklace tightly woven out of hair belonging to her late lamented husband. Most elderly women in her community wore black or gray dresses, but Granny Williams believed in wearing vibrant colors, because she enjoyed the beautiful colors of spring and loved living all her years of "borrowed time" as she called it.

Although she was past the century mark, she had fewer wrinkles than a sexagenarian, and her hair was still solid brown.

"I appreciate the compliments, dear Callie, but we're here to eat a late lunch."

"Callie, you're lookin' well. This is my husband, Dr. Elijah Benson. We were married the beginnin' of this month," stated Mollie.

"So good to meet you, Elijah. It ain't often you meet a colored doctor," said Callie.

"The pleasure's all mine! I find dear Mollie's family to be very kind so far," stated Elijah.

Cousin Callie was truly enthralled with the idea of Elijah being a Negro doctor. Her father and his parents were abolitionists who often encountered opposition from slave owners who intimidated them every opportunity that arose. Some store owners even refused entry to them and that forced them to travel farther distances to purchase staple foods and other farm supplies.

"Come on everbody! Let's go inside and I'll seat ya at one of our best tables near the winders," said Callie thinking about keeping Granny warm. She led them into an elegant spacious dining room containing twelve round tables with six chairs around each. Each table was decorated with a blue gingham tablecloth and cut-glass vases holding fresh wildflowers in them. Out of the twelve tables only two were occupied, because most of the lunch crowd had already left.

Phoebe came out of the kitchen with a coffee pot to refill the cups of the existing customers. She was surprised but pleased to see Mollie, her husband, Granny Williams, and Jacob. "I'll be right thar as soon as I serve these here people."

Not long after that she walked over to her family members' table. It astonished her to see how fashionably dressed Mollie looked and how nobly dressed Elijah appeared. She wondered if Mollie had suddenly inherited a large sum of money from someone. Nevertheless, Mollie, Elijah, and Granny Williams made everyone else seem poor in contrast.

"What can I get fer you folks to eat? I think we've got some pan fried steak, fried taters, and boiled carrots," said Phoebe.

"That sounds good! We'll all have some of that," cried Granny Williams.

"I'll be right back cheer in a few minutes. Come with me, Callie. I need yer help," said Phoebe.

While they were gone Granny Williams began to tell Mollie what was wrong with Nancy. Somehow, Nancy contracted an acute case of tuberculosis and was not responding to any treatments that Dr. Kinsler gave her. She had not personally seen Nancy in three weeks, because she was afraid of becoming ill at her advanced age. Jacob and Callie carefully took care of her according to the doctor's instructions to attempt to remain healthy. Thus far they exhibited no signs of any symptoms.

"Elijah, ain't there anything we can do to save her? I can't lose my mother too," stated Mollie worriedly.

285

"Darling, I've got to examine her first. I won't know anythin' until I see her," cried Elijah. Before they continued their conversation Phoebe and Callie returned with four plates of delicious-smelling food. Granny Williams said a short blessing, and they began to eat.

"When ya finish that we've got some apple pie fer dessert," said Phoebe. "If ya needs anythang else Callie and I'll be in the kitchen a finishin' up the dishes."

After they finished eating their lunch and ate their dessert they all got up from the table and started to leave the restaurant. Elijah left the money on the table and out the door they went. Then they all climbed into the wagon, ladies first, and went on their way.

All along the road back to Pine Mountain Township, Mollie admired the beautiful spring foliage and early wildflowers. She and Granny Williams talked about when she was a small girl and spent time on the farm helping plant flowers and milk the cows. They also discussed the times just after her father died and the spring and summers she spent there.

"This part of Virginia sure is lovely! I wouldn't mind livin' here if things was different," stated Elijah.

"That reminds me. I want ya both to come stay at my house. There's plenty of room, and I'd enjoy the company," said Granny Williams.

"Oh, Granny! We'd love to stay with you, wouldn't we, Elijah?"

"I think that sounds wonderful! I've heard all about that house. Mollie's described the inside and outside so well I almost feel like I've already been there," replied Elijah.

"However, durin' the day I know I wanna stay with Mother," said Mollie.

An hour later they began to pass through Pine Mountain Township. Hiram was in his livery stable busily hammering horseshoes, as he was an expert blacksmith. He did not notice them until Mollie called out, "Good afternoon, Brother dear."

"Vy Mollie Williams, it's so good to see you again! I taught you'd never come home again," stated Hiram.

Jacob stopped so that Mollie was able to climb down and greet Hiram. The others remained in the wagon and waited for them to finish conversing. Hiram looked up at Elijah and smiled, and then continued talking with Mollie. Elijah tipped his hat and smiled back at him. A customer arrived to get his horses shoed, so Hiram and Mollie bade each other goodbye.

"Ve'll talk again soon, Sis," stated Hiram.

On the way out of town they passed the Hatfield farm where Mr. Hatfield was working out in his fields. Then, a little down the road, they passed Nancy's homestead where they saw Dr. Kinsler's carriage parked in front. Jacob stopped and allowed Mollie and Elijah to get out and see about Nancy.

"Granny and I are goin' over to her place now. I'll be back later to pick yall up. Mother's inside with Grandma. She'll be happy to see ya, Mollie," cried Jacob.

287

"Thanks, dear Jacob! Elijah and I are exhausted, but I do wanna see Mother first. Don't worry. Elijah's a wonderful doctor, and he knows what precautions to take to keep us safe as possible," cried Mollie.

Mollie and Elijah walked inside without knocking into the sitting room. Carrie was sitting on a chair waiting for Dr. Kinsler to complete his examination. She told them that he had been in there with her for over an hour.

"Who's this with you?"

"This is my husband, Dr. Elijah Benson."

"Doctor? Whoever heard of a colored doctor? Well, I'll tell you one thing, Mollie. You're makin' a big mistake, and Mother'll never let him near her."

"I don't care what anybody says. I'm happy and Elijah's happy. That's all that counts. He saved my life. Didn't Granny tell you all about us getting married?"

"Granny never said a word. Jacob was probably just as surprised as I am to see a man by your side. You can stay here if you like, but your husband'll have to sleep elsewhere."

"Carrie! Of all people I thought you'd be the most understandin' of all. Do you forget that you married a man whose grandparents on both sides were Jewish? Remember how some of our neighbors acted for many years until they found out what a great man he is?"

"But this ain't the same. He's a Negro!"

288

"Do you realize my husband is standing right here while you're insultin' him? When you insult him you also insult me!"

"That's all right, darling. I'm use tuh this. I'll go outside," said Elijah.

"You'll do nothin' of the kind. Your place is beside me as my husband."

Suddenly, Dr. Kinsler came out of Nancy's room with a look of worry upon his face. He said, "Carrie, Mollie, I'm afraid there ain't much more I can do. I've practiced medicine in this town for o'er thirty-five year, and I ain't never seen a case like this. She gets worse for a while and then she seems to get some better. Well, from what I can see she's getting' progressively worse, and there ain't nothing more I can do. My medical knowledge is limited."

He looked over at Elijah noticing that he had his arm around Mollie's waist. Although he was displeased he did not complain about it. Mollie noticed his expression and said, "Dr. Kinsler. This is my husband, Dr. Elijah Benson."

"Pleased to make your acquaintance, my fellow physician," stated Elijah who then grabbed his hand and shook it.

"Hmmm, if you say so. Although I cain't believe any college would've admitted you," said Dr. Kinsler who wiped his hand on his coat as he said this.

"Sir, for your information I finished in the top five percent of my graduatin' class at Montpellier Medical School in France," said Elijah who opened up his doctor's bag and unrolled his diploma to show to Dr. Kinsler.

Dr. Kinsler was so shocked to see the diploma that he felt like he could swallow all of his teeth at any moment. Then he built up enough courage to say, "Dr. Benson, I apologize for a doubtin' what a fine physician you gotta be. All my years of study and practice could ne'er match yer prestigious European trainin'. I'm in awe to be standin' in the presence of a gifted man."

"This man saved me from a dyin' back in Kansas. I couldn't help but fall in love with a wonderful man. He neglected his own farm to be with me all day and night. Back home he's a successful cattle rancher because nobody'll trust his medical skills."

"She's the best thing to ever happen to me too. We know we'll have problems no matter where we go, but we love each other and won't let man put asunder what God has brought together," said Elijah.

"Dr. Benson, can we step outside together?" said Dr. Kinsler.

"Course, we can," said Elijah.

"I wanna discuss with you Nancy's condition. Carrie and Mollie wait fer us to return before yall go into your mother's room."

"Yes, doctor," cried Carrie and Mollie in unison.

Both doctors stepped outside and walked towards the kitchen. The Gehring twins were playing out front, and they did not want them to hear the conversation.

"Do you got any ideas what we can do for Nancy? Her consumption seems to be getting' worse."

"I haven't examined her yet, so I need you to tell me what you've done so far and her symptoms," exclaimed Elijah.

Dr. Kinsler began to explain all of his treatments and Nancy's symptoms. He stated that she had contracted consumption a month before from a family where she helped deliver a baby. Nancy was a midwife and this was the first time she had ever been infected with such a serious illness. For a while it seemed as though she were going to improve but two weeks earlier she no longer responded to treatments. Then he asked, "Dr. Benson, do ya know of anythang we can do to help her? With yer trainin' I feel like you may know somethin' I don't."

"It's true that I do keep up with the latest trends in medicine. I do receive monthly medical journals from New England. From what I recall I do remember somethin' that may help Mrs. Williams."

Chapter 19

"Elijah and Dr. Kinsler have been outside fer a very long time. Things hafta be far worse than we thought," said Mollie.

"I'm afraid so, Mollie. That's why we sent ya the wire. Granny told us war you were, but we had no idea you were a getting' married thar. Obviously, she knew all along," said Carrie.

"Of course, she knew it all along. Granny's the only person in the whole family who I can confide in my deepest thoughts and secrets. She never passes judgment on anyone," stated Mollie.

"You two have always been close. Believe me, I tried to, but she always seemed too busy when I was yer age. No matter now. I'll be polite to yer husband, but I don't hafta like him."

"You're darn right you'll be polite to him!"

Not long after that, Elijah and Dr. Kinsler reentered the house ready to tell the women their plans to attempt to treat Nancy. Dr. Kinsler still looked extremely worried and thought that nothing could cure her now. Elijah also appeared highly concerned and was not completely certain that his treatment would help. Together, they went into Nancy's room so that Elijah could examine her closely.

"We'll be right back, Darling. I'll let ya know when you can come in and see your mother," stated Elijah.

As both doctors entered the bedroom, there lay a woman appearing older than her years struggling to breathe as she slept. When Elijah drew closer to the bed he noticed small tear-sized bloodstains on her pillow. He knew that he had to take precaution because consumption was contagious. Listening closely to her breathing and looking at her frailty Elijah ascertained that there was likely only one thing they must do.

"Come on, Doctor. Let's go tell my wife and her sister the news," stated Elijah who genuinely felt sorry for his mother-in-law.

Mollie surmised by the expression on Elijah's countenance that her mother was gravely ill. She suddenly grew more worried. "What can ya tell us about Mother's condition, Darlin'?" stated Mollie.

"Your mother's condition's very critical and there's only one thing I know to do. She must be moved to a sanatorium immediately or some other arrangements. Dr. Kinsler tells me that the nearest one's too far for Nancy to travel, so we've got only one alternative," said Elijah.

"Only one alternative? What can we do? I cain't lose my mother. I've already lost too many people close to me," cried Mollie sadly.

"Listen to him, Mollie. He's got some news that just may help her," stated Dr. Kinsler.

"Although it's been a few years since I graduated from medical college, I do keep up with the latest trends in medicine; however, I gotta caution you."

"We're listenin', Elijah," stated Carrie.

"The best we can do for Mrs. Williams is to take her to a home where there's lots of windows and constant airflow. She needs as much fresh air as she can get. Again, I caution you that this treatment don't work for everyone. Does anybody know of such a place?" said Elijah.

Carrie and Mollie began to talk among themselves. They tried to think of such a place and could not think of anything suitable. Granny Williams's house would be perfect except they did not want to risk her health at such an advanced age. Then Dr. Kinsler spoke up,

"Ladies, I just happened to think of a place that's got lots of fresh air blowing through all the time. If you remember your Uncle David's got a summer vacation house on the very top of Pine Mountain."

"Oh, yes. I totally forgot about that place. It sounds perfect!" cried Mollie.

"We don't wanna get our hopes up. This regimen's solely a last resort," stated Dr. Kinsler seriously.

"When do we move her?" said Carrie.

"As soon as possible! I think we oughta take her there tomorrow afternoon at the latest," exclaimed Elijah.

"Who's going to stay with her? I know Dr. Kinsler has this whole community to attend to," said Mollie.

"You and I can look after her no matter how long it takes, and Dr. Kinsler said he'd be around ever other day for consultation. Tomorrow morning we can send a wire to Aunt Elsie

294

requestin' that Mr. Mullins look after all our farms until we return," stated Elijah.

"I love you so much, my darlin'!" shouted Mollie.

"And don't forget Dora's son Ephraim'll be there awhile anyway to help out," remarked Elijah.

"Then it's all set. We better go over to Granny's to get freshened up and rested before tomorrow comes," said Mollie.

They told Carrie and Dr. Kinsler goodbye. As soon as they went outside they signaled for Jacob to take them over to Granny Williams's home. Thankfully, her homestead was not too far away. As they pulled away Carrie said to Dr. Kinsler, "It's a big mistake letting that Negro even come near my mother, but if you can't be there I guess he's better than nothin'."

Dr. Kinsler uttered not a word for he knew in his heart that Elijah was a gifted and caring physician. Just talking with him for a half hour outside he knew that whether Nancy lived or died she had the best care anyone ever asked for anywhere in the whole state. Instead of anger or disgust towards Carrie he only felt sorrow for her ignorance.

Later on, Jacob, Mollie, and Elijah arrived in front of Granny Williams's abode. Coming out of the front door were smells of baked ham with pineapple, fresh buttered rolls, and hot apple pie right out of the oven. Jacob helped Elijah carry the baggage inside of the house. Then as they unloaded the trunk Mollie went inside and walked to the kitchen where she found Granny by the stove buttering the mashed potatoes and David

Junior's daughter-in-law Huldah Williams attending to placing the baked ham on the kitchen table.

"Can I help you ladies with anythin'?" said Mollie.

"Mollie! So glad you can join us for supper. Granny here insisted on helpin', so I think we can manage everythin' here. Just sit thar at the table and relax a few moments," said Huldah who grabbed Mollie and kissed her right cheek.

"Is anyone home?" called Jacob from the hall.

"You're so silly, Jake!" said Granny with a big grin on her face.

Elijah walked into the kitchen behind him. Huldah had a puzzled expression on her face as she did not realize Mollie's husband was a Negro.

Granny Williams walked over to Elijah, shook his right hand, and embraced him tightly. Then she motioned for him to bend down so that she could whisper something in his ear. "Thank you for takin' such good care of my dear Mollie."

"You're most welcome, Mrs. Williams," whispered Elijah into her ear.

"Supper's ready, so let's all sit down together," cried Huldah.

Jacob said the blessing and then they all began to eat. Everyone appeared to be happy at the moment except for Mollie who still appeared saddened.

Suddenly, Huldah worked up the courage to speak to Elijah, "So, Dr. Benson, I hear that you've come to help Aint Nancy."

"Please call me Elijah. We're family now. Yes, I'll do everythin' I can with God's help to treat Mrs. Williams."

"I'm glad to hear that you're a God fearin' man," stated Huldah.

"That's right. I was born and raised a Methodist. It's a good thing that Mollie's a Methodist too," chuckled Elijah.

After supper, Huldah arose from the table, cleared it, and put the dishes near the sink to begin washing them. Jacob went out the back door to return home and Granny, Mollie, and Elijah retired to the parlor.

"Now that Huldah and my grandson John live with me my duties are lighter. I like to help them now and then, because I wanna keep up what little strength this old body has."

"You're lookin' well, Granny. I just wish Mother was up and around," sighed Mollie.

"Mrs. Williams, if I didn't already know you I'd swear that you were in your late seventies or early eighties." stated Elijah.

"Call me Granny, Elijah, and I appreciate the compliment," said Granny with a huge smile on her face. "I plan to sit here for an hour or so and read. You two go on upstairs into my old room. Huldah's got it all fixed up for you."

"Goodnight, Granny!" said Mollie who hugged her tightly.

"Goodnight, my dear Mollie. I'll see you at breakfast," stated Granny.

Elijah kissed Granny's hand and then they ascended the stairs to their room. Upon the bed Huldah had placed one of Granny's prized hand woven coverlets. Near the bed on either side were washstands so that Mollie and Elijah did not need to share. Next, they washed off themselves, put on their night clothes, and climbed into bed. After a hard day they fell asleep almost immediately.

Early the next morning they woke up early to smells of fried bacon and fresh coffee wafting into the air. Granny Williams sat at the table drinking coffee while Huldah and John prepared the breakfast.

"Good morning, my dears," cried Granny as Mollie and Elijah entered the kitchen still in their nightgowns. They were glad to see that everyone else appeared in their bedclothes too.

"And a good mornin' to all of you," said Mollie.

"I trust you both slept well on my old bed," said Granny.

"We sure did, Granny. Neither of us moved all night," said Mollie.

"The only thin' that woke us up were those delicious smells comin' from the kitchen," stated Elijah.

Soon they all sat down together and after the blessing of the meal they began to eat. During the meal they explained to Granny, Huldah, and John their plans to try to help Nancy. They seemed relieved to know that whether she improved or not Nancy was receiving the very best of care.

After breakfast while Huldah and John cleaned the kitchen, Mollie and Elijah went upstairs to clean themselves and put on clean clothes. Then when they finished Elijah went into the barn to hitch one of the horses to Granny's extra phaeton carriage. He and Mollie planned to go into town to send a wire back to Aunt Elsie.

Not much later as they drove towards town, Mollie spotted Mr. Hatfield in his field. She called out to him and as soon as he saw her with Elijah he quickly turned back around pretending not to notice her.

"Mr. Hatfield's never been that rude before. I know he recognized me. It hasn't been that long since I left town."

"Mollie, you know good and well what's wrong. It's because *I* am with you and you know it."

"It don't matter because I love you and that's all that counts. Now let's go into town."

Soon they approached the small town of Pine Mountain. Visitors busily walked to and fro along the dirt paths leading in and out of town. When they stopped by the post office they noticed a crowd of teenaged boys standing near a produce stand outside of the mercantile. Just as Elijah helped Mollie down from the carriage the boys threw several tomatoes at Elijah. One of the boys said, "Get your hands off her, Boy! You don't belong in this town."

Elijah reached into his inside suit pocket for a handkerchief. The boys ran away hurriedly thinking he planned to pull out a pistol. As he wiped away the tomatoes and their juice, Mollie encouraged him to hurry on into the post office but not before saying, "I'm so sorry, Eli!" He knew in his heart that what just happened was nowhere near as bad as what Negroes endured before they were liberated.

Inside the post office the postmistress suddenly had a nervous expression on her face when Elijah entered. Naturally, she recognized Mollie but wondered why they were together especially since there were no other Negroes living in this community. Then when Elijah spoke to state their business she was in awe to hear how articulately he spoke and with a very slight French accent. She was not accustomed to hearing Negroes talk better than most Whites she had ever met.

Shortly, they rode on to Nancy's homestead. When they arrived they found Hiram and Jacob in front loading a mattress into the back of Hiram's buckboard. They had already attached the white canvas to protect Nancy from the elements for when they traveled to the top of the mountain.

"Oh, zere you two are. Elijah, you're just in time to help me carry Nancy from ze house to ze vagon. I zink it's time to go in," stated Hiram.

Immediately, Hiram and Elijah went inside to get Nancy. When they entered her bedroom she was fully awake but breathing heavily. Nancy had a look of uneasiness across her face, because she was not accustomed to having someone of the Negro race to touch her.

"You git away from me, you hair?" cried Nancy defiantly.

"Calm down, Mother. He's a doctor and he's Mollie's husband. As a matter of fact, he's a much better doctor zan Dr. Kinsler or any ozer doctor in ze state, I suspect," stated Hiram.

"I don't care who he is. No colored's gonna touch me," cried Nancy.

"That's all right, Hiram. Once we get her to the other house she won't have a choice. I'll go fetch Jacob," exclaimed Elijah.

"I'm so sorry for my mozer-in-law's behavior," stated Hiram.

"I do understand though. It's going to take a long time to change the minds of people in the South. Until then there's no way that Mollie and I could ever live here in peace," said Elijah.

Just as he was about to go outside Jacob came rushing in looking for them. "I was startin' to get worried. What's the hold up?"

"Your grandmother refuses to let me help carry her to the wagon, and I was comin' for you to help your father," exclaimed Elijah.

"Oh, all right," stated Jacob.

Elijah went outside to rejoin Mollie and Jacob went into Nancy's room. Before Elijah had a chance to explain the situation, Hiram and Jacob exited the house carrying Nancy bundled up in one of her blue, white, and red overshot hand woven wool coverlets. She had stopped yelling but looked at Elijah with ire.

301

"Don't pay attention to her, Elijah. Once we get her up on the mountain she'll have to cooperate," said Mollie.

Right after they loaded Nancy into the back of the wagon, Hiram said, "Elijah and Mollie, make sure and take vatever food you zink you vill need for today. Jacob and I vill bring you vhatever you need for ze next few days."

"Thanks! We appreciate it," exclaimed Mollie.

While Hiram and Jacob went along their way, Mollie and Elijah began to seek out supplies from the kitchen and root cellar. Although Mollie was aware of the fact that her mother might die she was still comforted in knowing that she was able to see her mother again before she did die.

Then after about an hour Mollie and Elijah placed the various supplies in the back of Nancy's wagon. Elijah decided to drive the larger wagon and Mollie drove the phaeton carriage. She explained to Elijah that it was likely that it would take at least an hour to travel to her Uncle David's house on the mountain.

Soon they began their journey to the top of Pine Mountain. All along the route Mollie recognized some of the early spring flowers she remembered as a young girl. The scents of the blossoms were almost overpoweringly sweet to the senses. Elijah had forgotten how spectacular springs were in the eastern states after living in Kansas so many years. They had already admired these signs when they arrived the day before, but they just could not stop being captivated by them.

After an hour without any consequences they made it to the top of Pine Mountain. Jacob was busily dusting the mattresses in the spare rooms. Prior to that Hiram had opened all of the windows to air out the rooms. They placed Nancy in one of the front rooms with the most windows. Since they were on the top of the mountain there were continuous breezes blowing bringing with them the freshest air. Hiram sat beside Nancy's bedside while he waited for Mollie and Elijah to arrive. When he heard the wagons approaching he stood up and walked outside.

"I see it didn't take you two very long to get here. Ve taught it might be a bit longer from now," stated Hiram.

"Now that we're here you two can go on. We can manage things from here," said Mollie.

"Are you sure, Mollie?" said Hiram.

"Everything'll be just fine. You go on so's you can check on Carrie and the twins," stated Mollie.

"All right, if you insist. Jacob and I vill be back tomorrow to bring you enough food supplies to last two veeks," cried Hiram.

"We appreciate it. Until tomorrow then," stated Elijah.

It was now later in the day just past noon. Hiram and Jacob knew they would be late for lunch so they took hardly any time at all preparing to go back down the mountain.

When Elijah brought the last of the supplies in he said, "I'm goin' to go check on your mother. Perhaps, you can start lunch?"

"That'll be fine, my love."

303

Elijah walked into Nancy's room as quietly as possible. Right when he grew closer to the bed Nancy's eyes opened wide. Then she screamed as loud as she could, "Help! Save me! Get this colored away from me! Help!"

Mollie came running into the room and walked quickly to her mother's side. "Mother, calm down! Elijah's a wonderful doctor and he's my husband. Me and him are here to help you get better."

"I don't care who he is. He ain't touchin' me!"

"My dear, could ya please hold her arms while's I examine her? I need to use my stethoscope to listen to her internally."

"Of course, Elijah."

Nancy was extremely annoyed with her daughter and gritted her teeth the entire time that Elijah listened to her heart and her breathing. He looked very worried after he listened this time.

"I think her breathin' sounds worse today than yesterday," he whispered to Mollie after she let go of Nancy's arms.

"What does this mean exactly?"

"It means that it may be way too late to help her now. The best we can do is keep ourselves healthy by boilin' everythin' that comes in contact with her. I'd advise you to wear a cloth in front of your face if you get any closer to her mouth than you already have. Also, I know it's goin' to seem extra chilly at night, but we gotta keep the windows open at all times. That's the very reason why I asked you to find as many blankets as you could find. Finally, I think as a precaution we oughta use separate dishes and utensils for our meals. We'll do whatever's humanly possible with God's help, of course."

"No matter how badly you're treated by people you still show care and concern for the sick," cried Mollie.

"My parents raised me to believe that someday things'll get better and to have sorrow instead of hatred for those who oppress us. We had a rather strict religious upbringin' even in slavery. Thankfully, we was also treated well by our masters."

Mollie walked over to her husband and embraced him rather tightly. Then she kissed him passionately. Nancy looked at them and just scowled. They both laughed out loud when she did that. "Sorry, Mother. We got a little carried away," said Mollie enthusiastically.

****

Throughout the following week there were times they thought they were about to lose Nancy. Jacob and Hiram regularly brought fresh supplies to sustain them and of course relayed the updates of Nancy's condition to the family and friends in the community.

Then one day at the end of the second week, Nancy began to show some improvement. Her breathing was a little less labored and she no longer coughed up blood. Also, as a result of the healthier eating regimen her strength was beginning to return. Nonetheless, Elijah felt that she still might be contagious and did not want to put anyone else at risk.

Poor Nancy was already thin enough as it was, but during the illness she lost a considerable amount of weight and appeared rather gaunt. This was one of the major reasons both doctors felt that she might not survive. She continued to run a low grade fever, and it was difficult to store any of the ice that Hiram and Jacob transported with them in order to help lower it to normal.

One evening, two months later, Nancy arose from her bed to go to the kitchen while Mollie and Elijah dozed off in their chairs. She hobbled slightly as she walked and knocked over a vase that sat on an end table in the bedroom. They both awoke and Mollie said, "Mother! What're you doin' outta bed?"

"I was hungry," cried Nancy.

Elijah went to Nancy and asked her to sit down on one of the chairs in the bedroom. Upon examining her closely he discerned that she was drenched all over from a cold sweat and her fever had left her. Her body temperature appeared to be normal and her breathing was even less labored.

"I suppose I oughta thank you, Doctor, for stayin' cheer to help," said Nancy.

"If it hadn't been for his expertise you probably wouldn't have made it. Mother, I don't mean any disrespect to you, but I think you oughta apologize to him for the way you treated him," exclaimed Mollie.

Nancy looked at both of them for the longest time saying nothing. She found it to be a struggle to find the right words to say. Because of her southern upbringing she was conditioned to regard

Elijah as someone a lot lower than herself. Finally, with slight hesitation she blurted out stammering, "I'm, I'm s- s- sorry. B- b- but I d- don't h- have t- to like y- you."

Next, Mollie led Nancy back to the bed while Elijah walked into the kitchen to boil water for tea and make a sandwich for Nancy. Then Mollie walked over to the washstand and poured water on a cloth to wipe away the sweat on Nancy's face, neck, and hands.

"Tomorrow, I'll help you bathe all over, Mother," said Mollie.

"I'll be glad to put on some clean clothes too," chuckled Nancy for the first time in months.

Moments later, Elijah returned to the room carrying a tray with tea and a sandwich for Nancy. Although she still did not approve of Elijah being her son-in-law, she did admit to herself he was the kindest Negro she had ever met. Regardless, she decided it was going to be a very arduous journey to keep from detesting him.

"May I speak with you for a moment in the room, Dear?" said Elijah.

"Is somethin' the matter?" exclaimed Mollie nervously.

"Oh, nothin' at all. I just had to tell you somethin' important," cried Elijah.

"How about if we go outside instead?" Together they went outside holding hands. Nancy was too busy eating to notice anything that did not directly involve her.

307

"Your mother's made great progress in the time we've been here. I suggest that we take her home in the next two days. We want to make certain she's strong enough after tomorrow to withstand the trip back down the mountain," stated Elijah.

"Whatever you say, my darling. I already love you more than life itself, but I love you more than that for what you've done for me and my family. In time I think my mother'll learn to accept you. I'll be doin' a lot of prayin' over that," cried Mollie.

Elijah grasped her hand and held it firmly in agreement with what she said. Mollie smiled at him again and together they went back inside holding hands.

Two days later, it was time to leave the house atop the mountain. Both Hiram and Jacob and even Carrie arrived very early to have a late breakfast with Nancy, Mollie, and Elijah. Carrie and Mollie bathed their mother in preparation for her trip back home. When it was time to leave and they had placed everything in the backs of the wagons, Hiram and Jacob assisted in lifting Nancy in the back of Hiram's wagon. Since they were going downhill Jacob rode with Mollie in the phaeton. This gave them time to talk about old times and any future plans.

"That husband of yours is quite a doctor, Mollie," said Jacob.

"He certainly is. Elijah don't get many chances to practice medicine other than with members of our family. After what he did to save my life and Mother's no one oughta ever utter a bad word or feel any hatred towards him," cried Mollie.

They followed behind the other wagons, because they rode in the smallest carriage. The road was extra steep going down, so they had to ride the brake all the way to the bottom. As soon as they all reached the bottom Mollie blurted out, "How does Uncle David stand livin' here durin' the summer? I don't think I could."

"Think about it, Mollie. Don't ya think it'd be worse in the winter with all that there ice and snow on the road?" stated Jacob.

"You're so right, nephew!"

The travelers rode in the direction of Granny Williams's homestead. With the help of John and Huldah, Granny Williams planned a spectacular welcome home dinner for Nancy. She invited all of the family members from near and far. When they finally arrived Mollie was shocked to see so many wagons parked in front of Granny's house. She had no idea what was transpiring but recognized some of the relatives sitting on the porch.

"What's goin' on? Why're there so many people here?" cried Mollie.

Granny Williams strolled out the front door to greet the convoy of newly arriving wagons. She was extremely pleased to see her daughter-in-law looking well. The one thing that was different is that as soon as she climbed down from the wagon with Hiram and Jacob, she hobbled so much that she needed a cane.

All of the women in the family, including Granny Williams's baby sister Aunt Helga Williams, wife of David Senior's baby brother, were busy cooking in the kitchen. The men were busily carrying long tables and benches from the barn to the shaded areas under the grove of cherry trees. Hand-in-hand Carrie and Mollie went inside to help the other women prepare the food for today's festivities.

"Oh, Nancy! I'm so pleased to see you up and around. You had me scared a few times. An old lady like me ain't supposed to outlive her children and their spouses," exclaimed Granny Williams just before she embraced Nancy.

Nancy kissed her mother-in-law on the cheek and then said, "Fer awhile I thought I was a goner too."

Hours later, the celebration dinner began. When Elijah sat down beside Mollie, several family members who had not yet met him stared a long time and stopped talking. Some of them even grimaced but others just looked surprised. Granny Williams being the eldest member of the family stood up from her chair and then asked everyone to lower their heads for prayer. She asked the blessing upon the food and after that asked for a special blessing upon Elijah and Mollie because of their unselfishness for helping Nancy. Again many of the family members just stared and murmured amongst themselves and then they began to eat.

Then later in the afternoon after most of the relatives left, Mollie and her sisters and their husbands began to clear off the tables and put the benches back in the barn. Next, the men carried the tables one-by-one into the barn. The women took all of the dishes into the kitchen to wash. Granny and Nancy sat on the front porch enjoying the refreshing breezes blowing and talked about when Nancy and Isaiah first married. Then they reminisced about their first child born during Jackson's presidency. "Eveline was a wonderful baby, wasn't she? My mother said she looked just like me when I was an infant," stated Nancy.

"Oh, yes. Dear Eveline was a precious young thing. I'm proud of all my grandchildren," cried Granny Williams.

"Poor thing took after my side. All of my brothers except for Charles died of brain tumors," stated Nancy sadly. "Even my mother's sisters died young of strokes."

Mollie came out to the porch and joined her mother and grandmother. She was pleased to see that her mother was not smoking now, because she had been too ill. It always smelled badly, and she coughed more then, than she did now. Since everyone else seemed occupied now was the appropriate time to reveal to Nancy why she originally left for Kansas. Also, she felt that Nancy was strong enough to withstand the news.

Chapter 20

All the men were still loading tables in the barn and the women were in the kitchen cleaning the dinner dishes while at the same time preparing for supper. Mollie now had the perfect opportunity to disclose her secret to Nancy. She waited until both women stopped talking and then said, "Mother, I've got somethin' very important to tell you. I know it'll be a complete surprise to you."

Granny Williams knew perfectly well what Mollie was about to say. She easily read the somber expression on Mollie's face. It was easy to see that she needed some encouragement to continue. "Go ahead, Darling. Yer mother and me are listenin'."

"If you remember, before I left I told you that someday I'd explain why I had to leave Virginia," said Mollie.

"I remember well, Mollie. I've always wondered what took my youngest away from me," cried Nancy.

"I'm sorry, Mother, but I had a secret affair with Robert. I was so afraid of what he might do to me or the family if I stayed here. Getting' away and startin' a new life was better than bein' miserable all the time. Plus, Robert started to become more violent and began strikin' me 'cross the face."

"Land sakes! If Robert weren't dead already I'd kill him myself," stated Nancy angrily. "Why didn't you come to me? Did Eveline know?"

"Joshua told her just before her death, but I think she knew before that. Mother, I really did believe he loved me and planned to divorce Eveline in order to marry me. The only reason he tried to gain my trust was to take my share of Father's land. He wanted control of the water rights in this part of the county."

"Robert was an evil man, indeed. He treated ya and Eveline horrbly, and I'm glad he's dead. If only poor Eveline coulda lived a life without him," said Nancy.

"Elijah's been a welcome relief to me. He treats me like there's no other woman on earth. Someday soon I hope you can grow to love him too," cried Mollie.

Here was where Nancy stopped listening to reason. No matter how much Elijah helped save her life and Mollie's, she still detested him because he was a Negro. Mollie hoped her mother's stubbornness would subside, but nothing like that was happening anytime soon. Unfortunately, Elijah was within earshot of Mollie when she said that and was close enough to observe the expression on Nancy's face. He knew that his mother-in-law may never welcome him into the family as long as she lived. Still, he remembered his religious upbringing and vowed to forgive her and pray for her.

"There's one thing I'm very curious about, Mother," said Mollie.

"Yes, dear?" said Nancy.

"What's it about Elijah that you can't like him? What's he done to you?"

313

"He ain't done nothing to me. I got my reasons, and I don't have to tell you anythin'. Remember, I'm your mother and respect me no matter what I say." Nancy grabbed her cane tightly and went inside looking for Jacob. She looked for him all over downstairs and then went back outside where she saw him returning from the barn. "Jacob, take me home. I'm ready to leave."

"Mother…" said Mollie.

"Don't say another word! I'm leaving immediately!"

"She'll come around. Just give her more time. Nancy'll realize just as you did what a wonderful man Elijah is," said Granny who grasped Mollie's hand.

"I'm sorry you had to hear all that Elijah," said Mollie as he ascended the steps to the porch.

Jacob helped Nancy climb into her buckboard and left right away. Nancy refused to look at anyone and looked down at her hands the whole time she was within sight of Granny's home. Many times Jacob tried to start a conversation, but each time Nancy resisted.

"There's one thing I can say about Nancy," said Granny.

"And what's that?" said Mollie.

"She's as contrary as ever, so I'd say she's pretty much back to her old self," remarked Granny heartily.

Both Granny and Mollie laughed together out loud. Elijah joined in their laughter and laughed out loud as well. "Come on.

Let's go inside and have some lemonade. Huldah made some fresh this mornin'," cried Granny.

Mollie and Elijah each grabbed one of Granny's hands and walked with her to the kitchen. As they walked to the kitchen, Granny told Mollie not to worry about her mother and just wait until the next day after breakfast to see her.

That evening after supper Mollie and Elijah decided to retire to bed early. Elijah wanted to discuss with her their plans for returning to Kansas. Mollie enjoyed the almost three months they spent in Virginia so well that she hated to leave. Being with her family made her feel like she had never left them; however, she was in love with Elijah and knew perfectly well that they could never live together in the South.

"When do you want to go back to Kansas? I'll leave that up to you, Mollie dear."

"It's now July, so I know I wanna be able to still enjoy some nice weather before the fall. Can we leave the end of the week?"

"If that's what you wish. We can stay until the end of next week too," said Elijah.

"No, no. That's fine. We can leave on Friday. I'm feelin' kinda tired right now. Can we go to sleep?" They both changed to their night clothes and climbed into bed. Elijah climbed out again and blew out the oil lamps. Then he returned to bed.

Very early the next morning Mollie and Elijah awakened and then heard the rooster crow. They both chuckled when they realized how funny it was to wake up before a rooster crowed. Mollie climbed out of bed and went downstairs to prepare breakfast. She wanted to repay Granny and the others somehow for all that they had done for them. Suddenly, she heard the dogs barking wildly outside. Elijah came running downstairs as did John and Huldah.

"We men will go outside and see what it is," cried Elijah.

Huldah went into the bedroom in the back to calm Granny Williams as she heard her calling out to find out what all the noise was about. She told Granny to go ahead and get ready for breakfast.

Meanwhile, Elijah and John searched the front lawn and then the backyard but found nothing amiss. Still, the dogs continued to bark uncontrollably. Then they discovered what the matter was. An unknown carriage approached at the very end of the lane of cherry trees. It was a very expensive-looking brougham coach. John had not even seen one of them in many years and the last time Elijah saw one was in Minneapolis. The driver looked rather weary, but he still sat erect on the driver's seat.

When the coach finally stopped near the porch the driver climbed down to open the door of the luxurious brougham. Out of the coach stepped a woman of about forty years and a man about the same age. What was odd about the woman is she wore a large scarf around her shoulders that looked very familiar to Elijah. The scarf looked a lot like one his sister wore the last time he saw her.

"Why's this white woman wearin' an African scarf?" thought Elijah to himself.

The woman looked at John and said, "My name's Kathleen Hairston and this is my husband Lawrence. We're a lookin' for Nancy Williams's farm. My ma sent us to locate her daughter Mollie and her husband Elijah."

John pointed to Elijah and said, "This is Elijah. Mollie's inside makin' breakfast. You're welcome to join us."

"That's most kind of you. We've been a travelin' since yesterday and feel very weary. I'm sure our driver's 'bout ready to fall off the coach," said Kathleen.

Elijah and John led them into the parlor to sit and rest awhile before breakfast was ready. Granny was in there sitting on her favorite wicker rocker near the fireplace working on her knitting. She looked up when Kathleen and Lawrence walked in and naturally she did not recall ever seeing them before.

"Greetings, Mrs. Williams. We've heard my mother talk about you all my life, but please forgive me for a sayin' this. I didn't expect you to still be alive," said Kathleen.

"That's all right, dearie. I realize I'm living on borrowed time. Now what did you say your name is?"

"I didn't. I'm Rebecca Patton's daughter, Kathleen Hairston. This is my husband, Lawrence. We're on our way to Aunt Nancy's, and I think we took a wrong turn."

"You didn't. Nancy's place is yonder down the road about a mile or two. But please have breakfast with us first."

317

"Thank you, Mrs. Williams."

Just as Kathleen said that Mollie came into the room and announced, "Breakfast's ready!"

Later on after breakfast everyone reconvened to the parlor. Mollie and Elijah were perplexed as to what reason Kathleen and Lawrence needed to see them. They told them they had something important to tell them after they ate. Then Kathleen spoke, "Ma was pleased to hear that you both returned east to care for Aunt Nancy. She'll be happy to know Aunt Nancy's a feelin' better now."

"Nothin' but the best for my mother," said Mollie.

"A week after you both left for Virginia Aunt Elsie sold her farm to Ma."

"What? Where's Aunt Elsie goin' to live? Did she send out a telegram?"

"Please let me finish, Mollie," said Kathleen patiently.

"I'm sorry. Continue on."

"Ma bought Aunt Elsie's farm just after she invited her to move with her to Tennessee. That's where both of them are now. We just left them a few days ago, but that's not why we're here."

"Now, we really are confused. Tell us why you're here then, Cousin."

"It was all Aunt Elsie's idea. She told Ma that if she bought her land she'd move to Tennessee on the condition that she gave you the land as a weddin' present, free and clar."

"I just can't believe it, Elijah. Imagine Aunt Rebecca and Aunt Elsie doin' this for us. Now ya can really live yer dream as a prosprous cattle rancher. Oh, Kathleen. We thank ya fer this wonderful news!"

"Kathleen, you tell your mother we're forever indebted to her," cried Elijah excitedly.

"Yes, I will, but first we gotta go see Aunt Nancy. We plan to stay with her a few days," said Kathleen.

"Nonsense! You'll do nothing of the kind. We've got an extra room for you here. Nancy's house is too small," stated Granny Williams.

"If ain't no bother. Lawrence, let's go see Aunt Nancy now. Won't she be surprised?" said Kathleen.

Mollie and Elijah persuaded their cousins to allow them to accompany them in their beautiful, luxurious brougham coach. As soon as they washed up, they proceeded to Nancy's homestead.

When they arrived, Nancy was sitting outside on her front porch. Jacob was sharpening his farm tools out in the barn. She was in awe as she sighted the brougham. No one she knew in the whole county could afford one of them.

The first person to climb out was Lawrence followed by Kathleen. Still, Nancy did not know who they were, because the last time she saw Kathleen she was a small child. Any trips Rebecca made to Virginia in recent years she usually traveled alone with a servant.

"Aunt Nancy! I'd recognize you anywheres. You resemble my ma quite a bit. I'm Kathleen Patton Hairston. This is my husband Lawrence."

"You do look like me sister Rebecca somewhat. It's good tuh see ya after all these yars. You was small when I saw ya last," said Nancy.

"My husband and I've brought you somethin' from Ma and Pa. It's a gift of $5,000 to help you keep yer farm a goin'. Father had an extry good yar in his business this yar. Just consider it an early Christmas present," said Kathleen.

Kathleen handed Nancy a small wooden box containing five thousand dollars. Nancy almost fainted when Kathleen told her this and almost dropped the box on the porch. Mollie and Elijah then climbed out of the carriage to visit with Nancy and make certain that she was feeling just fine after her shock.

Together, the five of them sat on the porch and talked about old times, the present, and the future. Nancy barely said a word to either Mollie or Elijah but spoke readily to Kathleen and Lawrence.

Finally, Mollie spoke up and said, "Mother, if you want, Elijah and I are goin' into town before lunch. We'd be happy to take yer money and put it in the bank for ya."

"You can if ya want. It don't matter much either way," said Nancy who then turned her attention back to Kathleen.

Mollie took the wooden box from Nancy and asked Elijah to go get the buckboard from the barn. Lawrence told his driver to take them in the brougham instead. He said, "You might as well use it since it's already parked in front."

Along the way to town Mollie grew sadder and sadder. Elijah noticed and said, "I'm sorry, darling that your mother's acting this way. We have to give her more time."

"Of course, we will, but I think I wanna go back to Kansas tomorrow instead of the end of the week. We've done our duty."

"Are you sure? Your granny will hate to see us go so soon."

"Yes, I know, but I can't tolerate my mother's attitude much longer. Besides, I've been feelin' sick the last couple days, and I'd rather be home in Kansas."

"If you've been sick then why didn't you say somethin'? I *am* a doctor, after all."

"I didn't say anythin' because I figured it must've been what I ate."

"As soon as we get back to your Granny's I wanna examine you closer."

Mollie rested her head on Elijah's shoulder as they reached the edge of town. He, too, was eager to return to Kansas. Although he enjoyed the captivating Virginia scenery he did not enjoy being reminded of what it was like living in the South as a slave. The Williams family treated him decently, except for Nancy, but the general southern population did not and he wondered if they ever would.

In the front of the mercantile Mrs. Mueller busily swept the dirt off the porch. She never once looked up and sang as she worked drowning out the sounds of the coach with her own voice. Mr. Mueller, at the same time, placed baskets of produce on the produce stand in front of the mercantile not once looking up to see who was traveling in the brougham. They both usually minded their own business before the crowds started coming into town.

The brougham stopped in front of the bank where a few people lined up waiting for it to open. One man called out angrily to his wife, "Here it's ten minutes after nine and no Mr. James."

"Maybe that's him in his new fancy coach," proclaimed another man causing the crowd of people to laugh.

Elijah climbed out first and then helped Mollie. The townspeople recognized Mollie but they were puzzled to see Elijah exiting the same coach as she. "What's that colored man doin' cheer? Do ya think he's har to rob us?" said the first man again to his wife.

After he said that the women in the crowd clutched their purses tightly in fear. Mollie and Elijah stood in line behind them and they grew silent. Soon after that, Mr. James arrived in his black phaeton carriage. The annoyed townsman remarked loudly, "It's about time ya arrived, Mr. James!"

"Sorry there, folks! My youngest grandbaby cried all night, and I couldn't get a wink a sleep. My daughter Hannah's visitin' me and forgot to wake me. So, I'm awfully sorry."

This appeased most of the townspeople except for the first man and his wife who had been waiting since nine o'clock. Because of the crowd of people ahead of them Mollie and Elijah decided to sit on the bench out front and await their turn, especially since they were carrying such a large sum of money, and they wanted to keep their transaction in private.

Later on when the others left the bank it was Mollie and Elijah's turn to see Mr. James. She walked to the counter and handed the small wooden box to Mr. James. When he opened the box he was astonished to find so much money inside it. "Where'd ya get all this here money, Miss Williams?" said Mr. James.

"I'm makin' a deposit for Mother and the name's Mrs. Benson. This is my husband, Dr. Elijah Benson," declared Mollie.

"I see. Give me a moment and I'll write ya a deposit slip."

Mr. James walked to his desk and sat down. The safe was beside his desk, and he placed the money inside and then closed it securely. Then he began to fill out the ledger making an entry for Nancy followed by writing out a deposit slip for Nancy. "Here ya are, Mrs. Benson. Do come again and give my best to yer mother," stated Mr. James coldly.

"Well, I guess that's that," stated Mollie as she and Elijah left the bank. She was completely annoyed with the treatment she and Elijah received in town. What made things worse is Mollie pondered a few moments and realized that if she had never left Virginia she could easily be one of the bigoted townspeople, and it made her feel sad enough to start to cry.

"My darling Mollie, whatever's the matter?"

"Please, just take us back to Mother's to get our wagon, so we can return to Granny's. I don't feel like talkin' right now."

Elijah perceived that as of late Mollie was becoming more emotional even in public. Normally, she kept her feelings to herself since he had met her. Still, he ascertained that not gaining her mother's acceptance disturbed her even more and more, and she remained unhappy the longer they stayed in Virginia.

Later on, they arrived in front of Nancy's home and no one was in sight. Mollie surmised that this was the perfect time for them to slip away and return to her Granny's home. She took a piece of paper out of her purse along with a pen. Then she dipped the nib in some ink and wrote a note to Kathleen. In the note she wanted to thank her for bringing the deed and for allowing them to use the brougham. Considering the circumstance, Mollie made no mention of their plans for the following day, as they did not wish to alarm Kathleen nor anyone else.

"Please hand this note to the Hairstons for me, Driver," said Mollie.

"Will do, Ma'am," exclaimed the driver.

Afterwards, they remembered they had ridden in the brougham and had no transportation of their own. Therefore, they proceeded to stroll back to Granny Williams's farm which was only a little over a mile down the road. Elijah had no trouble walking, but he worried about Mollie complaining about sickness earlier. At first, she seemed just fine, but as they drew closer to her

Granny's farm, Mollie once again started complaining about not feeling well.

"I knew we shoulda come back in the brougham. You're getting' sick again."

"Oh, Elijah! I'll be just fine. Just ask Huldah to get me some more lemonade. I'll wait for ya here on the front porch."

"As soon as ya finish your lemonade I wanna examine you."

"That's all right, darlin'. I think I'm probably just a little hungry, as I didn't eat enough breakfast."

"Well, it'll be time for lunch in a couple of hours. Until then I'll get ya a sandwich when I go in to get your lemonade. I'll be right back, my love."

While she waited for Elijah, Granny Williams came outside to sit with her favorite granddaughter. Looking at Mollie's face she ascertained that Mollie was tired and overworked. She held Mollie's right hand and said, "Is there anythin' the matter, my dear? You look like you ain't slept in days."

"We're leavin' tomorrow. I can't take my mother much longer."

"Tomorrow? I thought you was waitin' until the end of the week. Tomorrow's only Tuesday."

"I wanted to wait, but Mother's really workin' on my nerves. I hope you'll understand."

"This saddens me greatly, and I'll miss havin' ya around. But... you're a married woman, and you know what's best for you."

About twenty minutes later Elijah returned with three glasses of lemonade and a ham sandwich for Mollie. He then sat down to the left of Mollie and did not interrupt their conversation.

"Elijah, dear, I told Granny that we're leavin' tomorrow on the afternoon stage to Bristol," stated Mollie. "I hope that's all right."

"Granny, I hope you understand that I tried to make her wait. I know how happy she is when she's with you. You oughta see her eyes just light up when anyone mentions you back home. If she had her way she'd take you home to Kansas with us," said Elijah.

"If I were just ten years younger I might consider it. I feel like I did when I was sixty, but I know that on the outside I'm way too old. Maybe I'll live long enough to see your first baby."

"Now Granny, you remember what I talked about before I left. I don't think I'll ever have a baby and dear Elijah has accepted that because he loves me so much," said Mollie who grasped Elijah's hand and then leaned her head on his right shoulder.

Later that evening after supper, Mollie and Elijah were upstairs in their room packing things for their journey the following morning. Suddenly, there was a knock on the door. Mollie went to the door and discovered it was Granny. She normally did not ascend the stairs, but she was carrying a quilt in her arms.

"Granny, I'm surprised to see you up here. Is there somethin' ya need?"

She motioned for Mollie to sit down on the bed and she joined her. Then she unfolded the quilt and placed it on Mollie's lap. "I don't understand. Why are ya givin' this to me? It's absolutely gorgeous!" said Mollie.

"This is a quilt I made and gave to yer father when he was ten year old. Considerin' its age it's in perty good shape."

"Thank you, thank you! I couldn't have wished fer a better gift."

"I'll leave you two alone now to finish packin'. See ya in the morn, my dears," said Granny.

After Granny left and closed the door, Mollie walked back towards the bed but collapsed on a straight back chair near the bed. Elijah immediately dashed to her side. "Darlin', what's the matter?"

"I feel sick. I really don't think it was bein' hungry, 'cause I'm stuffed."

"Remember, I did say I wanted to examine you. Now's as good as a time as any."

Before he began he made sure the door was secured. Next, he cleared the bed and placed a clean sheet over the bed. Elijah took his time and examined her thoroughly. Afterwards, Mollie asked him, "Am I gonna be sick for very long?"

"It's nothing that you won't get over in six months," said Elijah with a slight smile on his face.

"What do ya mean?"

"What I mean is you're gonna have a baby."

"Are ya sure? When I was with Robert I never carried any babies to full-term. You know that!"

"There's no mistakin' it. We're gonna have a baby of our own."

"That's wonderful! Granny'll be so thrilled!"

"Yes, she will, but what'll your mother think?"

"We'll worry about that later. Now we hafta think about gettin' ready to go back home to Kansas."

"Are ya sure ya still don't wanna stay here? We *could* wait until after the baby's born. I can go alone back to Kansas and arrange for Mr. Mullins to hire extra men to look after our farms. Then I'll return in time to help ya in your difficult months."

"No, that won't be necessary. I'm ready to go home. Can I travel in this condition?"

"You'll be fine, my love. If this were your seventh or eighth month, then we'd worry. Now, you go ahead and try to sleep as we've got a long day ahead of us. I can finish packin' for both of us."

He kissed her and then she lay down to sleep. She felt too sleepy to take off her dress. Not long after she lay down, Elijah finished and climbed into bed too.

Early the next morning after breakfast, Granny, Mollie, and Elijah went into the parlor. Huldah and John cleaned the kitchen, so the three of them had time to talk privately. In a few hours, Mollie and Elijah were leaving for Kansas. "I'm sure you're wonderin' why we wanted to talk with you. I've, I mean, we've got somethin' important to tell ya," said Mollie.

"Go on, dear."

"Do you remember yesterday when ya said ya hope to see my first baby?"

"Yes, I do recall sayin' that."

"About next January or so, I'll have my first baby."

"My dearest Mollie! I'm so happy for the both of ya. Are ya goin' to tell your mother?"

"No, and we don't want you to tell anyone. After the baby's born I'll have Elijah send ya a wire. I want my baby to be born in Kansas."

"Anything ya say, dear. I wanna photograph of the three of you."

"Thank you, Granny! I know I can always count on you to be happy for me."

Hours later, it was time for Mollie and Elijah to board the stage in town. John planned to take them along with Huldah and Granny in the buckboard. The sun was scorching hot and fortunately, Huldah brought along a canister of water. Along the way, the wind blew lightly but made the warm air a little less troublesome.

329

Then when they stopped in front of the mercantile they saw the stage arriving. They expected to have about a half hour to talk, but the stage appeared earlier than normal. Hurriedly, John and Elijah climbed down to load the luggage onto the stagecoach. The ladies remained on the wagon and bade each other farewell.

"Now don't forget to war me when you get to Kansas," said Granny.

"We won't. I love ya, Granny! I'm so glad to see ya again."

"Just remember this. If I should die before ya get home I always loved ya dearly no matter what ya been through."

Mollie tightly embraced her grandmother for the last time. She held Huldah's hand and hugged her as well. Then Elijah helped Mollie down and together they boarded the stagecoach. Both parties waved to each other and then the stage drove away. Mollie and Elijah were on their way home to await the birth of their new baby. They knew that they expected to experience many obstacles, but they knew that with God's will they would live the best lives possible.